NOW HE WILL GET HIS REVENGE

"Joel, what are you doing?"

As Susan took three steps into the living room, Joel raised slowly out of the easy chair and turned to face her. She paused abruptly, horrified as he raised a large butcher knife slowly in his right hand.

As the light gleamed off the long blade, Susan bolted up the winding staircase. She swept Aggy up out of her crib and climbed another flight of stairs into the attic. She slammed the attic door shut behind her and quickly threw the bolt lock into position.

"Mommy, where are we?"

"Sh, honey, just be quiet."

Susan leaned closer to the doorway and listened carefully.

Suddenly, the silver blade of the butcher knife splintered through the thin wooden panels of the old door.

GHOST LOVER

GHOST
LOVER

Dennis M. Clausen

BANTAM BOOKS
TORONTO · NEW YORK · LONDON · SYDNEY

To the child born Edwin Moseng,
who became through adoption
Lloyd Augustine Clausen—my Dad

GHOST LOVER
A Bantam Book / March 1982

ISBN 0-553-20405-X

Published simultaneously in the United States and Canada

Bantam Books are published by Bantam Books, Inc. Its trade-
mark, consisting of the words "Bantam Books" and the por-
trayal of a rooster, is Registered in U.S. Patent and Trademark
Office and in other countries. Marca Registrada. Bantam
Books, Inc., 666 Fifth Avenue, New York, New York 10103.

PRINTED IN THE UNITED STATES OF AMERICA

0 9 8 7 6 5 4 3 2 1

GHOST
LOVER

Preface

The human spirit, confined for any period of time, grows inwards in strength. Like the river checked from its natural course, it will overflow all boundaries. For the river's relentless, unyielding search for the sea is eternal. The things that are meant to be— will be. . . .

1

Chapter One

I

October, 1926

Judd McCarthy tugged at the straps of the huge canvas bag he carried across his shoulders and looked down at his dirty leather shoes as they crunched through the gravel and small rocks alongside the railroad embankment. A leather holster and a large hunting knife were strapped around his waist, and the brim of a floppy black hat tilted awkwardly over his forehead. His right hand moved back and forth between the straps of the canvas bag and the .45-caliber Smith and Wesson revolver that protruded out of the holster. His eyes constantly scanned the surrounding terrain, searching for any movement in the brush and clumps of trees on both sides of the railroad tracks.

Earlier in the day he had been sent to Carson to bring the Hanley Brothers Construction Company payroll back to Danvers. He was now within a few miles of the construction camp, but the sun was bending into the western horizon, and he knew if an attempt was to be made on his life, it would probably be at dusk in the marshland just ahead of him.

It had occurred to McCarthy that there was something strange in Fred Hanley's decision to send him for the company payroll on a day when the trains were not running. Normally two or three heavily armed men went to Carson to accompany the payroll back by railroad car.

"The men are getting nervous about not being paid," Fred Hanley had said. "We can't wait for a day when the train's be runnin'. Besides, Mac, with your reputation no one'll mess with ya."

Judd McCarthy had the reputation of being one of the most violent men in Carver County. It was a reputation he had earned in numerous bar fights and wrestling matches during his two years as a laborer for the Hanley Brothers Construction Company.

He was a huge man, well over six feet tall, and his wide muscular shoulders easily bore the weight of the large canvas payroll bag. His hands were large and callused from years of hard labor in heavy construction projects. Only his eyes betrayed a gentleness and sensitivity that contradicted his otherwise menacing appearance. There was a twinkle of life and good humor in his large brown eyes, even as they moved apprehensively over the surrounding terrain.

Signs of Indian summer were all around him. The stubble of recently harvested wheatfields poked out of the parched earth. Dead leaves, propelled by steady autumn breezes, hopped and skipped across newly plowed fields. Hen pheasants clucked contentedly in the nearby brush, while an occasional cock pheasant emitted a shrill mating call that echoed across the desolate Midwestern landscape. In nearby sloughs and ponds, muskrats busily stockpiled reeds and fallen branches. And overhead a V-shaped formation of Canada geese flew gracefully southwards.

McCarthy paused briefly to watch the geese as the V-formation slowly opened and closed high overhead. Their loud honking echoed across the Midwestern prairies.

"Damn, if me soul don't feel like going south like that," McCarthy blurted out in a thick Irish accent. "But Kate said it's time to do somethin' else with me life. An' she's right."

The thought of Kate reminded him of the present he had brought back from Carson, and he reached into the front pocket of his canvas overalls and pulled out a small golden locket. The tiny piece of jewelry almost disappeared in his huge, callused palm.

As he admired the golden locket, he remembered the wrestling match in Carson. While he was waiting for the payroll to arrive, Farmer Tobin had challenged him to a wrestling match, winner take all. Tobin was the strongest man in Carver County, stronger and bigger even than McCarthy.

But McCarthy had managed to stay out of Tobin's hammer-lock long enough to wear him out. When it was over, Tobin was flat on his back, unable to move.

"Ah, Tobin," McCarthy laughed to himself as he admired the golden locket, "Ya ugly Norwegian. Ya jus ain't no match for an Irishman, lad. But I thank ya for the money to buy a locket for me Lady Kate." The thought of Kate brought the gentleness back into McCarthy's brown eyes. "I made a promise to ya, Kate, an I mean to keep it. Above all else, Judd McCarthy means ta keep that promise. I loves ya, lass, more'n anything else in the world."

He carefully placed the small locket back into his pants pocket, and again his dirty leather shoes crunched through the gravel and small rocks alongside the railroad embank-ment. Ahead of him, on both sides of the railroad tracks, was the last marshland he would have to pass through before reaching the wheatfields just outside of Danvers. He was almost home. He knew that Kate was waiting for him farther south, by the banks of the Little Sioux River, but first he would have to leave the payroll with the company paymaster and collect his wages. Then he was free.

"Got a locket for me darlin', for me darlin' Lady Kate." He sang the chorus of an old Irish folk ballad and then suddenly stopped as he entered the fringes of the marshland. The railroad company had been negligent in caring for the Little Sioux Line, and the weeds and brush grew almost to the edge of the railroad trestles. McCarthy proceeded cautiously, his right hand never more than a few inches from the .45-caliber revolver.

Suddenly there was a movement in the brush ahead of him. McCarthy stopped instantly, his right hand drawing the revolver out of the leather holster.

"Who be it there?" he yelled into the reeds and brush. "If ya be waitin' for me, ya best come out or get yur head blown off!"

The dried reeds swayed slowly back and forth on the fringe of the marshland, but there was no response to McCarthy's challenge. Slowly he knelt on the edge of the railroad embankment, his eyes never leaving the dried brush where he had spotted the movement. He picked up a huge rock and stood back up to his full height.

"I be warnin' ya. If ya don't come out, ya'll be a mighty sore lad!" he yelled again into the marsh.

Still there was no response. Suddenly McCarthy fired the rock into the brush and a shrill screech pierced the autumn air. There was a brief flurry of movement where the rock had entered the brush. Then there was again stillness and silence.

McCarthy crept up to the edge of the marsh and slowly, cautiously parted the reeds with his huge hands. In the middle of the dried vegetation a cock pheasant lay prone on the ground, its neck broken from the impact of the rock. The pheasant's eyes blinked twice, then remained open.

"Ah, no, me beauty. I only meant ta scare ya, not ta kill ya." McCarthy lay the revolver down on the ground and gently stroked the beautiful red and brown feathers of the cock pheasant. Beneath his hand he felt a convulsive movement in the animal's chest, then a shutter as the pheasant breathed its last and died.

"I only meant ta scare ya, lad," McCarthy repeated softly and sadly as he felt the bird stiffen and die beneath the stroke of his huge hand.

A few yards away, in the waters of the marshland, the early evening crickets began to chirp contentedly and a frog leaped off a fallen log and splashed into the shallow slough. McCarthy heard these sounds as he stroked the dead body of the cock pheasant.

McCarthy dug out a hole in the dark black soil with his sharp hunting knife and placed the bird in it. Then he piled dirt and weeds over the dead pheasant, picked up the revolver and canvas bag, and walked back to the railroad embankment.

The sun was dipping into the western horizon when McCarthy stepped out of the marsh and entered the wheatfields a few miles outside of Danvers. He paused briefly to watch the sun cast its shadows across the stubble of the wheatfields. In the distance, the Little Sioux River was curling southwards across the prairie. He remembered that Kate was waiting for him down by the river, and he walked faster in the direction of Danvers.

It was then that he saw something standing in the shadows of a small clump of trees a few hundred feet to the east of the railroad embankment. As McCarthy looked in that direction, a sudden gust of wind caused the dead autumn leaves to wave wildly in the thicket and tumble out into the prairie.

McCarthy's hand reached instinctively for the handle of the .45-caliber Smith and Wesson revolver. Something was hiding in the shadows of the trees. As McCarthy drew the revolver out of the leather holster and pointed it in the direction of the clump of trees, a human figure stepped out of the shadows and waved to him. McCarthy recognized who it was immediately, and he replaced the pistol.

He walked down the railroad embankment, entered the stubble of the wheatfield, and approached the figure. . . .

But it did not end there. It was days later. Maybe weeks. Maybe even months. It did not matter. Surrounded by the impenetrable darkness, time ceased to exist. Except as measured by his failing strength, his dying will.

At first he lashed out frantically, until the blade of the hunting knife shattered. When that failed he fired the revolver into the darkness. He watched the orange flames spit out of the barrel as the muffled gunshots echoed harmlessly all around him. Still it did not end.

And each time he fell, the rats would scurry over to sniff at his mildewed clothing. Bolder they became with the passage of time, until he would lash out with the butt end of the knife, sending them scurrying back into the darkness. But always they came back. Relentlessly. And he grew weaker.

Sometime, near the end, he heard the scream. Loud and shrill, it echoed in the darkness. First in anger, then in agony. Growing weaker as his strength failed him. When it too failed, he again heard the soft padding of tiny feet scurrying about in the darkness. Moving ceaselessly. Relentlessly.

When the end came, he was lying face down. The rats sensed that he had lost his will, his strength. He heard them padding softly across the ground to where he lay. They sniffed at his clothing and brushed against his cheek. Then a sharp pain tore through his arm like a thousand needles penetrating the flesh. But he was too weak to care. And he lay there, enduring the pain until it turned into a moist numbness.

As the life poured out of his body, he was filled with rage at the horror of how he had been duped. And even as his life yielded to the darkness that surrounded him, his soul held firm against the night and refused to accept what had been left undone.

It was then that he thought of the locket. He reached towards his pocket to see if it was still there. But the numbness had spread over his entire body and his arm would not move....

II

When Judd McCarthy failed to return to Danvers with the payroll, the Hanley Brothers Construction Company sent a search team out after him. At first they assumed McCarthy was the victim of foul play, but when no body was found alongside the Little Sioux Railroad, they concluded he had fled into the Dakotas with the payroll. A reward of $5000 was posted and McCarthy became a wanted man.

To the men who worked for Fred Hanley, McCarthy's disappearance was not exactly unexpected. He was a drifter, a man who lived for the moment, and it was not surprising that he would seize an opportunity to become wealthy, wealthy beyond their wildest dreams. The men on the construction crew cursed him because his disappearance with the company payroll meant they would not be paid for three months of work, but they also felt that Fred Hanley should have known better than to send a man with McCarthy's reputation after the payroll.

Within weeks after McCarthy's disappearance, the Hanley Brothers Construction Company abandoned the Little Sioux Water Reclamation Project. Fred Hanley moved to the East Coast, where he retired and lived for the next ten years until his death in 1936. Ben Hanley simply disappeared somewhere in Florida. Some of the construction workers stayed around Carver County for several weeks, hoping that McCarthy might yet return with the long overdue payroll. Then they too drifted away. Soon the memory of Judd McCarthy faded and his disappearance was forgotten by all except a few of the men who had worked for Fred Hanley and who decided to stay in the Danvers area after the company folded. The mystery of McCarthy's disappearance became only a minor footnote in the larger history of Carver County.

The Little Sioux Railroad line that connected Danvers and Carson was abandoned in 1927. As the seasons changed and the years passed, the vegetation alongside the railroad embankment crept steadily towards the railroad tracks. By 1930 the vegetation had buried the rusty tracks.

For thirty-three years the seasons passed with monotonous regularity. In winter the wheatfields were buried beneath the glistening white snows. In spring the waters of the Little Sioux River would break free from the ice-covered lakes farther north and drift slowly southwards towards the Mississippi River and the Great Sea beyond. In summer the tiny heads of grain would dance playfully above the wheatfields that now grew almost to the very edge of the abandoned Little Sioux Railroad Line. And in late fall, Indian summer would settle over the marshlands and newly harvested fields of wheat and corn, and the Canada geese would fly overhead in V-formation on their annual pilgrimages southwards.

The Great Depression of the 30s wiped out most of the farmers along both sides of the Little Sioux River, forcing entire families to abandon their farms to follow their shattered dreams westwards to California and Oregon. World War II and the Korean War came and went, and, by October of 1959, so much history had passed through Carver County that the name Judd McCarthy was buried in the memories of all but a few of the old-timers.

Like the thousands upon thousands of itinerant laborers who had passed through the Midwest in the 1920s and 30s, Judd McCarthy and his mysterious disappearance became a forgotten issue, another of the eternal secrets buried beneath the prairie soil. Certainly his life carried with it no special significance for most of those who continued to live in Carver County into the middle of the twentieth century.

But Judd McCarthy had made a promise in October of 1926 before he journeyed from Danvers to Carson. And, more than anything else, Judd McCarthy meant to keep that promise.

Chapter Two

I

October, 1959

When Joel Hampton awoke his body was drenched in a feverish sweat and his wife, looking puzzled and frightened, was staring down at him. She was shaking him by his shoulder.

"Huh?" he managed to whisper through dried lips. His eyelids were sleepy and heavy. They opened, then slowly closed again.

"Joel, wake up!" Susan insisted. She seemed to be calling to him from far away, pulling him out of the darkness. "You're having that nightmare again."

"Nightmare?" The word itself was only faintly recognizable to him.

"You're talking in your sleep."

Slowly he pushed himself up to a sitting position. His eyelids blinked twice, then remained open. "The nightmare?" He was beginning to remember.

"Yes," Susan said, the concern evident in her voice.

"Did I do it again?"

"Yes, Joel. God, you scared me half to death."

He knew then why she was afraid. He had been having the same nightmare since he was a boy. It had stopped during the years that he was in high school and college, but as soon as he became a junior partner in the law firm the nightmares started again. It was always the same. He was walking alone, somewhere out in the country. It was autumn and colorful leaves waved in the wind and blew out into the empty fields. He was happy, but he was also apprehensive about something. Something that was lurking out there in the shadows of a group of trees. Then he took a step out into an empty wheatfield and suddenly he was surrounded by darkness. There were strange noises in the darkness, strange and threatening noises that he did not understand. Then he felt pain and fear and he heard the scream as his body grew numb. The scream grew louder and louder and . . .

As a boy he would awaken to look up into the eyes of his mother. She would be staring down at him, looking puzzled and frightened. Now it was his wife who had pulled him out of the darkness.

"I'm sorry," he said to Susan gently as he looked into his wife's dark eyes. "What did I say?"

"You didn't say anything. You just started to sweat and then you began to scream, Joel . . ." Susan Hampton paused to sit up on the edge of the bed.

"Yes honey?"

"You've got to stop working so hard," she said wearily. "I know it's your first year in the firm and you feel you have to prove something to the others. But you can't kill yourself in the process. You're just trying to do too much."

"It isn't the firm, Susan. I've been having that nightmare for years, ever since I was a boy."

"Then I think it's time you see someone about it. Someone who can help you figure out what it means and why it keeps coming back to you."

"What are you suggesting?"

"I don't know . . ."

"Mommy!" The voice of a child drifted into the bedroom and Susan and Joel Hampton glanced toward the open doorway.

"Just a minute, Aggy," Susan yelled out to the hallway. "I'm coming."

Before she could push herself away from the bed, Joel reached over and grabbed her gently by the forearm. "Wait. Why have you started to call her Aggy?"

"It's just a nickname. The kids in the neighborhood

couldn't pronounce Seneca or Angela, so they scrambled the two together and came up with the nickname Aggy. She seems to like it."

"Mommy," the little girl's voice implored again from somewhere beyond the open doorway.

"I don't like it," Joel said firmly. "I think it's wrong to saddle her with a nickname when she's only four years old."

"Mommy, I'm hungry," the little girl pleaded.

"I'm coming, honey," Susan yelled in the direction of the open doorway. Then she looked again at her husband. "It's a harmless nickname. Besides, she'll outgrow it. But, Joel, please do me one thing."

"What's that?"

"See someone about that nightmare. There must be some reason why you've been having it for all these years." She kissed him gently on the cheek.

Joel watched the white linen nightgown and the flowing black hair disappear through the open doorway. After six years of marriage, he was still proud of his wife's radiant beauty.

Then he kicked back the covers with one foot and looked towards the bedroom window. The window had been left open an inch or two and a slight autumn breeze drifted lazily into the room, lifting the blue curtains as it passed over the window sill.

He walked over to the open window and pulled down hard on the shade. As the shade clattered upwards, light streamed into the bedroom. He stretched mightily as he looked out at the autumn landscape and felt the cool breeze against his bare skin.

In the east the sun was hovering above the horizon, pouring light through the autumn leaves that hung from the trees surrounding the house. He thought of how very much he loved autumn. He loved the colors and the sense of passing that he felt in the cool autumn breezes. Sometimes he thought of moving West, to Arizona or California, where he wouldn't have to face another winter. But he knew he would miss the autumns in the Midwest. More than that, he would miss the small towns. The thought of living in a large city made him claustrophobic.

Below him, he heard the sounds of activity in the kitchen. The clinking dishes, mixed with the quiet chatter of mother and daughter, drifted up into the bedroom. The sounds gave him a pleasant domestic feeling, and he knew that he was happy to be married.

As he walked toward the bathroom, he checked the clock on the bedstand; it was 7:30. He had to be in court by 9:00 to argue the Mallory case. Thomas Mallory had driven into the back end of a police car while he was drunk, and the county was trying to take his driver's license away. Since Mallory was a salesman, Joel planned to argue that this would be excessive punishment, since it would deny Mallory his livelihood and create undue hardships for both himself and his family. It wasn't exactly Clarence Darrow and William Jennings Bryant arguing the theory of evolution, but it was a start. As the junior partner in the law firm, he received the cases no one else wanted to argue.

In the bathroom, he quickly brushed his teeth and washed his face. As he was starting to shave, he heard the sound of footsteps on the carpet outside the bathroom door.

"She wants to watch you shave," Susan announced as she stepped into the bathroom carrying a little girl. Seneca had coal black hair and an impish grin on her face.

"Hi Daddy," she announced as she studied the strange assortment of brushes and colognes and shaving equipment scattered over the bathroom counter.

"Hi, honey," Joel replied as he leaned over to kiss her on the cheek. Then he applied the thick white shaving cream to his rough beard.

Susan set the girl on top of the bathroom counter and left.

Seneca studied her father as he moved the safety razor carefully through the white shaving cream. "Can I do that too?" she asked.

"Shave?"

"What you're doing, Daddy."

"Honey, little girls don't shave. They don't have to."

"Why?"

"Because they don't have beards."

"I want a beard, Daddy."

"Okay." Joel pressed the button on the aerosol can of shaving cream and squirted the white foam into his daughter's open palm. "Now rub it into your face."

"Like this?" the little girl asked as she smeared the white foam over her cheeks and into the long black locks that curled over her ears.

"Yes, just like that," Joel said as he finished the last swipe with the safety razor and inspected his chin in the mirror. Then he rubbed the green after-shave lotion slowly over his face.

"Me too, Daddy," the little girl insisted.

"This?" He held out the bottle to her. "You want some of this?"

"Yes, me too."

He poured the lotion into his open palm and rubbed it gently over his daughter's cheeks. Then he stepped back and studied her black hair, which was matted with white shaving cream. "You're a mess, Seneca," he laughed as he reached for a towel to wipe her off.

"My name is Aggy, Daddy," she said as she leaned over to admire herself in the mirror.

"Seneca!" he announced firmly. "I don't want you calling yourself Aggy. Do you understand me?"

"My name *is* Aggy," the little girl insisted as she turned away from the mirror and looked back at her father. Her eyes were wide and teasing.

He had seen that look before. But where? Or was it the name? Something in his daughter's eyes suddenly made him both fearful and angry.

He grasped the little girl by her tiny shoulders and spoke to her in a strong, menacing tone. "Don't you ever call yourself by that name again! Do you understand me, Seneca?"

"You're hurting me, Daddy," the little girl said, beginning to cry.

"Your name is Seneca! Repeat it!" He was breathing heavily now.

"Daddy!" the little girl moaned and sobbed.

"Repeat it!" he insisted fiercely.

"Aggy, come down here and finish your breakfast!" Susan Hampton's voice suddenly drifted into the bathroom from the parlor below.

His wife's voice made him realize how hard he had been squeezing his daughter's tiny shoulders with his huge hands. She was sobbing hysterically.

"Oh, honey, I'm sorry!" He pulled her close to his naked chest and tried to comfort her, but she wiggled out of his grasp and ran quickly out of the bathroom, still sobbing quietly to herself.

Within a few seconds, Susan stepped into the open doorway of the bathroom. "What happened?" she asked, puzzled.

"She . . . she got into the shaving cream," Joel stammered. "I punished her. I was probably too hard on her. I guess she's upset with me."

"Oh," Susan said complacently. She was accustomed to many such tear-filled experiences with her young daughter. "Hurry down. Your breakfast is ready," she said to Joel, then walked quickly out of the bathroom.

As Joel Hampton studied his features in the bathroom mirror, he took a deep breath and sighed nervously.

What was wrong with him? Was he going crazy?

He shuddered as he looked away from the mirror. For a few seconds, a moment earlier, he had felt as though he could actually strangle his own daughter. The thought terrified him and he shuddered again.

II

As Joel drove towards the County Courthouse, he decided that maybe Susan was right. He *had* been working too hard. He would have to speak with Jim Morris about taking a few weeks off. Perhaps he could go up north with Susan and Seneca? Rent a cabin, do some fishing, just be together. He hadn't taken a day off since he had joined the firm almost a year earlier. Surely he was entitled to a vacation after all that time.

The County Courthouse was on the other side of Kenyon. Large oak and willow trees hovered over both sides of the narrow streets that twisted through the Midwestern community. The red and yellow leaves flashed past the windows. He was trying to concentrate on what he planned to tell the judge about the Mallory case, but he found his mind drifting back to Seneca and the scene in the bathroom earlier that morning. He felt terribly guilty about what he had done. Seneca had kissed him good-bye, but not with her usual wet-lipped love and exuberance.

As the leaves continued to flash past the windows of the car, he forgot completely about the Mallory case. There were other things of much greater importance than defending a drunken salesman. The red and yellow leaves mesmerized him, sent his mind reeling backwards to a time long, long ago.

Who was he then? What was he doing? It was all out there, just a few inches beyond his reach. And yet he could not grasp it. It constantly eluded him.

He drove past the County Courthouse and continued down the narrow, two-lane road toward the empty fields in the surrounding countryside. Then he parked on a narrow shoulder next to an empty wheatfield, climbed out of the car, and looked out over the countryside. *It was out there, somewhere.*

He stepped off the gravel road and walked out into the empty wheatfields. . . .

It had started in a place something like this. Autumn. An empty wheatfield. And a thicket of trees colored with red and yellow leaves. Who was he then? Where was he going? What had happened to him? He was singing and he was happy. Someone was waiting for him. That's why he was happy. But who? But there was someone else too. It was almost night and something in the grove of trees was waiting for him. Still he felt no fear. Apprehension maybe, but not fear. Why? And then there was the darkness and he felt real fear. Fear because he was so helpless. And there were the strange, mysterious sounds in the darkness. And the screams. Oh God, the screams! But it had started in a grove of trees. And he was someone else . . .

Later, when he looked at his watch, it was four o'clock. In the distance the sun was falling into the Midwestern prairies. He knew then that he had been wandering all day among the empty fields looking for something he only vaguely remembered from somewhere in his past.

He had never made it to the County Courthouse. Mallory had probably lost his driver's license and he, Joel Hampton, was most likely out of a job.

What was happening to him? He was going insane. Now he was certain of it.

III

When he returned home, Susan was already cleaning up in the kitchen. A small bowl of peaches and an untouched plate of pot roast and potatoes were on the kitchen table.

"Hi, honey," Susan greeted him. "Did Jim Morris get ahold of you?"

"Morris?"

"He called right after you left. He told me to tell you the Mallory case had been postponed until Friday. He said there was no need for you to hurry into the office."

"Did he call back?"

"No," Susan replied, somewhat puzzled. "Didn't you talk to him?"

"Yes," he lied, not wanting to explain to her what had happened to him that afternoon. "I just didn't know if he had called back. I spent the day at the law library." He looked around the kitchen and the adjacent living room. "Where's Seneca?"

"I put her down early," Susan said as she placed a plate of food in front of him. "She hasn't been feeling too well. She didn't want to go outside all day. She spent the afternoon upstairs in the attic playing in her doll house. I think she's coming down with something."

"Did you call the doctor?" he inquired as he toyed with his food and looked out the window at the oak trees. The departing rays of sunlight were flashing through the dead leaves.

"No. I thought I'd wait until tomorrow morning to see if

it's anything serious. One of these days those tonsils will have to go. But I don't know if now is the right time, even though Dr. Lawler thinks we should do it as soon as possible."

He remembered the leaves waving back and forth in the wind. Orange and red and yellow and brown leaves twisting listlessly next to a small road. Or was it a road? No, it was more of a . . . hill of some kind. And he was walking. Walking beneath a clear blue sky . . .

"Did you hear me, Joel?" Susan looked away from the dishes she was washing in the kitchen sink. Joel was staring out the window, seemingly mesmerized by the autumn leaves swaying listlessly in the oak trees. "Joel?"

"What?" he replied without taking his eyes off the oak trees.

"I asked if you thought we should let Dr. Lawler take Aggy's tonsils out. He's been after us to do it for a couple of months now."

It was an oak tree and it was early morning. She was swinging under the branches of the oak tree as the sun caught her golden hair and her laughter rang out.

"Joel, are you all right?" Susan walked over to the kitchen table and studied her husband's face as he continued to stare out the window. "Joel . . ."

She had on a white dress but her back was turned toward him and he could not see her face. But she giggled as she threw herself into the clear blue autumn sky and the ropes creaked against the overhanging branch of the oak tree.

"Joel, what are you talking about?"

He remembered it. How could he forget that name? It was burned into his soul. . . .

"Joel?" Susan implored her husband as she shook him by the shoulder.

"What?"

"Who is Katharine?"

Joel slowly turned and looked into his wife's eyes. "*Katharine?*" he asked, puzzled.

"You were just talking about someone named Katharine. You repeated the name three times."

"Katharine?" Joel glanced in the direction of the oak trees, then quickly looked back at his wife. "I don't know anyone by the name of Katharine."

"You repeated her name three times."

"I don't remember..."

"Joel, are you seeing another woman? Is that what's been wrong with you?"

"Of course not, Susan. Why do you ask?"

"You just haven't been yourself lately. Your attitude towards Aggy and me.. Well, it just isn't the same."

He pulled her close to him. "There's no one else, honey. I must have been daydreaming."

"I still think you should see someone, Joel. Sometimes I feel like I don't even know who you are anymore. You seem like a different person."

"In what way?"

"In little ways. You seem so frustrated. And when you start repeating another woman's name, what am I to think?"

"You're right about one thing, Susan, but it doesn't involve another woman. Today I decided that we're going to take a vacation. Go up north, get a cabin. Just you and me and Seneca. It'll be beautiful up there this time of year. I was thinking about it and you're right. We need a vacation."

"Is that a promise?"

"Yes."

"I'd like that," she whispered to him as she leaned against his shoulder.

Joel glanced quickly out the window as the last rays of sunlight streaked through the autumn leaves. Then there was darkness.

The promise? He remembered that too. The darkness and the screams and the soft footsteps padding around ceaselessly, relentlessly in the night. But most of all he remembered the promise....

IV

Susan Hampton knew there was something terribly wrong as soon as she opened her eyes and reached over to where her husband should have been sleeping. The warmth of his body still clung to the sheets and she could smell his after-shave lotion on the crumpled pillow next to her. But as the moonlight filtered through the half-opened window, she could see that Joel was not in the semi-darkened bedroom or adjacent bathroom.

She sat up in the bed cautiously, leaning on one elbow as she gazed into the darkness. Something was definitely wrong. She felt her stomach tighten as she slowly pushed herself out of bed and crept toward the open doorway leading into the hallway. Below her there was an eerie silence. She paused briefly outside of Aggy's room. A small battery-powered night light glowed weakly in the far corner of the room, illuminating three rag dolls that were propped up against the wall. Susan paused beside the crib and placed her hand gently on the sleeping child's chest. The little girl was breathing strongly beneath her gentle touch.

Susan carefully placed another blanket over Aggy. Then she walked back out into the darkened hallway. She crept cautiously over to the narrow staircase that circled into the parlor below. On the main floor, a weak light filtered out of the living room and spread across the oak floor of the parlor.

"Joel, are you down there?" she whispered into the darkness. "Are you all right?"

When there was no response, she walked slowly and cautiously down the winding staircase, peering constantly into the shadows and the darkness. At the bottom of the staircase, she paused and looked apprehensively around her.

Then she crept slowly toward the open archway of the living room. Joel was sitting in an easy chair with his back towards her, a dim light glowing on a small table in front of him.

"Joel, what are you doing?"

As Susan took three steps into the living room, Joel lifted himself slowly out of the easy chair and turned to face her. She paused abruptly, horrified as he raised a large butcher knife slowly in his right hand. As the light gleamed off the long blade, she bolted quickly back into the parlor and raced up the winding staircase. She swept Aggy up out of her crib and ran back out into the hallway, then climbed another flight of stairs into the attic. She slammed the attic door shut behind her and quickly threw the bolt lock into position. She leaned against the door for a moment, panting.

"Mommy," the little girl whispered sleepily as she rubbed her eyes and stared into the darkness of the attic. "Where are we?"

"Sh, honey, just be quiet," Susan admonished her daughter. She tried to control her own breathing so she could hear the sounds on the other side of the doorway. But she could hear nothing.

The moonlight filtered gently through a gable window at the other end of the attic, illuminating children's toys that were strewn across the wooden floor. A large dollhouse, big enough for a child to play inside, was hidden in the shadows between two large rafters.

Susan leaned closer to the doorway and listened to the sounds on the stairway below. Suddenly the silver blade of the butcher knife splintered through the thin wooden panels of the old door. The knife was quickly extracted, then it flashed again through the wooden panels.

She heard her husband's heavy breathing on the other side of the doorway.

"Mommy, I'm scared," the little girl whimpered as she pressed her face into her mother's neck.

Susan Hampton ran across the wooden floor to the large doll house and pushed her daughter through the open door. Then she crawled in after her.

"Mommy!" the little girl whimpered again.

"Hush, honey, you mustn't cry."

"What's wrong with Daddy?"

Susan held Aggy close to her as the sound of the butcher knife slashing into the door grew louder and more frenzied. Then, unexpectedly, the sounds ceased altogether.

Susan peered through one of the windows of the dollhouse, expecting the attic door to come crashing down at any minute. But the heavy breathing on the other side of the doorway had ceased, and the only sound was the occasional whisper of wind whistling gently around the chimney.

"Go to sleep, honey. Pretend this is all a game. Won't it be fun to sleep in a dollhouse?" Susan said, trying to steady her voice as she placed Aggy's head in her lap.

As the little girl whimpered off to sleep, Susan Hampton kept her eyes focused on the tiny door at the other end of the attic.

V

Susan awoke as the first rays of sunshine filtered through the tiny windows in the gables of the attic. Aggy was asleep beside her. Somehow the little girl had found a doll and was cuddled up to it on the wooden floor.

Being careful not to awaken her, Susan crawled through the narrow opening of the dollhouse and walked over to the door. The thin panel of the door was destroyed by knife slashes. Susan cautiously opened the rusty bolt and stepped out onto the steep stairway.

She couldn't hide in the attic forever. Sooner or later she'd have to face him.

She walked cautiously and silently down the steps toward the parlor on the first floor of the house.

As she peered around the corner into the living room, she saw Joel sprawled out next to the brick fireplace. The knife blade had shattered against the hard stone, but he still clenched the handle firmly in his large right hand.

On the floor next to him, one of Aggy's rag dolls lay crumpled in a heap. Its stomach had been slashed open and the stuffing was strewn across the living room floor.

Chapter Three

I

"Joel," Susan called softly across the living room to where her husband lay collapsed next to the fireplace. "Joel, are you all right?"

Joel stirred, then sat up slowly and looked around the room. There was fear and confusion in his eyes. "What happened?" he finally asked, looking first at the knife handle and then at Susan. "What am I doing down here?"

"You had a nightmare again last night." Susan sat down on a nearby couch and nervously clenched and unclenched her hands, trying to remember that this was the man she'd loved for eight years, a kind and gentle man. "You came down here and did this in your sleep," she said, gesturing around the room.

Joel's eyes moved slowly around the room, surveying the damaged furniture and the chunks of mortar and rock that had been chipped out of the stone fireplace. Then he looked again at the handle of the knife in his open palm. "Did anyone get hurt?" he asked, his voice hollow with fear.

Susan shook her head slowly. "Joel, you have to see someone about those nightmares." She started to sob as she spoke. "We just can't go on like this, not knowing what . . ."

"Mommy," a voice suddenly called from the staircase behind her. "Are you okay?"

Susan quickly composed herself and looked up. Aggy was staring at her from between two of the wooden bannister poles. "Yes, honey, I'm okay," Susan said reassuringly. "You go back to your room. Mommy will be right up."

Suddenly the little girl's eyes grew wide as she spotted the mutilated remains of the rag doll on the living room floor. "Mommy, what happened to Tina?" she shrieked as she raced down the stairway into the living room. She stared in horror at the mutilated doll, then gently picked it up off the floor. "Tina, Tina!" she cried hysterically, clutching it.

"It's okay, honey," Susan said as she picked up the little girl and hugged her. "It was an accident," she stammered unconvincingly. "Mommy will get you a new doll."

"Tina's dead, Mommy," Aggy cried as Susan carried her back up the staircase.

Susan tried to comfort her daughter, but each time Aggy looked down at the crumpled remains of the rag doll, she would start sobbing hysterically. "Tina's dead and Daddy did it," she whimpered.

II

Outside Ned Finley's office, an autumn storm was whipping the oak trees into a frenzy of activity. A light mist had settled over the dead grass and fallen leaves in the small park next to the County Health Center. As the mist fell, it collected on the rear window of Finley's office, and tiny rivulets of water streamed down the glass pane, dissolving the autumn scene in the park outside. A poor caulking job enabled the water to seep through the sash, and soon two tiny puddles of water formed on the window ledge.

Doctor Finley was seated at his desk. Behind him, he could hear the steady dripping of water as it collected around the window ledge and either fell to the oak floor or rolled down the plaster wall. Finley had long ago given up on trying to patch the leak in the window. He was content to mop up the puddle on the oak floor whenever it rained.

Light and shadows intermingled throughout the comfortable clutter of the room. Finley was a collector of things, not in the traditional sense of those enthusiasts who have a patterned and disciplined need to collect stamps or coins or rocks. Finley was a collector of junk. Even he would not find a pattern to the many objects that littered his office walls and floor. Small stuffed birds and predatory animals, ancient muskets and ammunition pouches, old books and magazines, a turn-of-the-century thermos jug—these and other worthless objects were scattered randomly throughout the room.

Finley lived by the axiom that "an organized man is a dull man." He preferred his surroundings to be cluttered, full of surprises and mysteries. He liked to think his office reflected the human psyches he worked with every day. They too were full of hidden surprises and mysteries, possessing depths unfathomed by even the most skilled psychologist or psychiatrist. But this too was a rationalization. The truth of the matter is that Finley was a bit of a slob—and he just liked junk.

Finley's appearance was equally unconventional. He was an exceptionally tall man, well over six feet, with prematurely snow white hair. He refused to wear suits, preferring instead comfortable old sweaters and tan cotton pants, complemented by an ancient brown beret he had won from a drifter in a buck euchre game. Finley was convinced the beret gave him a rakish look, and he wore it constantly. But, in moments of candor, his friends informed him that the beret made him look like a lost seaman in search of his ship. Finley liked that image of himself even better, and he continued to wear the beret at all times, even indoors.

He studied the face of Susan Hampton who was sitting on the other side of the desk. In two decades as a clinical psychologist, Finley had become a keen student of human nature. At the nearby Farmington State Mental Hospital, he had worked with all forms of deviant behavior, ranging from mild paranoia to criminal insanity. He prided himself on his ability to size people up quickly. Normally his first impressions were accurate.

Susan Hampton, he had decided, was a beautiful young woman of poise and stability, but also one who had never before been exposed to the darker side of life. Perhaps that was for the best, he thought. God chooses to spare some people the real agony of human existence so their innocence can serve as a beacon to others who have been hardened by time and circumstances. As one who had spent a good part of his life working with the mentally ill, Finley found it occasionally refreshing to share the company of those who remained relatively unscathed by the traumas of human existence.

"Does your husband have any previous history of mental illness?" Finley asked gently after they had exchanged small talk and he was certain she was comfortable in his presence.

"No."

"Is there anything in his family history that reflects abnormal behavior?"

"Not that we know of..."

"Anything..."

"Dr. Finley, I should explain that Joel was adopted. We know nothing about his real mother or father. His adopted parents were very secretive about his past."

"Where are they now?"

"Joel's adopted parents?"

"Yes."

"They're both dead."

Finley glanced briefly at the light autumn storm that was rattling the window casing behind him. Then he looked again at Susan Hampton. "Tell me *precisely* what your husband has been doing that makes you think he needs psychiatric help."

Susan sighed deeply. "Well, first of all there's the nightmares. He had them as a boy and he's starting to have them again."

"What kind of nightmares?" Finley asked.

"It's always the same one."

"Has he ever described it to you?"

Susan nodded. "He says he's walking out in the country. It's autumn and he's surrounded by empty fields and groves of trees. He remembers the colors of the leaves and he's happy. Then he starts to feel apprehensive about something. Suddenly he takes a step out into one of the empty fields and he's surrounded by darkness and strange, threatening noises. He feels fear and pain. Then he starts to scream. That's when he wakes up, or I wake him up."

Finley made several notations in a small, blue notebook. "You say he had this nightmare as a boy?"

"Yes. When he joined the law firm, about a year ago, the nightmare started again."

"Has your husband been under a lot of pressure in his new job?"

"Yes."

"That could account for part of it," Finley mused. "You indicated in your phone call that there are other things your husband has been doing lately that concern you. What are they?"

"Joel came home later than usual last night. I had already put Aggy to bed. . . ."

"Aggy?"

"Our daughter."

Finley nodded. "Go ahead."

"When he left for work that morning, he was kind of strange. He was still strange when he came home that evening."

"Strange in what way?"

"It was as if he were locked up inside of himself, almost in a trance. He just wasn't the same towards Aggy or me."

"Was he angry or frustrated? Did he display any outward signs of resentment or aggression?"

"No. It was more like he was in a trance. Almost . . . like he didn't know what he was doing or who he was. I was washing the dishes and Joel was sitting by the kitchen table toying with his supper. He was staring out the window at the trees. Then he mumbled something like, 'Katharine, what happened?' I couldn't hear the rest of it. He mumbled the name Katharine twice more. When I asked him what he had said, he looked dazed. I asked him who Katharine was and he said he didn't know anyone by that name."

"Maybe he was daydreaming?"

"At first I thought that might be the case, but it happened again just this morning. He was looking out the living room window at the trees—something in the dead leaves seems to trigger it. He had his back to me when I came down the staircase, but I distinctly heard him ask the same question, 'Katharine, what happened?' He denied it, but I know I heard him mention that name again."

"Does your husband know *anyone* by that name?"

"You mean, does he have a girlfriend?"

The question surprised Finley. His first impression of Susan Hampton was that she was one of the innocents of the world, perhaps too naive and vulnerable to want to admit that possibility to herself. Yet she had not hesitated at all to confront the unthinkable. "Yes," he asked gently. "Do you think your husband has another woman?"

"No, I'm almost positive that he doesn't."

"Was there anything else?" Finley asked.

"Only that last night I awoke to find Joel missing. I found him in the living room. He had destroyed some of the furniture and was passed out on the floor."

"Has he ever threatened to harm either you or your daughter?"

Susan toyed with the idea of telling him what had happened in the attic, but decided against it. She still found it hard to accept that her husband could have done that. "No, he's never threatened to harm either of us," she stammered.

Finley paused thoughtfully. "Your husband is not epileptic or subject to convulsions is he?" he finally asked.

"No, he's in perfect health."

"Would he be willing to come in to see me?"

"Yes, I think so. He promised me this morning he would come in if I arranged an appointment."

"Bring him by tomorrow. About four o'clock, if you can. And in the meantime, see if you can find out anything more about Joel's adoption—any papers or pictures that he might have in the house."

Susan promised she would and left the room, and afterwards Finley sat at his desk for a time toying with a ballpoint pen and pondering his conversation with her. He dropped the pen and it rolled over to a plastic paperweight next to a note pad. Inside the paperweight, imprisoned in a plastic cube, an eagle raised its wings in a seemingly futile effort to launch itself into the sky. Finley studied the paperweight briefly, then walked to the window.

The mist had stopped falling from the gray sky, but the wind still rattled the window casing. Outside the window, dead leaves were hopping and skipping across the park. Finley watched the leaves as they skimmed over the dead grass and were caught against a concrete retaining wall.

III

As Joel drove home from work that afternoon, he thought of his upcoming vacation. Jim Morris had told him there would be no problem, just so long as he waited until later in the month when the Mallory case and several other smaller lawsuits had been settled. Morris had even suggested that they use his cabin on Lake Salizar, some 120 miles north of Kenyon. Lake Salizar would be beautiful in late autumn. It would be quiet and peaceful—a perfect place for the three of them to take long walks and go on picnics.

Joel knew Susan would be pleased. In the meantime, he decided he would stop the nightmares by taking sleeping pills. He knew that both Seneca and Susan had been terrified by whatever had happened the previous night. The memories in his own mind were vague. He remembered moving around in the darkness and he remembered lashing out at something hard, but then, suddenly, it was morning and Susan was calling to him from across the living room. Susan wouldn't tell him exactly what happened, but she was still terrified. That was obvious.

Joel parked his car next to the small drug store. He bought some non-prescription sleeping tablets that were guaranteed to produce "eight hours of comfortable sleep in any adult male or female." He also picked up a big box of gumdrops for Seneca. They were her favorite. Susan wouldn't let her have them very often, because of her teeth, but this was kind of a special occasion. He wanted Seneca to forgive him. Hopefully the candy would be an effective bribe. Joel loved his little daughter so much he couldn't bear the thought of her being mad at him.

As he walked to his car, Joel remembered that Susan also needed some reassurance from him. If he had some small present to give her, at the same time he told her about the vacation, perhaps that would make her feel better.

There was a small jewelry store several shops down from the drug store. He knew that Susan wasn't much for fancy jewelry, but maybe a small charm or ring would please her? At the very least, it would show her that he still cared, that there was no one else in his life.

He studied the watches, charms, necklaces, and earrings in the window. Probably an inexpensive pair of earrings would be the best present? She already had a beautiful watch. He had given it to her as a wedding present. He'd had it inscribed, "With love always." Maybe the earrings? Or perhaps a charm? Or even a locket?

A locket? Once . . . he had bought a locket. No, he had won it. Somehow he had won a locket and was bringing it back with him as a present. And he was singing a song. A locket for . . . He could almost hear the song. It had been a long time but he still remembered the melody. . . .

"Mommy," a voice behind him said, "who's that man talking to?"

Joel turned to find a small boy pointing at him. "Now, Peter," his mother admonished him, "you mustn't point at people. It's terribly impolite. Come along now." The woman grabbed her small son by the hand and pulled him down the street. The little boy's head turned and looked curiously back at Joel as his mother dragged him down the sidewalk.

Embarrassed, Joel turned again to study the window. *So he had been talking to himself. About what this time?*

His mind made up, he entered the jewelry store. A short, elderly man was standing behind the glass-enclosed counter next to a cash register. He was tinkering with the mechanism of a large, pendulum-operated clock. "Yes?" he asked, smiling cheerfully at Joel. "What can I do for you today?"

"That gold locket . . . in the display window," Joel explained nervously, pointing toward the front of the store. "How much is it?"

The clerk walked quickly over to the front window and removed the locket from its black felt pad. "This one?" he asked, holding it up as he walked behind the glass counter. "This one retails at $170, but, for you, $130."

One hundred thirty dollars? Had it cost him that much? He had never made that much money in his life, except maybe once or twice gambling. He worked with his hands then. He was strong. Very strong. He had won the locket with his hands and his strength. But who was he then?

"Say, are you all right?" the clerk asked suspiciously.

"What?" Joel asked as he reached for the locket. He held it gently in his hands.

"Nothing. You looked very pale there for a moment. I thought maybe you were going to pass out."

"How much did you say this was?" Joel asked, still admiring the locket as the chain dangled from his open palm.

"One thirty. It's genuine fourteen karat gold. See, on the back." The clerk reached for the locket to turn it over.

What happened to the locket? He had won it and he was going to give it to someone. He knew the name... But something happened. Something terrible. And he was never to get there....

Joel stepped back from the glass counter. His huge, sweaty palm encircled the tiny piece of jewelry protectively as he glared back at the clerk.

There was always someone. Everytime he tried to... But not this time. This time he would do it. No one would stop him....

"Hey, where are you going with that?" the clerk asked as he scrambled around the glass counter and positioned himself between Joel and the front door. "You can't take that out of here without paying for it. There are laws. The police will arrest you."

He had a knife and a gun. So why was he afraid? There was nothing to be afraid of... What was that? The loud ticking of a pocket watch. It didn't work too well and... She was going to buy him a new one. She said his made too much noise. And he was going to get her the locket. But then there was the darkness. He heard the watch ticking away in the darkness. Tick. Tick. Tick. Tick. It was driving him insane. He could not stand the loud ticking. He had to stop it. He put the watch on the ground and stomped on it with his leather boots. Still the ticking did not stop. Tick. Tick. Tick. Tick. He held his hands up to his ears to shut out the relentless ticking of the pocket watch....

"You're drunk, right? You're drunk! Or are you crazy?" the jeweler asked excitedly as Joel stood with both hands raised to cover his ears. On the counter, the large clock chimed merrily away. "Either you give me back that locket and get out of here, or I call the police," the clerk threatened.

Joel slowly lowered his arms and unclenched both fists. He held his hands out, palms upwards. As he did so, the clerk snatched the locket and quickly retreated behind the glass counter.

Joel paused to study the lines in his open hand. He had clenched the small piece of jewelry so hard that the imprint of the locket was sharply outlined in his sweaty palm.

"Now get out of here, or I call the police!" the clerk shouted. "Out! Out!"

Joel's eyes moved slowly around the small store. Then he walked toward the front door.

This wasn't the place. It was something like this. But, no, this was not the one. The other store had the smell of tobacco hanging heavily in the air. And there was a card game in the back. At first, he had thought of joining the card game, but he knew he would not leave until the money was gone. And he had made a promise to buy the locket. That much he knew for sure. The rest was confusion and pain and an impenetrable, lonely darkness. . . .

IV

The next afternoon Susan Hampton escorted Joel into Dr. Finley's office. Finley exchanged small talk with them until he felt Joel had relaxed enough to discuss his problems. On the surface, at least, Joel Hampton appeared to be in complete control of his moods and emotions. But Finley knew that appearances could be deceptive.

"Joel," Finley said, "your wife tells me you've been under some stress lately. She also tells me you've had temporary blackouts and losses of memory."

Joel looked cautiously at his wife, then back at Finley. "Well, I have felt some stress, yes," he replied blandly. "But I suspect it's the same with every young lawyer who's first starting out."

"Do you remember having temporary blackouts?"

Joel looked again at his wife. "Yes," he admitted. "But I don't know what importance to place on them. I think they're more daydreams than blackouts."

"Your wife tells me you've been having the same nightmare ever since you were a small boy. Tell me, does this nightmare ever intrude on your waking hours?"

"In what way?"

"Are you ever walking along and suddenly visual impressions from this nightmare flood into your mind? In other words, do you have the nightmare when you are awake as well as when you are asleep?"

"I don't know," Joel confessed sheepishly.

"What do you mean?"

"I daydream a lot. And sometimes I can't seem to control the daydreams, but I don't know if they're connected to the nightmare. I don't remember what I daydream. I remember the nightmare vividly."

Finley made several notations in the blue notebook in front of him. "Joel, does the name Katharine mean anything to you?"

"No," Joel responded emphatically.

"Your wife tells me you have mentioned the name Katharine while you were daydreaming. Do you remember any of those times?"

"No, I think that's a figment of Susan's imagination," Joel said, looking at his wife reassuringly. "I know absolutely no one by the name of Katharine. I never have."

Finley paused to make more notations in the blue notebook. As he did so, Joel patted his wife's hand comfortingly. Then the movements of the dead leaves in the trees outside the rear window caught his attention and he stared wistfully in that direction.

"Joel," Ned Finley said quietly as he looked up from his notebook, "how would you feel about seeing me on a regular basis? At least until we can get to the source of these nightmares and daydreams you've been having. We might even try regressive hypnosis. . . ."

As Finley spoke, Joel Hampton's gaze fixed on the dead leaves waving in the wind and tumbling across the yard.

Then he remembered it. It was a long, long time ago,

next to an oak tree like the one outside the window. A young woman in a swing glided gracefully back and forth, propelled by some unseen force behind her. She wore an old-fashioned white dress. He could not see her face because her back was turned toward him. But she laughed as the sunshine sparkled off her golden blond hair and she soared gracefully through the autumn sky, propelled higher and higher by some unseen force. . . .

"Come, *Katharine*, we must go!" There was a note of urgency, almost panic in Joel Hampton's voice as he reached for his wife's hand.

"What did you just call your wife?" Finley quickly asked.

"I told *Katharine* it was time for us to go!" Joel's response was firm, almost menacing.

"Joel, you just called your wife Katharine," Finley replied softly.

Joel Hampton glanced in disbelief, first at Finley, then at his wife. Then he stood and stalked out of the room.

V

Joel took one of the sleeping tablets that night, but still he was unable to sleep. Instead, he tossed and turned until the sheet was wet beneath his body. The sun was already filtering through the eastern window of the bedroom when he finally fell asleep.

As his eyelids closed, he felt the same frustration. It was out there, just beyond his reach. If only he could . . .

He remembered it again. The girl with the golden hair and the white linen dress soared higher and higher into a blue sky, propelled by some unseen force behind her. The sunlight sparkled off her hair and her laughter rang out as she soared back and forth in graceful arcs. Then the swing turned into a piece of jewelry, swaying back and forth on the end of a large gold chain, like a huge pendulum, while a clock ticked loudly in the background. Two large hands reached through the gold chain as though to strangle someone. Then a

*door slammed and there was complete darkness. A scream
pierced the darkness and grew louder and louder....*

VI

The next day, when he walked into Finley's office, Joel
Hampton was obviously frightened and exhausted. Finley
made him comfortable in a reclining easy chair and then
listened carefully while Joel related the details of his latest
nightmare.

Afterwards, Ned Finley asked him gently, "Joel, have
you ever heard of regressive hypnosis?"

"Isn't that where you take someone back through the
various stages in their life?" Joel Hampton asked nervously.

"Yes. If these things you've been seeing in your dreams
are a part of your past, maybe we can find them. Maybe we
can also find out who Katharine is."

"How does it work?"

"Through the powers of suggestion and concentration.
You must allow your mind to be totally relaxed while I create
an image of time. You must concentrate completely on that
image as I describe it to you."

"Okay."

"Joel, your wife tells me something in the dead and
dying leaves seems to trigger these nightmares you are
having in your subconscious mind. So I want you to relax
completely while I describe for you the seasonal changes in
a single tree. Do you understand me?"

"Yes."

"I want you to picture this tree in fall. I want your
imagination to provide color and detail while I describe the
tree to you. I want you to create the strongest visual impression possible. Do you understand me?"

"Yes," Joel Hampton answered softly.

"Joel, it is mid-autumn and this tree is filled with leaves
of all different colors. There are orange, brown, red, and
yellow leaves waving in the breeze. Some of them tear loose

from the tree and blow away with the wind, but most of these leaves sway gently in the light breezes. Orange, brown, red, and yellow leaves swaying against a blue sky. Can you see them?"

"Yes," Joel Hampton whispered.

"Concentrate on the leaves," Finley said soothingly. "Orange, brown, red, and yellow leaves swaying in the autumn breezes. Swaying ever so gently in a blue sky. Orange and brown and red and yellow leaves swaying against a blue sky. Do you see them, Joel?"

Joel Hampton took a deep breath and sighed, "Yes, I see them . . ."

"They are swaying, swaying against a blue sky," Finley said softly as he leaned over to switch on a tape recorder. "Orange and brown and red and yellow leaves . . . Allow yourself to relax completely, Joel."

Joel Hampton sighed but did not speak.

"Now, Joel, we are going backwards in time. I want you to visualize the seasonal changes in the leaves on the tree, only in reverse order from fall to summer to spring to winter. We are going to reverse the seasonal cycles. Do you understand me?"

Again Joe Hampton did not speak.

"The oranges and reds and browns and yellows are now changing and blending together, Joel. They are very gradually turning into a deep green as the white clouds drift faster and faster overhead against the blue sky. The leaves are turning the deepest, darkest green against the blue sky and they are filling the tree, covering the branches and swaying in the breeze. Huge summer leaves turning a dark green beneath a blue sky. Do you see them?"

Finley looked closely into the face of Joel Hampton. "Yes, I see them," Joel whispered.

"Now the leaves are turning a lighter green as the clouds move rapidly overhead and the sun moves backwards across the sky from west to east. As the sun moves more and more rapidly across the sky from west to east, the leaves on the tree shrink in size and turn a light green. Then they fold into the branches on the tree and disappear. Now it is winter and the tree has no leaves. It stands alone in an empty field. Can you see the tree standing alone in an empty field in winter?"

"Yes," Joel Hampton whispered softly.

"Good," Finley said gently as he quickly took Joel's pulse, then placed his arm back on the side of the black reclining chair. "Now, I want you to see how fast you can make the leaves on that tree change color as the seasons move in reverse order from autumn to summer to spring to winter to autumn again. Make your mind work to change the colors of those leaves as the clouds float rapidly by overhead and the sun swirls around the earth from west to east. Make them go faster and faster, Joel. Red and orange and brown and yellow leaves turning dark green, then light green, then disappearing into the branches of the tree and reappearing as red and orange and brown and yellow leaves . . ."

Ned Finley reached for the microphone on the tape recorder and placed it on top of the reclining chair within inches of Joel Hampton's head.

"The sun is moving across the sky and the changes in the leaves are taking place so fast that the colors are becoming a blur, a spinning whirlpool of color that blends together as it sucks you into its depths. Do you see the spinning whirlpool of colors on all sides of you, Joel?"

"Yes," Joel whispered sleepily.

"Now, I want you to reach out to stop the whirlpool, Joel. I want you to stop it momentarily while I ask you some questions. Just place your hand against the spinning wall of colors."

"Yes."

"What year is it, Joel?"

Joel Hampton paused momentarily. "1950," he finally said.

"Where are you in 1950?"

"College."

"What is your name?"

"Joel Hampton."

"Did you know a Katharine in 1950, Joel?"

Joel Hampton hesitated for a moment. "No."

"Did anything happen to you in 1950 while you watched the autumn leaves blow away in the wind?"

"No."

"Then let's go back further yet. Start the whirlpool of color spinning again, Joel. Make it spin faster and faster until the colors blend together and you are sucked deeper and deeper into the swirling tail of the vortex. Make it spin faster and faster, Joel." Finley paused momentarily, then peered closely again into the face of Joel Hampton. "Now, stop the whirlpool. Stop it and tell me what year it is."

"1935," Joel Hampton whispered almost incoherently.

"1935, okay, you're a young boy. Did you know anyone by the name of Katharine in 1935?"

"No."

"Are you standing next to a tree filled with dead leaves?"

"Katharine," Joel whispered sleepily.

"Did you know a Katharine in 1935?" Finley asked, leaning forward and listening closely.

"Katharine? No."

"Then start the whirlpool spinning again. Make the reds and browns and oranges and yellows of the autumn leaves change to a dark green, then light green, then disappear altogether as you are sucked into a prism of color, moving closer and closer toward the center of the vortex..."

Finley glanced briefly out the window at the light mist that was settling on the dead grass. Then he turned his attention back to Joel Hampton.

"Joel, I want you to stop the whirlpool again. Stop it from sucking you deeper into the vortex. What year is it?" Joel Hampton mumbled something and Finley leaned closer to hear him. "What did you say, Joel?" Finley asked.

Joel Hampton did not respond.

"What year is it?" Finley asked again.

"1926," Joel whispered softly. "October, 1926."

"October of 1926," Finley said, leaning even closer to the reclining chair. "What is your name in October of 1926?"

"No name. I have no name..."

"Who is Katharine, Joel?" Finley asked.

Her blond hair caught the golden rays of sunlight as they filtered through the red and orange and yellow leaves in the oak tree overhead and she arched higher and higher into a blue sky. Her laughter echoed across the landscape as she threw her head back and held on tightly to the ropes of the swing as her feet almost touched the dead and dying leaves on the lower branches.

"Who is Katharine, Joel?" Finley repeated.

"Kate, Kate, me lass," Joel suddenly blurted out cheerfully, his voice taking on a thick Irish accent. "You are such a lady."

"Who is Kate, Joel?" Finley asked eagerly.

"Such a lady . . ."

"What is your name?" Finley asked again. "Who are you? What happened to you in October of 1926?"

"Ah, Kate, ya just tamed the toughest man in Carver County," Joel replied tenderly, still with a strong Irish accent. "Have ya no pride, girl?"

"Joel, who are you talking to? Where are you in October of 1926?"

His shoes crunched through the gravel and the rocks while he walked beneath a clear blue sky. Walking and singing beneath a clear blue sky . . .

"Got a locket for me darlin', for me darlin', Lady Kate," Joel Hampton whispered slowly, dreamily. Then he chuckled softly to himself.

"What happened to you in October of 1926?" Finley asked.

"Ah, Kate," Joel whispered dreamily.

"What happened to you in October of 1926, Joel?" Finley repeated the question.

The leaves were blowing off the trees and drifting into the nearby fields while the crickets chirped contentedly behind him. The sun was drifting into the western horizon and he heard the sound of water. He took one long step and then there was darkness. A deep, impenetrable darkness and a scream that rose up out of the darkness and grew louder and louder and . . .

VII

That afternoon Ned Finley met Susan Hampton in the playground behind the elementary school where she occasionally worked as a substitute teacher. Overhead, the first of the Canada geese were flying southwards in V-formation. Their honking sounds echoed across the playground and mingled with the sounds of children laughing and playing.

"Did you find out anything at all about Joel's adoption?" Finley inquired, as a volleyball bounced across their path.

"Nothing. The Hamptons must have destroyed the adoption records. All I found was this. In a box of old baby clothes that belonged to Joel."

Susan Hampton handed Finley a large envelope that had yellowed with age. The return address in the upper left hand corner had been torn off, though the names "Mr. and Mrs. Tom Hampton" were still legible on the face of the envelope. The address of the Hamptons on the front of the envelope was also smeared and illegible.

Finley extracted a lock of hair and an old sepia photograph of a farmhouse from the envelope. He examined them for a few seconds, then placed them back into the envelope.

"When a child is adopted, aren't the permanent records sent to the state capital?" he inquired.

"I would think so. But aren't they sealed?"

"Maybe a court order would release them?" Finley paused momentarily to watch the Canada geese pass overhead. "Susan, what do you know about Carver County?"

"Only that it's some miles northwest of here. Why?"

"I put Joel in a hypnotic trance yesterday and took him back to 1926. He said he lived in Carver County in 1926."

"Joel wasn't born until 1927, Doctor."

Ned Finley stopped watching the geese and looked directly at Susan. "I know!"

Chapter Four

I

The red granite walls and turrets of the Farmington State Mental Hospital rose out of the Midwestern prairies like an ancient Gothic fortress. Built out of granite blocks hauled by horses from the quarries in nearby Archer County, Farmington had served as an asylum for the mentally ill and the criminally insane since the early 1850s. Somehow, in spite of its Gothic design, Farmington had managed to blend into the surrounding landscape during its one-hundred-and-ten years of existence. Nonetheless, residents throughout the adjacent communities eyed the red granite walls and turrets with suspicion. The lost souls of the insane who had been housed there for over a century still roamed through the basement catacombs of Farmington and haunted the nearby farmlands at night, or so it was rumored. Tales of the hideous deeds of these madmen were still told around hearths and coal stoves in the surrounding farms and small towns.

Ned Finley pushed hard on the heavy oak doors of the hospital and stepped out into the bright sunshine. He paused momentarily at the top of the steps to view the beauty of Indian summer as it settled lightly over the countryside. Then he walked down the long flight of granite steps and crossed the lawn toward a far corner of the hospital grounds where a small, elderly man was busily examining and rearranging the vines that clung to one of the tall granite walls. Aurther Schlepler was totally preoccupied with his work and did not turn to acknowledge the approaching footsteps.

"Your plants look healthy today, Aurther," Finley said at last, after watching the old man inspect the vines.

"They are dying. Any fool can see they are dying," Schlepler responded impatiently, as though not wanting to be disturbed.

"They look healthy to me," Finley repeated somewhat sheepishly.

"That's because you spend too much of your time probing into the depths of the human psyche, Ned," Schlepler admonished him. "You have lost touch with the essential rhythms of nature."

As Schlepler turned to face him, Finley was once again struck by how much he resembled Albert Einstein. Schlepler had the same patches of downy white hair on both sides of his balding head, and he wore a shirt and trousers that were several sizes too large for his small frame. But it was his eyes, more than anything else, that reminded Finley of Einstein. Schlepler's eyes were large, deep, full of wisdom and compassion and sadness. Aurther Schlepler was a psychic. He had carefully studied the human race for over seventy years and found it produced in him only deep sorrow. So, for the past eight years of his life he had turned to horticulture, preferring the simpler pleasures and surprises of plant life to the more foreboding and dangerous insights into the human soul.

"Aurther, I need your help," Finley said after Schlepler had turned his attentions back to the vines and dying flowers that clung to the red granite walls. "A patient of mine is having problems that don't seem to fit into anything I've ever encountered before."

"I'm retired, Ned. You know that," Schlepler said emphatically. "My plants are my life. I have seen enough of man and his capacity for evil to last me several lifetimes, not to mention the one I am now finishing and plan to complete in great peace and tranquility."

"Aurther, do you believe in reincarnation?"

"Why do you ask?" Schlepler kept his back to Finley as he spoke.

"My patient is taking on the personality of someone who lived in Carver County in the 1920s."

"Has your patient ever lived in Carver County?"

"No. He's never been there in his entire life."

"How old is he?"

"Early 30s."

"Come over here," Schlepler said. He pointed at a piece of sheet metal that separated the tendrils of a climbing vine. "See this? I have been experimenting with the growth patterns of these vines. Would you venture to say, Ned, that the tendrils of this vine have been completely separated by this piece of sheet metal?"

"They appear to be, yes," Finley said awkwardly, not knowing what was expected of him.

"Wrong!" Schlepler said, pulling away the piece of sheet metal and discarding it on the dead grass. "That is what appears to be the case on the surface. But, as you can see, the tendrils have managed to creep beneath the sheet metal by following the tiny grooves where the granite blocks are joined together. Thus, they have established all kinds of intertwining connections." As he spoke, Schlepler moved his finger carefully along one of the tendrils to illustrate his point.

"I don't understand what you are trying to tell me," Finley said, bewildered by Schlepler's explanation.

"Nature obviously never intended for this vine to be separated at this point, so it found other ways to circumvent the tiny obstacle I placed in its path."

"What does that have to do with my patient?"

"Probably nothing. I simply find it to be fascinating, that's all."

"Aurther, *will* you help me?"

"We must remember," Schlepler continued, ignoring Finley's question, "that what we see on the surface, in the present moment, is only an illusion. The reality is that all living things are connected to a common past. There are many lessons to be learned from nature, Ned, lessons that men like you should understand before you even attempt to probe into the human psyche. It is first of all a lesson in fate. These vines teach us that the barriers men place in the path of fate are ultimately meaningless, for the vines will continue to circumvent all obstacles until they have completely covered this wall. The things that are meant to be—will be. You must remember that."

"You're not going to help me, Aurther. Is that what you're trying to say?"

"The other lesson to be learned from these plants is that there is beauty in the death of the flower, for it reveals the common root from which we all sprang and the common future to which we all aspire through successive lifetimes. These plants are not yet done with their work, Ned," Schlepler said softly. "They will lie dormant for a time and in the spring they will continue to spread over this entire wall. The same is true with men when they have not finished with something in one lifetime. Let's go back to my room and discuss your patient."

Finley looked perplexed for a few seconds. Then he followed Aurther Schlepler inside. Tranquilized patients were sitting on wooden benches and in wheelchairs alongside both walls of the narrow, poorly lit corridors. Some patients stared out blankly at the two men as they passed. Others sat motionless on the edge of narrow benches and stared at the dirty floor. Still others babbled incoherently or waved their hands and fingers frantically in the air, trying desperately to communicate.

"Why do you insist on living here?" Finley asked. "Certainly you could find someplace where you'd be more comfortable." No matter how many times Finley visited the hospital, he couldn't get over the shock of seeing all these lonely, lost souls locked in their own peculiar, tormented worlds.

"Because the truly insane people are the ones like yourself, Ned. The ones living on the outside who think they're sane. I feel much safer in here with people who suffer from no such illusions about themselves."

Schlepler turned suddenly and entered the open doorway of his tiny room. A partially completed jigsaw puzzle of a landscape was laid out across the coffee table. Small potted plants and trays of seedlings were scattered randomly throughout the room, and a library of horticulture books was jammed into one corner, its contents spilling out onto the threadbare carpet that covered the floor.

"So, you think you have another Bridey Murphy on your hands?" Schlepler said somewhat impishly.

"Bridey Murphy?"

"The woman who under hypnosis remembered some previous existence in Ireland."

"I don't know," Finley admitted. "At this point, I honestly don't know what I'm working with. Most likely, there's some simple, logical explanation. But it might be something else. Something much more profound."

"What is it you want from me?" Schlepler asked, folding his hands and sitting back in his chair.

"My patient's name is Joel Hampton," Finley explained. "He's been having losses of memory which are becoming progressively more acute. During these times, he speaks of a Katharine and a life he knew earlier in the century. I finally put him in a hypnotic trance and took him back to the 1920s. He told me he lived in Carver County at that time. He talked again of a Katharine. Then he began screaming hysterically until I was forced to take him out of the trance. I was afraid there might be permanent damage if I kept him under any longer."

"And you are absolutely certain he has never lived in Carver County?"

"Yes. He has never been near it."

"What can I do to help you?"

"I have something here," Finley said, reaching into his shirt pocket and pulling out the envelope Susan Hampton had given him earlier. "His wife found this. I just want you to see if you can tell me anything about his past by studying these."

Finley dumped the lock of hair and the faded picture of the old Victorian farmhouse on the coffee table. He placed the envelope next to them.

Schlepler closed his eyes and gently held the lock of hair in his right palm. After several seconds he said, "This comes from a child . . . a very small child . . . he . . . he is happy . . . there is love, warmth. . . ."

"You say 'he.' Is it a boy?"

"Yes. He is surrounded by love and warmth, but he feels different. Something inside of him is not right. It is too much sadness for a child to bear."

"What about the envelope?"

Schlepler opened his eyes and carefully studied the yellowed envelope. "There is no return address on it."

"Apparently someone tore it off."

Aurther Schlepler again closed his eyes and ran his fingers lightly over the handwriting on the front of the envelope. "Oh, there is much sadness here too . . . great and overwhelming sadness . . . and pain . . ."

"Whose handwriting is it?"

"A young person . . . a young woman, I think," Schlepler said sadly. "Oh, the sadness is overwhelming."

"Is there a connection between the envelope and the lock of hair?" Finley asked, placing the lock of hair in Schlepler's open palm.

"Yes. Yes and no. There is a connection, but her life is sadness and pain. His is love and warmth."

"Joel Hampton was adopted. Could this envelope have been addressed by his real mother?"

"Maybe. There is a connection. But wait . . ."

"What is it?" Finley asked eagerly.

Schlepler paused momentarily. "Nothing. There was something else, but I no longer feel it."

"What was it, Aurther?"

"Confusion. Just confusion."

"What about the picture?" Finley asked, handing Schlepler the picture of the old Victorian farmhouse.

Aurther Schlepler placed the picture in his right palm. He studied it for a few minutes, then again closed his eyes. His kindly face grew rigid. "This is . . . oh, this is vicious . . . this is . . . horrible. . . ."

"What is horrible, Aurther?"

"This house is horrible!" Aurther Schlepler suddenly stood up, dropped the picture on the coffee table, and shuffled quickly over to a nearby window where he stood with his back to Finley. "I must finish my work on the plants now," he said tersely as he looked out the window.

"What did you see, Aurther?"

"There is so much to do before the winter frosts."

"Aurther, please, what did you see?"

"Don't go near that house!" Schlepler said firmly as he shuffled toward the doorway. "It is a place of madness! Not the harmless insanity you have seen sitting in the wheelchairs and benches just outside this room! That house is filled with a madness that destroys everything that is pure and good about life."

II

As he drove from the Farmington State Mental Hospital to his office in Kenyon, Finley ran through in his mind the salient features of the Joel Hampton case. He was well aware that what had begun as a matter of professional curiosity was rapidly becoming something far more complicated. He had an appointment with Joel that afternoon, and he wanted to bring everything he could to it in the hope of making some kind of breakthrough.

Joel's whole demeanor, he reflected, was changing, becoming increasingly sullen and morose. Frequently, as he stared out the window or focused on one of the many objects in Finley's cluttered office, he would become lost in thought and oblivious to his surroundings. At other times his eyes darted nervously around the room, like a cornered animal looking for a way out of a trap. Finley had seen that look before in those patients at Farmington who were ultimately labeled "psychopaths." He had also seen that look in the eyes of the prisoners of war he had worked with after their release from the Japanese and Korean prison camps. One could not apply psychological labels to these men. The labels simply did not fit. It went much deeper than that. These men had seen something so horrible that they themselves were driven to suicide—or to outrageous acts of violence against one another, almost as if in imitation of what they had seen and experienced. Finley saw that same look in the eyes of Joel Hampton, and he knew it signaled the beginnings of a complete nervous collapse, followed by a period of potentially violent and uncontrollable behavior.

Joel was a few minutes late for his appointment, and Finley lost no time in putting him under hypnosis. However, before taking him deeper into the hypnotic trance, he checked Joel's pulse. The pulse rate registered much too high for a man his age who appeared to be in the peak of condition and who was in a resting position. Clearly something was happening inside Joel Hampton that defied conventional psychological labels.

"Joel, can you hear me?" Finley asked, placing Joel's right arm back gently on the black arm rest of the reclining chair.

Joel Hampton did not respond.

"Joel, what year is it?" Finley asked as he checked the tape recorder. "Concentrate on the whirlpool of color and tell me what year it is."

"1933," Joel whispered, the words barely escaping from his lips.

"Good, now let's go back even further. Follow the whirlpool of color back to 1926. You live in Carver County in 1926 and you know someone by the name of Katharine. Can you tell me your name?"

Joel Hampton's lips moved slowly, but he did not respond.

"It's 1926. You live in Carver County and you know someone by the name of Katharine. What is your name?"

"No name," Joel mumbled softly.

"What are you doing in Carver County in 1926?"

"Walkin'," Joel said softly after a slight pause.

"You are walkin'?" Finley asked.

"Walkin'," he repeated.

"Where are you walkin' to?" Finley inquired gently.

"Walkin'. Walkin'. Got a locket for me darlin', for me darlin' Lady Kate." Joel suddenly blurted out the lyrics of a song in a thick Irish accent.

"Who is Kate?"

"Kate. Kate. Such a lovely lady," he replied cheerfully.

"What happened to you in 1926, Joel?"

Joel Hampton moved his lips but again he did not respond.

"Did something happen to you in 1926, Joel? What was it?"

"Killed . . ."

"Who was killed?" Finley asked eagerly.

He remembered it again. His hand reached slowly, steadily, into the dried reeds and brush on the edge of the marsh-

land. The beautiful red and brown bird was lying in the middle of the dead vegetation. He stroked its magnificent plumage. The bird gasped and shuttered and died under his gentle stroke . . .

"Who was killed?" Finley repeated.

"Killed . . . killed," Joel whispered softly.

"What happened to you while you were walking in 1926?"

"Cock pheasant," Joel whispered sadly. "Killed 'em with a rock."

Finley paused. "Where are you walking to, Joel?"

There were sounds all around him. The crickets chirped contentedly in a nearby pond and a frog leaped off a fallen log and splashed into the shallow water. Overhead, the Canada geese honked loudly as they flew southwards. Dead leaves rustled in the nearby trees and he was walking. Walking beneath a clear blue sky.

"Who is Kate, Joel?"

"Such a lady . . ."

"Were you killed while you were walking in 1926?" Finley asked boldly.

The thicket of trees was only a few hundred feet away from where he stood. Dead autumn leaves waved wildly in the wind and tumbled out into the open fields. Something was in the thicket of trees, waiting for him. He did not want to go over there, but his legs started walking in that direction. He stepped off a small embankment, entered the stubble of a wheatfield, and approached the small clump of trees. Don't go in there, he told himself! Two arms reached out of the thicket and gestured for him to enter it. Don't go into the thicket, he told himself again! Don't go! But he went in anyway.

"Get away! Get away from me!" Joel screamed loudly as his arms flailed out, desperately fighting the air.

"Who are you fighting, Joel?" Finley asked quickly.

"Get away from me!" Joel Hampton screamed as he sat up and looked directly at Ned Finley. "Get away from me or I'll kill you!"

"Joel, I'm Dr. Finley. It's 1959. You're okay. Please lie back!"

"I said I would kill you!" Joel repeated fiercely.

"I'm taking you out of the hypnotic trance, Joel. Your name is Joel Hampton and you are a lawyer. You live in Kenyon. You have a lovely wife and daughter." As he spoke, Finley looked deeply into the hate-filled eyes of his young patient. "Concentrate on the whirlpool of color as I count off the years. 1939, 1940..."

Joel Hampton closed his eyes and leaned slowly back in the reclining chair as Finley counted off the years.

"When I reach 1959, I want you to open your eyes, Joel. 1957, 1958, 1959..."

When Joel Hampton opened his eyes, the look in them had changed from anger to confusion. He lay back in his chair for several seconds before speaking. "Dr. Finley, am I going insane?" he finally asked softly as he stared at the ceiling.

"No, but something's going on inside of you that neither one of us understands."

"What's wrong with me? I seem to drift between two worlds. This one, and a nightmare world I only vaguely remember and have no power to control."

"I wish I could give you an easy answer. But there are none," Finley said gently. He reached into his shirt pocket and pulled out the photograph Susan had given him earlier. "Joel, have you ever seen this house before?" Finley asked, handing the picture of the old Victorian farmhouse to Joel.

Joel studied the details in the photograph, then handed it back to Finley. "No," he said, shaking his head.

"Are you certain?"

"Yes. Why do you ask?"

"Your wife found it in a box of old clothes your parents gave her. It was in an envelope with a lock of your baby hair."

Joel looked at the photograph again, then shook his head. "Nope. I've never seen it before."

Finley pushed himself slowly out of his chair and walked over to the rear window. Outside, a lone hawk was floating serenely in a clear blue sky. Finley watched the hawk soar in ever-widening circles until it gradually disappeared from sight. "Joel, do you believe in reincarnation?" Finley asked hesitantly as he searched the skies for any sign of the hawk. He turned and looked back to where Joel was sitting in the reclining chair. "Do you believe that people can live more than one life?"

"Why do you ask?"

"Because something is happening inside of you that cannot be explained by anything in the psychology textbooks. It's much more complicated than that. You . . . you seem to be taking on the personality of someone who lived thirty or forty years ago."

Joel stared pensively at the ceiling. "Dr. Finley, I know that I died once before, a long time ago."

"Do you remember who you were or how it happened?"

"No," Joel uttered softly as he turned his head toward Finley. "But I felt myself die just before you took me out of the trance."

III

Susan Hampton had just placed a tray of cookies in the oven when the telephone rang.

"Susan, this is Jim Morris," a loud, deep voice boomed across the telephone line. "Do you have a few minutes?"

"Yes, of course, what is it, Mr. Morris?"

"I've been meaning to talk to you for several days now. But I've just been too busy . . ." There was a sudden, awkward pause at the other end of the line.

"I've wanted to talk to you too, Mr. Morris," Susan interrupted him. "I wanted to thank you for giving Joel the two weeks off. We're looking forward to the vacation."

"Yes, well, my pleasure, of course," Morris stammered at the other end of the line. "Susan, can I speak to you candidly about some things?"

"Yes, of course," Susan replied nervously.

"It's about Joel. As you know, I think very highly of your husband. He's one of the best young attorneys we've ever had in this firm. And I think he has a tremendous future in front of him. But some things have happened recently." Again, there was an awkward pause.

"What kind of things?" Susan asked apprehensively.

"For the past month Joel just hasn't been himself. His legal briefs are sloppily written, he forgets appointments, and there are entire days when he doesn't show up in the office. He tells the secretary he's been in the law library, but the other attorneys in this office spend a lot of time over there and they've never seen him. I was wondering... Well, I was wondering if things were all right at home? Or, if not, if there was something I could do to help?"

"I don't know," Susan said softly. "I think Joel just needs a vacation. He moved directly from law school to the law firm without a break. I think he's just exhausted."

"I hope that's all it is, Susan. It's just... Well, listen, if there's anything I can do, anything at all, just let me know. You know how the wife and I feel about both of you. We really want to see Joel make it in this law firm."

"Thank you, Mr. Morris. We appreciate that. Incidentally, would you tell Joel to call me before he comes home from work?"

There was a nervous pause at the other end of the line. "Susan, I haven't seen Joel in this office for three days. That's primarily why I called."

"But I thought he was to argue the Mallory case..."

"I had to send another attorney over to represent Mallory. Joel didn't show up either time he was to meet Mallory at the County Courthouse," Morris said, almost apologetically.

Susan vaguely heard Jim Morris say something else at the other end of the line. Then there was a loud click and a buzzing noise as the connection was broken. She placed the receiver slowly back on the hook and sat down at the kitchen table to ponder the significance of what Jim Morris had just told her.

Had her suspicions been correct? Was Joel seeing someone else? Or was it...

She stood up quickly and walked to the foot of the staircase. "Aggy," she yelled up to the attic. "Aggy, get your things. I'm taking you across the street to play with Robin."

After dropping off Aggy, Susan drove toward the law library. She thought about her earlier conversation with Dr. Finley. She hadn't been completely honest with him about Joel's behavior. She couldn't tell him about the mutilated doll or the episode with the butcher knife in the attic. She had been too embarrassed. Or possibly she didn't believe it herself. The strong, gentle man she had married seemed incapable of such things. To reveal it would seem like she was being unfaithful to Joel.

The next time she met with Dr. Finley, she would tell him everything. Joel's career, their marriage, and possibly even their lives were obviously in grave danger.

Susan accidentally spotted Joel's light-blue, Ford station wagon next to a small city park about three miles from the law library. Relieved, she parked the Chevrolet next to it. She found Joel sitting on a bench, his eyes fixed on several old Victorian homes on the street across from the park. "Condemned" signs hung from two of them and work crews scurried around on scaffolds, tearing the roofs off.

"Joel, what are you doing here?" she asked him angrily. His gaze remained fixed on the row of Victorian homes. "Joel, answer me. Why aren't you at the office?"

He had known such love and such hate in that house. There was a windmill and two huge silos. And a large oak tree with a swing hanging from one of the branches. He had been happy there. Many times. But if he had been so happy, why did he also feel such fear?

"Joel, can you hear me? Do you know who I am?" The anger in Susan's voice had been replaced by concern. "Joel . . ."

And there was a river. As he stood on the banks of the river he could see the house in the distance. And he could hear her voice laughing beside him. Laughing as the river gurgled behind them. Why, then, did he feel such fear and anger and sadness when he saw the stately old house rising out of the prairies? What had happened there? And who was he?

"Joel, do you know who I am?"

He heard the voice pulling him out of the darkness and he looked up at his wife. "Susan?" he muttered faintly.

"Joel, are you all right?"

Joel's eyes moved slowly around the park. Then he looked up again at his wife. "What are we doing out here?" he asked weakly.

Susan sat down beside him. "What were you just thinking, Joel?"

"I don't remember."

"How long have you been here?"

"I don't know. I'm sorry, Susan, I don't know. I just don't know." He leaned forward until his head was buried in his hands and his body began to shake.

Susan felt his back muscles quiver as she ran her hand gently along his spine. Then she saw the half-empty vial of sleeping pills in the grass next to his foot. "Joel, Joel—did you take these?" She half-choked the words out.

Joel shook his head slowly without looking up at her.

"Are you sure you didn't take these?" she demanded of him.

"I was going to but I didn't have the courage," he whispered hoarsely as he looked across the park at the row of old Victorian homes.

Susan held him hard. "God, Joel, what is it? What is doing this to you?"

IV

The first thing Susan heard was the metallic pinging of the rain drops against the aluminum gutters outside the bedroom window. Then a sudden gush of cold air blasted into the room and the blue linen curtains billowed toward the ceiling. It was followed by the ping, ping, ping of tiny hail stones against the glass panes.

Susan rolled sleepily out of bed and half-walked, half-stumbled over to the open window. She pulled it down with a loud thud.

Suddenly the thunder flashed and roared in the skies overhead, sending brilliant streaks of light into the bedroom and across the empty bed. "Oh my God! Not again!" she gasped, peering nervously into the darkness of the bedroom and hallway. "Aggy," she whispered weakly as she rushed toward the darkened hallway.

The battery-operated night light glowed dimly in the corner of Aggy's bedroom and a lone rag doll slumped forlornly next to a toy telephone. Susan reached into the crib and felt blindly for the small body as the thunder again crashed overhead.

"Aggy," she called nervously to the darkness of the room as she reached for the light switch on the wall. She flicked the switch up and down several times. The lights were out. Where was Aggy?

Susan cautiously descended the staircase into the parlor. "Aggy," she whispered into the living room. "Aggy, are you in there?"

A small candle was burning in the middle of a coffee table in the living room. As the light flickered in the darkness, it fell across the form of her daughter lying on the floor.

"Aggy!" Susan cried as she rushed to her, placing her hand gently on the little girl's chest. "Aggy, what are you doing down here?" she asked, her voice relieved.

The little girl sat up and rubbed her tiny hands sleepily across her eyes. "Mommy?"

"Yes, honey, what are you doing down here?"

"I think Daddy brought me down."

Susan searched into the darkness of the living room for any sign of her husband. "Where is your Daddy?"

"I don't know, Mommy," Aggy yawned.

"Let's go back upstairs, honey," Susan said as she picked up Aggy and looked apprehensively behind her into the darkness. There was something back there. But what?

As she walked back toward the stairway, she heard it, a soft rustling noise coming from the basement. Then she heard the slow, steady sound of footsteps on the basement staircase. It was followed by the soft shuffle of feet across the linoleum kitchen floor.

As the flickering light from the tiny candle fell across her husband, Susan saw that Joel was holding a long, thin fishing knife in his right hand.

"Oh my God!" she gasped as she turned and ran back up the flight of stairs toward the attic. Behind her she heard the slow, steady sound of footsteps on the carpeted staircase.

She wrenched the attic door open and slammed it shut behind her in the same motion. She quickly slid the bolt lock into position and leaned against the nearby wall.

Almost as soon as she pulled her fingers away from the metal lock, the long, thin blade of the fishing knife slashed through the new panels of the door. The knife was extracted quickly. Then it slashed through again as the thunder exploded outside the attic window and the lightning flashed off the shiny metal blade.

Susan stumbled over toys and dolls as she carried Aggy over to the dollhouse. She pushed the little girl through the open door.

"Mommy," the little girl whimpered.

"Aggy," she said to her daughter. "Get as far in the back as you can."

"Mommy," the little girl whimpered again.

"Please, honey, do as I say. And don't say a word."

As Aggy crawled into the depths of the doll house, Susan heard the sharp, splintering sound of wood breaking behind her. An arm suddenly smashed through the thin wooden panels of the door, and a hand began fumbling with the bolt lock as the lightning again flashed across the room.

Susan shut the door of the dollhouse and quickly crawled across the attic floor to the darkness on the other side of the room. She pressed her body as close as she could into a narrow recess beneath one of the gables.

In the darkness, she could not see the door of the attic. She could only hear the creaking hinges and then the slow shuffle of feet across the attic floor. She tried to control the pounding of her own heart, but it raced wildly out of control and beat madly in the darkness.

Then she heard another sound, like a puppy crying in the night. She listened to the shuffling feet as they paused, then moved slowly toward the doll house on the other side of the room. What had first been a whimper became a quiet, uncontrolled sobbing from the interior of the doll house. Then the thunder exploded outside the gable window, and bright light flooded the room, illuminating Joel as he reached for the door of the small doll house.

"Joel, what are you doing?" Susan screamed across the room as she stood up. "What are you trying to do to us?" she sobbed.

In the darkness, she again heard the feet shuffle across the attic floor, moving in her direction. As the thunder exploded and light again flashed into the room, she saw the knife raised in Joel's hand. She began sobbing uncontrollably. With one hand she groped madly for something to protect herself. But she found only a large, locked trunk.

"What are you trying to do to us? God, what is it you want?"

Then something clattered across the wooden floor. As the lightning flashed again, she saw that the hand was empty.

"Ah, Katharine," she heard a voice with a thick Irish accent call in the darkness. "What is it ya be cryin' for, girl?"

"Joel, what are you trying to do to us?" she sobbed again.

"Ah told ya I'd be back, now didn't I?" the voice continued. "So why so sad now, girl?"

Susan felt two hands caress her cheeks in the darkness. They were gentle, loving.

"Didn't ya have no faith in me, lass?"

"Joel, please. Who are you? What do you want? Please, for God's sake . . ."

"I got a present for ya, Kate. I brought it all the way from Carson. Do ya want to see it?" The hands continued to caress her cheek.

"Joel . . ."

"It's right here," the voice continued.

Suddenly she felt one of the hands stiffen.

"I put it . . . Where did it . . ."

The tone of the voice was changing, growing more angry and menacing.

"It's . . . it's . . ." Suddenly the darkness was filled with a loud scream—a deep, mournful lament that slowly blended in with the exploding thunder outside the attic windows.

The hand was withdrawn from her cheek and the darkness quickly swallowed up the sound of footsteps as they scurried across the attic floor and descended the staircase.

Susan heard the sound of the basement door as it was flung violently open two stories below her. Then she slumped to the floor, sobbing quietly in the darkness of the attic.

V

Finley had very little to work with, only the name "Katharine" and a picture of an old Victorian farmhouse. He knew that wasn't much to start searching for someone who had possibly lived in Carver County earlier in the century, someone whose memory still lived on inside the subconscious mind of Joel Hampton.

Finley was concentrating on replaying the tapes of his sessions with Joel when Susan Hampton slipped quietly into the room. He didn't notice her at first.

"That was Joel, wasn't it?" she asked, gesturing towards the tape recorder.

"Yes," Finley said gently.

"But it wasn't his voice."

"No. It's someone else's voice," Finley agreed.

"He talks with that voice in his sleep," she said nervously. "He talks of strange people and stranger events in a voice that is not his own. Dr. Finley, what is happening to my husband?"

"I don't know, Susan. I'm going up to Carver County tomorrow to see if I can get some answers."

"I hope you find something soon," Susan Hampton said tiredly. "It's getting worse. Much worse. I haven't been completely honest with you, Dr. Finley. I don't know why. I guess there were just some things I didn't want to admit to myself."

"Such as?"

"You asked me, the first time we talked, if Joel had ever threatened Aggy or me."

Finley nodded. "Has Joel threatened you?"

"Twice now," Susan sighed. "In the middle of the night. He came after us with a knife. He was speaking in the voice you just heard on the tape recorder. He was completely out of control. We had to hide in the attic."

"Were either of you hurt?"

"No. I'm not really sure he meant to hurt us. I know that sounds insane. But he had the chance to kill me. Instead he threw the knife away and gently caressed my cheek. He called me Katharine and talked as though he had been trying to get back to see me for a long time."

"Are you willing to have him committed?"

"I don't know. I'm afraid that would destroy him."

"You have to think of your daughter."

"She's with her grandmother. I drove her over this

morning. She's safe there. I don't know if Joel would really try to hurt her. I know he won't try to hurt me. He had his chance and... Instead he expressed his love for me, or at least for Katharine."

"I'm leaving for Carver County first thing in the morning," Finley said. "I'll leave a phone number where you can get ahold of me if anything happens—but I think you should consider having him committed."

"Dr. Finley, there's just one other thing," Susan Hampton said quietly, pulling a small, folded legal document out of her purse. "I found this behind Joel's baby picture, in an old photo album the Hamptons apparently put together years ago."

Finley unfolded the document and studied its bold print. "It's the adoption certificate," he said, looking up.

"Yes."

"No father is listed, but the mother's name is Katharine McCarthy," he whispered as he looked up again at Susan Hampton.

Chapter Five

I

Ned Finley drove his 1953 Studebaker along the smooth concrete surface of Interstate 111 and turned west on the bumpier asphalt surface of County Road 16. According to the map, Danvers was approximately 55 miles from Kenyon and 45 miles from the Farmington State Mental Hospital.

A faded sign soon announced "Carver County Line." A smaller sign announced "Danvers, 10 miles." An old bum sat at the base of the sign, his legs sprawled out across the gravel embankment and his hands folded across his baggy, navy-blue trousers. His eyes and face reflected a profound weariness as he lay indifferently spread out over the gravel shoulder of the narrow road. He stared straight ahead as Finley's Studebaker passed the sign and continued in a westerly direction toward Danvers.

Most of the small grain crops had been harvested, and bales of hay and straw littered the parched fields and ditches on both sides of the narrow road. A few clusters of trees also dotted the landscape. Their colorful leaves swayed gently in the mild autumn breezes. And in some fields, the jagged, brittle stubble of corn stalks protruded above the baked earth.

Finley wasn't quite sure how to proceed now that he was in Carver County. But since Danvers was the County Seat, he decided he would start with the County Building.

As Finley approached the city limits of Danvers, he

passed a small sign that said "Danvers, pop. 212." Another sign reminded him that Danvers was the "Carver County Seat." The town itself was located between several gently sloping foothills. A church steeple, an old water tower, and a grain elevator rose high above the small village. Nearby, the Little Sioux River curled through the small foothills and prairielands.

As Finley entered Danvers from the east, the other end of town was visible as it opened up onto the recently harvested corn and wheat fields in the west. Main Street itself was laid out over no more than five or six blocks.

The buildings on Main Street were old, seemingly untouched since the early part of the twentieth century. Many of the small shops and stores were obviously abandoned, and dust had collected heavily on the display windows. A few forgotten, faded items still sat in some of the windows. Other windows were boarded up, although signs advertising the wares and services of past tenants hung over Main Street.

He stopped in the middle of the street, next to an abandoned drug store. A thin, bearded man in a blue and white shirt and a matching baseball hat was inserting a long thin pole into the frame of the faded green awning that ran the length of the drug store. Finley parked the Studebaker diagonally against the curb and stepped out of the car into the bright sunlight. He paused to look down both ends of Main Street.

There was something strange, mysterious, almost ghostly about the abandoned stone and brick shops. A strong, pervading sense of death and decay clung to the brick facades, dusty windows, and ancient signs.

As Finley looked down the street, a small brown and white mongrel dog suddenly leaped out of a nearby alley, veered sharply to its right, and raced along one of the crumbling brick storefronts. A few feet ahead of the dog, a large rat scurried along the base of the brick wall. The rat's thin, pointed tail stuck out sharply behind its fat brown body as it disappeared into a hole where a brick had fallen out of the foundation of one of the buildings.

The mongrel dog came to a skidding halt in front of the hole. It lowered its nose and barked loudly into the darkness.

Then it sniffed along the entire wall of the storefront, paused once more in front of the small, dark hole, barked again and, defeated, walked slowly back down the sidewalk.

Finley watched the dog disappear down the alley. Then he approached the man who was cranking the awning out over the sidewalk.

"Can you tell me where I might find the County Building?" Finley asked him politely. The man extracted the awning pole and turned to face Finley.

His Brooklyn Dodger baseball hat, the brim tilted upwards, shifted comically to the right side of his head. He smiled strangely at Finley and placed a stick of chewing gum in his mouth. Then, without speaking, he walked across the street and began cranking the awnings up against the brick walls.

Finley paused for a moment, puzzled by someone who would crank the awnings out over one side of Main Street and then crank them back up on the other side. There was no threat of rain. The sky was clear blue and the only clouds looked like distant wisps of smoke hanging in the north. And, even if it did rain, the awnings were obviously too tattered to offer protection.

Finley shook his head, decided it wasn't worth pondering in the first place, then looked up and down the street, searching for the County Building.

As Finley was looking down the street, an old woman shuffled past him carrying a small grocery bag. "Where might I find the County Building?" he asked her politely.

"At the end of the street," she replied cheerfully, pointing toward the largest building on Main Street. "Right down there."

"Thanks," he replied as he prepared to cross the street.

"New in town?" she asked.

"No, just on vacation. Might do a little fishing."

"Not much else to do around Danvers. Town's pretty much dead. 'Cept for us old people who find it too painful to leave."

"What happened?" Finley inquired. "From the looks of these buildings on Main Street, Danvers was once a prosperous little town."

"They opened up a soy bean factory and four huge grain

elevators over in Tyler. Pretty much killed off everything around here. Farmers shop over there now. Barney tries to keep his elevator open, but he's not making much money. When the elevators go in these small towns, everything else dies right behind them."

"Tell me," Finley said, pointing at the thin man cranking up the awnings across the street, "why does he do that?"

"Benny? Ah, don't pay no mind to him. He's retarded. They used to pay him a nickel or a dime to crank out the awnings when it rained. Crank them back up again when it was over. He probably don't even know most of these shops are closed. Anyhow, it keeps him busy and we all got to do something, now don't we?"

The old woman switched the small bag of groceries from her left arm to her right arm. "Good talking to you," she said. "Hope you have a nice vacation."

"One other thing," Finley insisted. "Have you ever heard of someone by the name of Katharine McCarthy who might have lived around here?"

"McCarthy?" She pondered the name carefully. "Nope. Not too many by that name in Carver County. Irish settled quite a bit north of here."

"You're sure you've never heard of a Katharine McCarthy?"

"Nope. Sorry," she said, walking away.

The County Building was constructed out of red brick and even redder granite blocks. Unlike the other buildings on Main Street, the County Building had pillars next to the arched portico. Above the portico, an American eagle clenched a bronze flagpole firmly in its beak, and its sharp talons gripped a stone ledge protruding out of the brick wall. Someone had neglected, however, to place a flag at the end of the dark green pole. A flag flew instead in the upper right-hand corner of the building, next to a stone nymph reclining on the wall just below the roofline.

"Yes?" a fat, middle-aged man with thick glasses asked as he looked up from the yellowish-brown pages of an old ledger lying on the counter inside the County Building.

"Is this the County Recorder's Office?" Finley asked.

"That's what the sign says, now doesn't it?"

"I need some information. Birth certificates, death certificates, anything like that on a Katharine McCarthy who might have lived in Carver County in the 1920s or earlier. Do you have that information here?"

"Well, if she was born here or died here, I might have it. When was she born?"

"Sometime between 1890 and 1915, I would think."

"You don't know the exact date?"

"No."

"Are you a relative?"

"No, I'm doing a genealogy," Finley lied, knowing the man would never believe the truth.

"Well, wait here a minute," the County Recorder said. He walked toward a huge steel vault in the back of the room.

"Thanks," Finley said.

"Katharine who?" the County Recorder yelled back as he paused at the entrance to the vault.

"McCarthy," Finley said loudly. "Katharine McCarthy. I think she was born sometime between 1890 and 1915."

After the County Recorder had disappeared into the steel vault, Finley stood by the front desk and let his eyes wander over the small room behind the counter. A large photograph of a distinguished, white-haired man in a dark blue business suit was prominently displayed on one of the walls. Finley was trying to remember where he had seen the photograph before when the County Recorder stepped out of the steel vault. He was carrying a large brown book.

"No Katharine McCarthy ever born in this county," he said, flopping the book down on the counter. "Course that don't mean nothin'. Records weren't that good back then."

"Were there *any* McCarthys born in Carver County around that time?" Finley asked.

"Let's see," the Recorder said, paging through the thick volume. "There was a Kevin McCarthy born in 1906. And a Jody McCarthy born in 1903. None of the mothers' names is Katharine. That's about it. Not too many Irish in Carver County. Mostly British and Scandinavians, even to this day."

"Did either of those two McCarthys die in Carver County?"

"Well, now I don't know. I'll have to check the death certificates. Just a minute," he said, disappearing again into the steel vault.

"While you're back there, would you check to see if a Katharine McCarthy was ever married in Carver County?" Finley yelled after him.

The County Recorder reappeared in a few seconds carrying two large brown books. He flopped the larger of the two volumes on the oak counter and began paging industriously through it. "No one named Katharine McCarthy was ever married in Carver County," he proclaimed, scratching the top of his head and pushing his large eyeglasses farther back on his nose.

"How about the death certificates?" Finley asked.

The County Recorder flipped through the pages of the second book. "Well, it says here this Jody McCarthy died three days after he was born. Diphtheria. An awful lot of that back then."

"And the other McCarthy?"

"Kevin McCarthy? Let's see. Killed in a farm accident in 1919. Fell out of a silo and broke his neck. That's a shame. Those silos can be awfully dangerous."

"That would make him thirteen," Finley speculated. "You have nothing on a Katharine McCarthy dying in Carver County?"

"Nope. But like I said," the County Recorder repeated, shutting the second volume and setting it carefully on top of the other two books, "it don't mean nothin'. A Katharine McCarthy might've lived in Carver County back then. But unless she was born here, died here, or married here, we'd have no record on her. Might not even have a record on her then. People weren't quite so particular 'bout filing legal documents back in those days."

"Where else might I look?"

"Well, I can think of two places. You could try the high school. She might have graduated from Danvers High. In which case her picture would be up there someplace. Or you could try the hotel. Some of the old boys over there might've heard of her."

"Can I go up to the high school on a school day?"

"No such thing as a 'school day' anymore. Young people in Danvers, at least what's left of them, are bused over to Tyler. Be movin' the county seat over there soon. Probably turn Danvers into a ghost town."

"Danvers seems awfully small to have been the county seat in the first place."

"It was."

"Then how come it became the county seat?"

"That fella over there on the wall, John J. Sylvester," the County Recorder said, pointing toward the large picture Finley had studied earlier. "He had a lot of political pull back in the 20s. Became governor in the 30s. Good man, John Sylvester. One of the best to come out of Danvers."

II

Joel Hampton was driving to work that same morning when he saw the little group of pre-school children on their hands and knees frantically peering into a storm sewer. Fearing that maybe one of the children had somehow fallen into the sewer, Joel parked his car and walked over to them.

"What's wrong?" he asked as he approached the group of children.

"Samantha's puppy," the oldest boy said as he pointed down into the dark hole. "It fell down there."

Joel knelt down and peered into the darkness of the storm sewer. A tiny, shivering ball of fur was curled up on a concrete ledge some five or six feet below the surface of the street. Below the ledge, a stream of dirty water flowed sluggishly across the concrete floor of the sewer.

"Stand over there on the sidewalk," Joel said to the children. "I'll see if I can pull the grate off."

As the children retreated to the safety of the nearby sidewalk, Joel leaned over and curled his large fingers around the heavy iron grate that covered the sewer opening. He pulled hard on it, but it would not move.

He paused for a moment, then curled his fingers around the grate and lifted again. This time the grate groaned against its iron housing and slid off onto the asphalt surface of the street. The group of children edged closer to peer into the dark hole.

"Now, stay away," Joel admonished them as he lowered

himself onto the iron ladder that was bolted into the concrete wall of the sewer. "I'll be right back."

Joel climbed down the ladder until his feet were resting on the last rung, some six or seven inches above the dirty stream of water. Then he reached out and gently lifted the puppy off the concrete ledge. He stroked and comforted the puppy as he stood on the bottom rung of the ladder. . . .

He had worked with animals before. A long time ago. He had delivered a tiny foal as the mare lay dying on the straw-covered floor of the barn. He had pulled the foal out of the mare with his bare hands. Then he had cleaned it and wrapped it in a heavy blanket and held it tight against his chest as the mare gasped and kicked and died and the blood flowed thick on the floor of the barn. . . .

"Is he okay?" a tiny girl's voice asked nervously overhead, outside the sewer opening.

"Ya, he be okay," Joel answered, his voice taking on the strong Irish accent. "He jus' be plenty scared, that's all."

Joel placed the tiny puppy in his coat pocket and climbed back up the iron ladder. A fresh breeze blew gently across his cheeks as he stepped out of the damp sewer. He sat down on the edge of the sidewalk and dangled his feet in the dark hole.

"Ya see," he admonished the girl gently in the Irish accent, "ya shouldn't be takin' a young pup like this one away from its mother. He ain't even been weaned yet."

"Can I have him?" the little girl asked as she reached out with her tiny hands.

"Inna minute, lass, but first ya gotta promise me ya won't take him out again. Not 'til he's older."

"I promise," the little girl said, still reaching for the puppy.

"Wait, lass. First I gotta know the names of these hooligans here. What be yur names now?"

"Samantha. . ."

"Bobby. . ."

"Alan. . ."

"Frances. . ."

The children obediently gave out their names as Joel pointed at each one of them.

"Well, Samantha an' Bobby an' Alan an' Frances, those

be some mighty pretty names. An' what be the pup's name?"

"He doesn't have a name yet," the little girl who had identified herself as Samantha answered shyly.

Joel handed her the tiny puppy. "Now you leave him home 'til he has a name and gets bigger. Ain't no one should go out in the world without a name."

"Thanks, mister," the older boy said.

"You're mighty welcome, lad."

The group started to leave. Then the older boy turned and asked boldly, "What's *your* name, mister?"

His name? He should know that. That very simple thing . . .

"My name?" Joel was uncomfortable with the question.

"I want to tell my mother," the boy said, "in case she asks."

"I don't know . . . I don't know, lad. I'm sorry. Jus' take care of the pup now. Ya hear?"

The older boy looked puzzled. Then he turned and walked after the rest of the group.

Joel pulled his legs out of the sewer and stood up. Then he leaned over and lifted the grate off the asphalt road. This time it seemed lighter, almost light enough to pick up with one hand.

He easily slid the grate over the hole until it fell with a dull thud into its iron housing. Then he peered through the grate at the sluggish stream of water flowing at the bottom of the sewer.

A name? That simple thing. Everyone had a name. Yet he could not remember his. He knew only that it had been a long time ago. And he was someone else. And he had once delivered a foal while the mother died and the blood flowed thick on the straw-covered floor of a barn. . . .

III

The thick metal door opened with a loud groan and Finley stepped into a dark hallway lined on both sides with dark green metal lockers. His footsteps echoed in the empty hallway as the door groaned shut behind him.

The hallway of the high school was lined with glass trophy cases. Two neat rows of black-and-white graduation pictures hung on the walls above the trophy cases.

Finley walked slowly down the hallway, studying the faces and names of the graduating classes from earlier in the century.

"What year did you graduate?" a voice behind him suddenly asked.

"What?" Finley asked, turning quickly.

A thin, bald-headed man with a half-filled bucket of water in one hand and a push broom in the other stood in the middle of the hallway. "I asked you when you graduated from Danvers High School," he said, setting the bucket of water on the floor.

"I never went to school here," Finley responded.

The janitor paused and pulled a cigar butt out of his front shirt pocket. "If you didn't graduate from Danvers, how come you're studying those pictures so carefully? Only reason people come back here anymore is to look at their graduation pictures. Or to point out their names on one of the trophies over there."

"I'm looking for someone. Someone who might have graduated from Danvers High School forty or fifty years ago."

"What's the name?" the janitor asked, lighting the cigar butt and puffing hard on it.

"Katharine McCarthy."

"Nope," he proclaimed emphatically, waving the cigar butt at the pictures on the wall. "Been dustin' those pictures for over twenty years. Never seen anyone by that name up there."

"Ever hear of *anyone* by that name living in Carver County?"

"Nope. Never even heard of a McCarthy livin' in Carver County." He leaned the push broom against the wall. "Like ya to see somethin', though."

The janitor walked over to one of the trophy cases in the middle of the hallway. Finley followed closely behind him. The trophy case was built into the wall and framed with four pieces of oak trim stained to the color of walnut. Several athletic trophies were located behind two sliding glass doors. The janitor carefully removed a slight smudge from one of the glass doors with a large rag he carried in his back pocket. Then he stepped back, puffed on the cigar, and admired his handiwork.

"See that?" he asked, pointing at the trophies behind the sliding glass doors.

"Which one?" Finley asked.

"That one there," the janitor said. He pointed the cigar in the direction of one of the trophies. "The one with the basketball player on top."

"Yes."

"Danvers won the regionals that year. 1937. Made it to the state basketball tournament. My boy was on that team. He was the captain."

"You must have been proud of him."

"Yes. I was. He was killed in World War II."

"I'm sorry," Finley said softly.

"We never made it into the state tournament again," the janitor continued sadly. "Never even made it out of the district."

"Listen," Finley said softly. "I have to leave. But let me know if you remember anything about a Katharine McCarthy. I'll be staying at the hotel."

"'Course we lost the first game in the state tournament," the janitor continued. "But that didn't make no difference to us. That year everyone heard of Danvers. Made us proud to go into the big cities and tell people where we were from."

IV

Finley walked slowly down the gently sloping foothill that separated Danvers High School from the Main Street of the town. As he looked up at the ancient gabled homes that towered above the narrow street, Finley had the sensation that he was being watched. He had felt that way almost from the very moment when he had first stepped out of his car on

Main Street. Now, surrounded by the ponderous old Victorian homes that were half-concealed in the deep shadows of late afternoon, he felt even more uncomfortable.

He glanced frequently at the small gable windows, some of which were half-buried behind thick autumn leaves clustered in tall trees. The gable windows reminded him of eyes looking down at him and following his movements through the narrow streets of the tiny prairie town.

Finley made his way to the Danvers Hotel and climbed a short flight of stairs which led to the outer lobby. Several old men were sitting by the window overlooking Main Street. Gold-leafed, framed photographs and daguerreotypes lined the walls of the outer lobby. Buffalo heads and deer antlers were prominently displayed on every wall. Brass spittoons were scattered randomly among the large, padded easy chairs, and a long bar with a brass footrail was visible in an adjoining room.

Finley approached the desk clerk in the back of the room. "Do you have any rooms available?" he asked.

"How long ya gonna be stayin'?" the desk clerk asked.

"Probably a few days."

"Well, we got rates. The longer ya stay, the cheaper the room. A dollar for one day. Six-fifty for a week."

"Make it a week," Finley said, thinking of the four weeks of vacation time he had coming to him.

"Fill this out then." The desk clerk slid a small white card across the counter. "Here's your key. Room 307. Looks right out onto Main Street. If ya leave early, be sure to return the key."

Finley filled out the registration card and handed it back to the desk clerk. "One more thing. I need information on someone who might have lived around here. Back in the 1920s."

"I've only been here ten years myself," the desk clerk said. He gestured towards the group of old men sitting by the front window. "You might talk to Oscar over there. The one lighting his pipe. He's been here most of his life."

"Thanks."

"Hey Wally, your turn!" a voice yelled from across the lobby.

"Just a minute!" the desk clerk yelled back to three men

sitting around a card table. "I'll be right over. Just don't look at my hand until I get there."

Finley walked over to the group of old men sitting by the front window. The man who had been identified as Oscar was carefully packing tobacco into his mahogany pipe. He went about the task in a very ritualistic manner, attending to every detail with loving care.

"Excuse me," Finley said after the old man had finished inspecting the bowl of his pipe to make sure everything had been properly attended to. "I was told you might be able to help me."

The old man lit his pipe and puffed on it several times. When he was certain it was lit, he looked up at Finley. "What is it you need?" he said, leaning back in his chair and drawing contentedly on the stem of the pipe.

"I need some information on someone who might have lived in Carver County in the 1920s."

"What's the name?"

"Katharine McCarthy."

Oscar considered the name carefully. "No Katharine McCarthy ever lived in this town. Not that I know of leastways."

"Are you sure?"

"I'm pretty sure." Suddenly he yelled across the lobby at another old man meditating next to a cigarette machine. "Fred, you ever hear of a Katharine McCarthy living around here?" The other old man looked up and shook his head feebly.

"Nope. Sorry," Oscar said.

"Was there *anyone* by the name of McCarthy living around here in the 1920s?"

"Well, McCarthy's a pretty common name in most places, I suspect. But not around here. Not anywhere in Carver County that I know of."

"You've never heard of a McCarthy in Carver County?"

Oscar puffed thoughtfully on his pipe. "Seems to me there was a construction crew that came through here in the 20s. There was a McCarthy among them."

"Was he married?"

"No, no, heavens, no. Those people never settle down.

Finish one job and move on to the next. It's in their blood. They can't help themselves."

"Do you know where I can find out more about this McCarthy?"

"You could try Harmon over in the newspaper office. He knows something about almost everyone in Carver County. He might be able to help you. That is, if he's sober, which isn't very often anymore."

Finley looked out the window at the Main Street of Danvers for a few seconds. "Do you have any idea what happened to this McCarthy?"

"Oh, I suppose he just left with the rest of the crew once they were through here. I was in and out of the area during much of the 20s. I probably wouldn't be the one to ask that question."

"Who might I ask?"

Outside the window, a fire siren suddenly screamed and all the old men who were nodding off to sleep raised their heads slowly and smiled knowingly at one another.

"What's that?" Finley asked.

"Ah, it's nothing," Oscar said, banging his pipe into a metal ashtray.

"Harmon's on a toot again," another old man cackled gleefully.

"Ever have a real fire in this town, no one'll ever know about it," another laughed.

"They'll just think Harmon is hittin' the sauce."

Within a few seconds, the notes of "Alexander's Ragtime Band" were playing on the fire siren and whistling through the streets and alleys of Danvers.

"It takes some gettin' used to, I guess," Oscar chuckled. "But after you've been in Danvers long enough, ya kind of look forward to Harmon gettin' drunk and playin' music on the fire siren."

"He does this often?" Finley asked.

"Just about every day. Guess he's drunk just about every day now." Oscar giggled, then once again began the ritual of packing his pipe. "You were askin' me something before Harmon started playin' his music."

"I was asking you what happened to McCarthy. The one

you said worked for the construction crew in the 1920s."

"Oh, yes. Gus," he yelled at another old man sitting by the front window, "whatever happened to that McCarthy who worked and wrestled back here in the 20s?"

"He disappeared," Gus said quickly.

"Just like I thought," Oscar said, turning back to Finley. "They leave right after they finish. . . ."

"No, he disappeared," Gus said, interrupting Oscar. "Just didn't show up for work one day."

"What was McCarthy's first name?" Finley asked Gus.

"Judd. Judd McCarthy. A powerful man. Probably the strongest man in Carver County. But no good."

"Why do you say that?" Finley asked.

"He disappeared with the company payroll."

"Are you sure?"

"Should be," Gus said, rising from his chair and shuffling toward one of the brass spittoons. "Cost me three month's wages."

"How well did you know this McCarthy?" Finley asked.

"Hardly at all," Gus answered, spitting into the brass spittoon. "We were assigned to completely different parts of the county. I just know I didn't get paid. That's all."

"When did he disappear?" Finley asked.

"Oh, it was in the 1920s sometime," Gus answered. He shuffled across the lobby and sat back down in the easy chair. "I suppose 1925, 1926. It's been a long time. But it's somewheres in there."

"Are you certain?" Finley asked eagerly.

"Yup."

"Do you have any idea where he might have gone?" Finley asked.

"We don't know," Gus repeated slowly as he lowered his head and closed his eyes. "He just disappeared."

V

Jim Morris glanced up at the clock in his office. It was 3:30. He had been at his desk all day and he was tired and stiff. He stood up from the desk and stretched to relieve the ache in his cramped muscles and back. At the age of 64, he was finding it difficult to devote an entire day to working over his desk. Retirement, just one year away, was beginning to look better all the time.

But there were compensations. Morris was proud of his paternalistic role in the law firm. He received far more satisfaction out of developing a young attorney than he did out of arguing a case in court. He hoped, in his retirement years, to continue to guide the younger members of the firm. But, thank God, he would never again have to write another legal brief.

He was looking out the window, thinking of perhaps getting in a hole or two of golf before sunset, when one of the secretaries appeared at the door of his office.

"Mr. Morris, I think you'd better take a look at something downstairs," she said. There was a troubled look on her face.

"What is it?" Morris asked.

"I don't know how to describe it," she stammered. "It's Joel. He's... he's in the vault."

"Yes, I know. I sent him down there to find some files for me. What's the problem?"

"He's talking in there," she stammered again.

"So?"

"It's not his voice. It's... Please, you'd better come downstairs with me."

"Okay," Morris said reluctantly.

Morris followed her out of his office and down the flight of stairs to the main floor of the building. Several offices had been created out of what had once been the main lobby of the Kenyon First National Bank Building. Several secretaries and attorneys were gathered around the old bank vault where the law firm stored valuable legal documents.

"What is it?" Morris asked as he moved into the center of the group.

"Listen," someone said. "Something awfully strange is going on in there."

Morris placed his ear close to the door and listened to the garbled tones drifting out of the vault.

"Who's in there?" Morris asked. "Is it Joel?"

"Yes," someone replied.

"God, it sure doesn't sound like him."

Morris grasped the huge handle of the steel door and pulled hard on it. The door pivoted on its well-oiled hinges and slowly opened.

Toward the rear of the vault, Joel Hampton stood with his back to the outer lobby. He was indiscriminately pulling folders and legal documents out of filing cabinets and flinging them across the vault.

"Joel, what the hell is going on in here?" Morris asked as he stepped through the open doorway.

Joel turned slowly to face him. "Ah, so it's you, is it?" he asked in a thick Irish accent. "Ah should've known ya had somethin' ta do with it." His eyes were fierce, threatening.

"Joel, what's wrong with you?" Morris asked the question cautiously, but firmly. The look in Joel's eyes was something he had never seen before, at least not in the eyes of any sane man.

So he had been right. Even as he felt the life slipping out of his body, he knew who had set him up.

"Joel, what's wrong with you?" Morris repeated the question apprehensively. He stared at the large arms and shoulders of Joel Hampton who was glaring back at him from the other end of the vault.

Joel Hampton, breathing heavily, started walking slowly across the metal floor.

"Ah shoulda known," Joel muttered in the strong Irish accent.

"Lucy," Morris whispered without turning around. "You'd better call the police."

In the darkness he had waited for that face, any face. He had waited for days. Weeks. Months. Maybe even years. There was no way of knowing. But the rage had grown until there was no way of controlling it.

"Joel!" Morris yelled as the younger man suddenly leaped on him and wrestled him to the floor.

Morris lay on his back, looking up into the angry, violent eyes above him. Then Joel Hampton clamped both huge hands around the older man's throat.

"Jesus Christ, he's trying to kill him!" someone yelled.

"Help him . . ."

"My God, he's too strong..."

"Get help, quick..."

"Grab him around the throat. Pull him back."

Morris felt the pressure on his throat increase, and a violent pain shot up into his brain and down into his chest.

"Jesus..."

"Hit him over the head with something..."

"I can't move his arm. He's too strong."

Jim Morris heard the police sirens screaming somewhere in the distance. Then he heard another sound, like the noise a large animal makes when it is cornered and about to die.

The scream blended in with the sound of the police sirens, and a deep numbness penetrated his body and he was surrounded by flashes of light and color and finally darkness....

VI

Finley was asleep in his hotel room when he heard a sound outside his door. As he turned in that direction, a shadow passed slowly over the sliver of light that had slipped beneath the crack at the bottom of the doorway. The shadow remained motionless for a few seconds, then it slowly passed across the light and disappeared. Finley heard two feet shuffle over the carpeted hallway and descend the flight of stairs.

Finley lay back in his bed and watched the shadows created by the lamps in the street below as they flickered across the ceiling of his hotel room. He thought back to his discussions with the old men in the hotel lobby. He had wanted to ask Gus some more questions about the Judd McCarthy who had disappeared in the 1920s, but the old man was obviously in poor health and in need of an afternoon nap. Gus had fallen asleep before Finley could pry any deeper into McCarthy's disappearance. Later that evening, Finley had searched the hotel lobby, but there was no sign of Gus or of any of the other old men.

As he stared at the shadows flickering across the ceiling

of his hotel room, Finley began to feel somewhat foolish for coming to Carver County in the first place. What was it he hoped to find in this virtual ghost town? More than likely Joel Hampton had read about Carver County somewhere, and under the hypnotic trance the name simply drifted out of his subconscious mind. And the thick Irish accent? Joel Hampton could have picked that up anywhere—books, movies, perhaps an old acquaintance. Finley remembered having read that accents leave permanent impressions on the subconscious mind. Hypnotic suggestion could easily have removed Joel's inhibitions, and perhaps he was simply mimicking an accent he had heard during some earlier experience.

Still, there was the adoption certificate, the name Katharine, and the disappearance of Judd McCarthy. And there was something strange, almost ghostly about the small town dying in the middle of the Midwestern prairies. As he *lay* in his hotel room staring at the ceiling, Finley could think of many plausible explanations for Joel Hampton's strange behavior. But as he *walked* the streets of the small town, Finley felt in his guts that there was some ghostly, almost supernatural connection between Joel Hampton and Carver County. . . .

Suddenly, Finley remembered that he had forgotten to call Susan Hampton as he had promised. He reached for his watch on the nightstand and held it up to the dim light filtering in from the street below. It was 12:15. Late, but still he felt he should make the phone call.

He put on his robe and slippers and padded out into the semi-darkened hallway. A few lights still glowed beneath the doorways of several of the hotel rooms, but most of the rooms were enclosed in darkness. In the lobby a single light was glowing and the desk clerk was asleep on a small cot behind the counter. The light from the street lamps outside the front window sent shadows flickering across the old photographs.

Finley stepped into the wooden phone booth next to the bar. The door of the booth creaked slowly shut behind him.

"Operator," a shrill female voice responded at the other end of the line as he placed the receiver to his ear.

"Yes, I would like to place a long distance phone call to Kenyon. The number is 589-1333," Finley said.

"Thank you." There was a slight pause. "Please deposit twenty-five cents for the first three minutes."

Finley dropped the quarter into the metal slot and listened to it jangle to the bottom of the pay telephone. The telephone rang three times. On the third ring, a female voice whispered a sleepy "hello" into the receiver.

"Susan, this is Ned Finley. I'm calling from Danvers. I'm sorry. I forgot to leave a phone number with you this afternoon."

"Dr. Finley, I'm so glad to hear from you," the voice said nervously at the other end of the line.

"What is it, Susan?"

"Joel went . . . he went berserk today. . . ."

There was a pause, then a stifled sob at the other end of the line.

"Susan, what happened?"

"Apparently, sometime in the middle of the day, he went crazy and destroyed a bunch of legal documents," Susan Hampton continued slowly. "When they tried to stop him, he almost strangled Jim Morris. God, it was awful . . ."

"Is Morris okay?"

"Yes. He's in the hospital. He has all the symptoms of a stroke, but he's going to be okay."

"Where is Joel?"

"He's at Farmington. They have him in restraints."

"Susan, I'm coming back. I'll meet you at Farmington in the morning. At ten. Do you hear me?"

"Yes."

"Please get some sleep, Susan. I'll see you in the morning."

Finley hung up the telephone and sat in the booth thinking about what Susan had said. When he finally stepped out of the phone booth, the desk clerk was still asleep behind the counter. A radiator hissed beneath the windows overlooking Main Street. He walked quietly up the two flights of stairs, down the semi-darkened hallway, and into his hotel room. He closed the door behind him and turned on the light.

As he turned around, he saw that the contents of his suitcase were strewn across the threadbare carpet of the hotel room and his watch had been smashed on the night-

stand next to the bed. When he picked up the watch, tiny
screws and gears and springs spilled out and disappeared into
the carpet.

Finley carried the watch over to the window and sat
down in a small desk chair. The radiator next to the window
belched once and clanged as the noise echoed through the
ancient plumbing system. Outside, two lights next to the
County Building illuminated the American eagle, its beak
clenching the metal flag pole and its talons gripping the brick
outcropping with fierce strength.

Finley lay the watch down on a vanity and looked back
out the window. He stared at the lampposts and signs and
stone façades of the buildings on the Main Street of Danvers.

Then he looked back at the bed. Something was not
right. He remembered having kicked back the covers before
going downstairs to the hotel lobby. But now the bedspread
was pulled back neatly over the rumpled blankets and sheets.

As he walked over to the bed and cautiously lifted the
bedspread, a tiny stream of blood trickled off the mattress
pad and dribbled to the floor.

He recognized the dog as the one he had seen chasing
the rat earlier that morning on the Main Street of Danvers.
The dog's body had been gutted and spread out across the
blood-stained sheets.

Chapter Six

I

"Where do we go from here?" Susan asked Ned Finley as she slumped down on one of the stone benches in front of the mental hospital.

"They'll be doing tests to see if it's anything physiological," Finley said, sitting down beside her.

"Physiological?"

"Brain tumors, things like that." Finley looked out over the hospital grounds. "But I don't think that has anything to do with it."

"On the hospital chart, they refer to Joel as a 'psychopath.'"

"I know. But Joel's not a psychopath." Finley picked up a dead leaf lying next to the bench and began crumbling it into little pieces in his open palm. "A psychopathic personality develops over a long period of time. Generally the symptoms are evident in early childhood. Joel seemed to develop these symptoms almost overnight. It's something else. Right now, he's dangerous, but I don't think he's a psychopath. It's probably closer to some form of schizophrenia. Maybe even something more complicated than that. Still, we have to get some answers as soon as possible. I've worked with schizophrenic personalities, of course, but never one who has retreated from reality as rapidly as your husband. He is plunging into some subconscious level of existence that I've never encountered before. Unless we get some answers and pull him out in the next few days or weeks, we may lose him

81

altogether. We've got to find out what demons Joel is fighting before we can help him deal with them."

Susan shifted nervously on the bench and glanced back in the direction of the mental institution. "You mean, Joel may never get out of there?" she asked solemnly. She looked so beautiful, so young, so helpless. Suddenly Finley realized he wanted to help Joel more than he'd ever wanted to help a patient before. His life was at stake.

"There's always that possibility. We never fully understand what forces work in the human mind, or whether they are permanent or temporary. But we'll get some answers, and I think we'll find them in Carver County."

"And you?" Susan inquired softly. "You can't just drop your practice to search for the ghosts in Joel's past. You have other responsibilities."

"I have my reasons. What I'm doing is not completely unselfish. I also have ghosts in my past, Susan." Finley paused momentarily. "Besides, I have almost a month's vacation time coming. I've been planning to use it sometime this fall. Now seems like as good a time as any. My case load is pretty light."

Neither Finley nor Susan spoke for a time. Finley stripped the tiny leaf and held the skeleton up to the gray sky.

"Tell me something, Susan," he said finally. "Was there any reason at all why your husband would have tried to kill Jim Morris?"

"No," Susan said emphatically. "Mr. Morris is like a father to all the young attorneys in that office. Joel idolized him."

"Maybe he thought it was someone else." Finley threw the skeleton of the leaf into the wind, then folded his hands and leaned forward on his knees. "How's your daughter?" he asked, changing the subject.

"I'm going over to my mother's this afternoon to pick her up. At least she's in no danger now that Joel's in there. I'm not accepting any more substitute teaching assignments until Joel gets better. I want to spend more time with Aggy. This has been too hard on her already."

Finley nodded. "We'll keep him sedated. In the meantime, I'll be going back to Carver County."

Both Finley and Susan remained silent for a time. Finley

leaned over, picked up another dead leaf, and began stripping it.

"You know, Susan, I'm convinced that something almost supernatural is driving Joel to do the things he does," Finley said. "Something happened a long time ago, something so horrible that it's still being acted out in your husband's subconscious mind. I'm convinced of that."

"Why Joel?"

"I don't know. But now that I've been to Carver County, I feel it too. I don't know what it is. But it's there." Finley paused briefly. Then he stood up and looked back in the direction of the hospital. "Whatever it is is also working on me. I felt it every second I was walking the streets of Danvers. Something's very wrong in that town."

II

Susan watched the heavy iron gates being locked after Ned Finley had walked through them. Then she stood and walked toward the stone stairway leading up to the front door. She pulled hard on the huge iron handle bolted into the thick wooden door. The door swung open, and she stepped into the cool shadows of the first floor.

The stale smell of urine and perspiration clung heavily to the air in the poorly ventilated halls and corridors. Heavily sedated patients sat on plain wooden benches and gazed at the floor as hospital orderlies and nurses moved among them distributing pills. Other patients, propped up in wheel chairs or strapped to large wooden chairs, sat along the outer walls.

As Susan approached the foot of the stairway leading up to the second floor of the hospital, an elderly woman in a green hospital gown suddenly appeared in a nearby doorway. The woman curled one arthritic index finger and gestured through the open doorway for Susan to enter the room. Susan could see that toys and dolls were scattered across the tile floor. Elderly male and female patients sat cross-legged on the floor, hugging the dolls or holding the toys up in the air for inspection.

"Come see," the old woman whispered as she stepped toward Susan. "Come see," she repeated.

One side of the woman's face was paralyzed, and the flesh had folded over into circular layers that dropped below the chinline. The eyeball was frozen open in the middle of the mass of flesh.

The old woman took another step toward the staircase. "Come see," she repeated again.

Susan stared at the unblinking eyeball as the old woman took still another step toward the staircase, all the time curling her crooked finger and gesturing for Susan to enter. "Joel doesn't belong here. They can't keep him here," Susan thought to herself hysterically.

As the old woman reached out to touch her forearm, Susan gasped and rushed up the stone staircase. At the bottom of the staircase, the old woman fastened her eyeball on the retreating form and repeated, "Come see, please come see . . ."

At the top of the staircase, a thick wire screen had been stretched across the entrance leading into a long, narrow hallway. The words "RESTRICTED AREA" were painted in black letters on a sign above the screen. Several muscular orderlies patrolled the hallway, and a young nurse sat at a small wooden desk just outside the wire enclosure.

"Who do you want to see?" the nurse asked coldly.

"My husband, Joel Hampton," Susan said.

"Do you have identification?"

"Yes." Susan reached into her purse and took out her billfold. "Here," she said, holding out the driver's license.

The young nurse studied the driver's license. "Okay, but you'll have to leave that here."

"Leave what here?" Susan asked.

"The purse," the nurse said as she stood up. "And I'll have to check your pockets."

"Why?"

"We can't let people bring things in that the patients could use to hurt themselves or someone else. Even a simple set of keys can do a great deal of damage in the wrong hands."

Susan placed her purse on the table, then lifted her

arms. The young nurse felt along the contours of Susan's body and thrust her hands deeply into her coat pockets.

"Okay," the nurse announced as she sat back down at the desk. "Sign here and be sure to sign again when you leave."

Susan obediently signed the register.

"Your husband is in room 216, in the middle of the hall," the nurse said, reaching for a key on the wall behind her. She stood up and inserted the key into the lock of a thick metal door in the middle of the wire meshing. "Please don't go into any of the other rooms if the doors are open."

As Susan stepped into the long, narrow hallway, the metal door clanged shut behind her. She heard the key scrape against the metal lock as the bolt slipped into place.

The smell of urine, perspiration and fecal matter was even stronger than it had been on the first floor of the hospital. Groans, stifled screams and other unidentified animal noises drifted out from behind the metal doors along both sides of the narrow corridor. Susan tried not to think of the horrors they hid.

A large, muscular orderly met her at the doorway leading into room 216. He inserted a key into the lock and turned it slowly counter-clockwise. "We keep the doors locked during the day," he said, sensing that some explanation might be necessary. "Some of the patients are occasionally allowed out into the halls. We don't want them stumbling into the wrong rooms."

"Are you going to lock it while I'm in there?"

"How long do you plan to be?"

"Not long."

The orderly sensed the nervousness in Susan's voice. "No, I'll leave it open. Just let me know when you leave."

Susan nodded and stepped through the doorway into the hospital room.

Joel was stretched out across a hospital bed in the rear of the room. A single window with thick iron bars was located next to the bed. Except for the bed and two small wooden chairs, the room was barren.

Susan walked over to the bed and looked down at her husband's face. He was dressed in a faded green hospital gown, and his arms and legs were secured to the sides of the bed by thick leather straps. His eyes were closed and the black stubble of a beard was spreading across his face and neck.

"Joel," she whispered softly.

There was no response.

"Joel, it's me, Susan. Can you hear me?" she asked gently.

Joel continued to breathe evenly and deeply, but there was no response to her gentle prodding.

As Susan sadly looked down at the still, sleeping form of her husband, she began sobbing quietly to herself. It was incomprehensible to her that the strong, gentle man she loved could be capable of murder—or even attempted murder. During the years that she had worked to support him through law school, Joel had baby-sat for Aggy and for other children in the apartment complex. He loved children and animals and people. Never before had he demonstrated even the slightest violent tendencies. If anything he was too gentle, too accepting, and people frequently took advantage of his kindness. But now, he had tried to kill a man. . . .

Susan wiped the tears from her cheek with a soiled white handkerchief. Then she reached down and gently stroked the top of her husband's muscular forearm. . . .

"It's a terrible thing, isn't it?" she heard a soft voice behind her ask suddenly.

Susan turned quickly and found herself looking into the large eyes of a small, elderly man standing just inside the doorway. He wore a large overcoat and his hands were plunged deeply into his pockets. "Who are you?" she asked nervously.

"Don't worry, child," he said softly and warmly. "My name is Aurther Schlepler. I'm Ned Finley's friend. He told me about your husband."

"What are you doing here?" Susan asked.

"I live here."

"Are you a patient?"

"No, child, it's a matter of choice. I live here because I want to."

A loud scream suddenly erupted from the end of the hallway and echoed into the hospital room. The scream was followed by a litany of garbled curses and profanities.

Schlepler approached the bed and looked down at Joel Hampton. "There is so much sadness and pain inside that young man. So much that he cannot understand or control," he said sadly.

"What do you know about my husband?" Susan asked.

"Only what Ned told me. And what I feel," Schlepler answered gently. "Come, child, let's go down to my room. I'll make you a cup of coffee. Then we can talk."

Susan looked into Aurther Schlepler's large, compassionate eyes.

"Don't be afraid," he said reassuringly. "The nurse out there will tell you who I am."

Susan felt her reservations vanish under the gentle, soothing tone of Aurther Schlepler's voice, and she followed him out of the room.

As they left, the orderly stepped quickly into the open doorway and pulled the large metal door shut, sending dust particles swirling across the few rays of sunlight that entered the room through the small rear window. Then the leaves from a large tree outside the window sent shadows flickering across Joel Hampton's beard and matted hair. . . .

He remembered the streets and the brick buildings and the large stone eagle. Especially the eagle with the flagpole clenched in its powerful beak. It was the last thing they had done to the building. He had stood on a ledge and guided the eagle as it was raised in the air by thick ropes attached to horse-drawn pulleys. And the men in the street below had cheered as the eagle was attached to the side of the building. And he had grinned down at them. And laughed. And felt alive under the clear blue sky. If only he could find the eagle. Maybe then he would remember . . .

III

When Finley arrived back in Danvers, he parked his car across from the County Building. He shuddered when he recalled the dreadful circumstances of his last night in town; but he was determined to keep calm and see things through.

With a glance up at the stone eagle above the portico, he walked across the street to the hotel.

Most of the old men were still sitting around the outer lobby, either playing cards, looking out the window, or dozing in easy chairs. Oscar was puffing on his pipe and watching a nearby card game when Finley sat down next to him.

"Have you seen Gus today?" Finley asked.

"Nope. He's in Tyler," Oscar responded.

"Do you know when he'll be back?"

"Hard to say," Oscar said, reaching into his shirt pocket and pulling out a nail. "Could be a day. Could be a couple days. Could be he'll never come back."

"Why do you say that?" Finley asked.

"Ambulance took him away this morning. Gus has a bad heart. Turned all blue last night."

"Do you think if I went over to Tyler, they'd let me see him?"

"Nope," Oscar said, thrusting the nail into the bowl of his pipe. "He was in pretty bad shape when they took him out of here. Unconscious. Half dead, really. What da ya need from him?"

"I was going to ask him some questions about this Judd McCarthy who disappeared in the 1920s."

There was a sudden uproar from the men seated around the card table. As Finley and Oscar looked in that direction, one of the players threw his cards down in mock disgust, shoved several match sticks across the table, and folded his hands behind his head.

"Well, I don't think Gus is gonna be much good to ya, at least for awhile," Oscar said as he finished scraping the burnt tobacco out of the bowl of his pipe.

"Where else might I find some information on this Judd McCarthy?" Finley asked.

"You could try the newspaper office. Harmon might be able to help you. That is, if he's sober."

"Where is the newspaper office?" Finley asked.

"One block west of here."

"Thanks," Finley said. Then he rose from his chair and walked across the dirty carpet toward the front door of the hotel lobby.

Finley walked one block west and crossed the street. The newspaper office was located in a small wooden building wedged tightly between two larger brick buildings. The windows overlooking Main Street were thick with dust and grime.

"Just a minute," a voice yelled from somewhere in the back as Finley entered the office. "I'll be right with you. God damn it, I don't know about this thing..." The voice trailed off into a series of garbled profanities.

Harmon soon emerged from behind one of the old printing presses. He was a short man with a huge pot belly, and he wore a visor that was much too large for his head. His shirt and arms were covered with printer's ink, and, as he walked towards the counter, he wrestled with a tray of printer's type. Finley could tell by his unsteady, wobbling gait that he was drunk.

"Want to place an ad?" he asked, stumbling up to the counter.

"No, the fellas in the hotel sent me over. I need some information on someone who might have lived here in the 1920s. Have you ever heard the names Judd McCarthy or Katharine McCarthy?"

Harmon pushed his visor back higher on his forehead and considered the two names. "Nope," he said, returning his attentions to the tray of printer's type. "Never heard either of those names before. Listen, you sure you don't want to place an ad. We got a special this week."

"No thank you..."

"You name the price. We'll take it."

"Listen, an old fella named Gus told me this McCarthy disappeared with a company payroll. Back in the 20s. Think the newspaper would have reported it?"

"Possible. I didn't have the paper back then. But I suppose if it was big news, they would have reported it. Shit, I can't seem to get this thing right," he said, referring to the tray of printer's type.

"Would you have copies of the papers from 1925 and 1926?"

"Might have," Harmon said, looking up from his struggle. "I know they'd be on microfilm in the state capital. But we could have them in the basement too."

"Do you have any idea where the papers from the 1920s would be located?"

"Hell, I don't know. Could be almost anywhere. I've never had time to sort them out. Try the west wall. Ah, shit," he said as the tray suddenly fell out of his hands, spilling the type all over the floor. "Ah, the hell with it. Maybe we'll just publish the headlines this week."

Finley walked quickly down into the basement. Beneath the harsh glow of a single light bulb located in the middle of the ceiling, Finley could see piles and piles of yellowish-brown newspapers stacked on makeshift wooden shelves around all four walls. He walked over to the western wall and began sorting slowly through the old newspapers.

IV

Hours later Finley uncovered a bundle of newspapers tied neatly together with string and labeled "1926." He walked to the center of the room and placed the bundle on top of a small table located directly beneath the overhead light bulb. He broke the two strings and began paging through the old newspapers.

As his eyes moved carefully over the newsprint of the October 14, 1926, *Danvers Sun*, he found what he was looking for. Under the small headline, "Payroll Stolen," the article read:

> Sheriffs in four counties have been searching for three days for a certain Judd McCarthy who disappeared with the Hanley Brothers Construction Company payroll.
>
> McCarthy, who is well-known throughout Carver County as a barroom brawler and ruffian, was last seen leaving Danvers early Saturday morning, October 12. Company officials say he was on his way to Carson to pick up the payroll and return it to the construction site of the Little Sioux Water Reclamation Project.

Deputies who have retraced his route from Danvers to Carson have found nothing unusual. Due to his size and reputation, there is little reason to suspect he ran into foul play. The search is now extending into the Dakotas. A $5000 reward has been posted by Ben and Fred Hanley for any information leading to the arrest of Judd McCarthy.

Citizens of the four county area are to be reminded that this same Judd McCarthy is a man of extremely violent temper.

Finley lay the newspaper flat on the small table and looked up at the few rays of sunlight filtering through the lone basement window. At the bottom of the window-well, a salamander was buried beneath a pile of dead leaves. The salamander was straining mightily against the glass pane to free itself from its prison.

Finley opened the blade of a small pocketknife and ran it along the outer boundaries of the newspaper article. He extracted the account of McCarthy's disappearance from the yellowish-brown page, folded it carefully, and placed it in his wallet. Then he retied the bundle of newspapers, placed it on the wooden shelf, and walked back up the narrow stairs.

As he stepped through the basement door into the front office of the *Danvers Sun*, he glanced out the front window. He could see that the shadows were creeping out into the Main Street of Danvers. He guessed it to be mid-afternoon.

"Harmon," he called into the back of the room. He waited for a few seconds, then called again. "Harmon."

Finley stepped out into the street and walked toward the Danvers Hotel. Behind him, the shrill notes of "Alexander's Ragtime Band" built to a crescendo, then faded into a deep, mournful wail, and finally died out altogether.

He paused to look back in the direction of the newspaper office. As he turned around again, he glanced down at the rear tires of his Studebaker. The left rear tire was flat, the black rubber folded neatly under the metal rim. Again he felt himself shudder involuntarily.

Finley leaned over and examined the tire. Two tiny, circular holes had been neatly punched in the top of the blackwall tire.

V

On the way back from Foley, Susan had stopped by the law office to pick up some of Joel's things. She had cleared his desk, cramming everything that would fit into the briefcase. Then she had made a hasty exit from the building.

The secretaries and attorneys who saw her walk toward the front door smiled politely and sympathetically, but still she felt uncomfortable. She hurried down the hallway so she would not have to talk to them. She wanted only to get home and hide.

As soon as Susan got back she sent Aggy across the street to play with her friend Robin. Then she put water on to boil for coffee. As she was waiting, she reached over to where she had set down Joel's briefcase on the kitchen table and idly popped the lock. Then she lifted the top of the briefcase and spread the contents out over the table. Anything was better than sitting by herself and letting her thoughts run wild.

At the bottom of the briefcase, she noticed a large notebook with a light green cardboard cover. The single word "WHY?" was boldly printed across the cover. Susan recognized it as Joel's handwriting. She slowly opened the notebook.

On the first page, Joel had drawn the picture of a young woman swinging from the branch of a huge oak tree. Only the back of the young woman was visible. At the bottom of the page, he had scrawled the name "Katharine" two times.

Susan slowly paged through the rest of the notebook. Subsequent pages revealed drawings of an old Victorian home, a large thicket of trees in an empty field, two unattached arms reaching out as though to strangle someone, and other strange, unrecognizable doodlings. The last page of the notebook had been completely blackened in with bold, violent strokes from a lead pencil. That page was torn in several places from the force of the pencil sweeping back and forth across the legal paper.

Susan studied the bold pencil strokes for several seconds.

Then she set the notebook back down on the kitchen table. She shuffled through the other contents of the briefcase and extracted a college yearbook that Joel had, for some reason, kept on his office desk. Susan flipped idly through the yearbook, looking at the pictures of the football team, the debating team, and the spring formal.

Joel had been an end on the football team, and his size, strength, and speed had attracted the attention of several professional scouts, even though he was playing small college football. But a knee injury in his junior year had ended any dreams he might have entertained of playing professional football.

For several weeks after the injury, Joel retreated into a shell. He even seriously considered dropping out of college. Then a mutual friend lined him up with Susan. She remembered how, on their first date, Joel had limped up to the dormitory, his knee strapped securely into a canvas brace. At first he seemed almost reluctant to be with her. But, by the end of the evening, he was laughing and talking freely about himself.

Several days later she talked Joel into joining the debating team with her. Together, they practiced their debating techniques in the rear of Bannister Hall, and Joel began to tell her of another of his dreams—law school. It was also in Bannister Hall that he had kissed her for the first time. His kiss was awkward, but gentle and strong. Then Professor Holliman, the debating coach, suddenly strolled into the room. Susan remembered how Holliman had mumbled something about "failing to develop the killer instinct in his debaters." As Holliman hung up his coat in the rear of the room, Joel glanced awkwardly at her. Then Joel started to laugh. His was a laugh that came from deep in his throat, filling the room with its good-natured masculinity. She loved Joel's laugh ... What wonderful times they'd had together. Then courtship, the early years of their marriage, and finally sharing the joys of parenthood.

Susan was studying the picture of Joel and her in the middle of the debating squad when she heard the sound of screeching brakes in the street outside. The sound was followed almost immediately by a loud scream. "Aggy," Susan whispered.

She leaped up from the kitchen table and rushed toward the front door. "Aggy!" she screamed as she threw open the screendoor.

A late model Ford coupe was stalled in the middle of the street. Two long, black streaks of burnt rubber curled out behind the car, marking the swerving course of the automobile as it had come to a skidding halt. A few feet in front of the car, a teddy bear was sprawled out across the road. Inside the car, an elderly woman was resting her forehead on the steering wheel.

Across the street, another old woman was staring in horror at the stalled automobile. A small bag of groceries lay at her feet, the contents of which were spread out over the sidewalk.

Aggy was standing a few feet in front of the black Ford coupe. She turned slowly in the direction of her mother. "Robin had to take a nap. I was coming home," she said penitently.

VI

Finley stood beside the water tank inside the DX Service Station as the attendant carefully examined the flat inner tube. A mongrel dog lay nearby, its head and tail curled lazily against the concrete floor of the service station.

The service station attendant filled the inner tube with air, then submerged it quickly in the water tank. Two tiny streams of bubbles sputtered quickly to the surface. The attendant pulled the tire out of the dirty water and carefully marked the two holes with a yellow crayon.

"Just as I thought," he said as he carried the inner tube over to a nearby work bench and began patching the two holes.

"What'd you find?" Finley asked.

"You didn't run over a nail," he said, scruffing the rubber surface and applying glue to the two holes. "These tires were deliberately punctured. See, the holes are on the side of the tube. Not on the bottom."

"Who'd do something like that?"

"Kids probably. Aren't too many left in Danvers. Ones that are here are pretty bored. Have too much time on their hands."

"Tell me," Finley said as he watched the attendant patch and then reassemble the tire, "who around here would know the most about the early history of Carver County?"

"How early?"

"First thirty years or so of this century."

"Lot of the real old boys are dead now. What is it you're trying to find out?"

"I'm looking for a Katharine McCarthy and a Judd McCarthy. Ever hear of them."

"Nope."

"Know of *anyone* who might have heard of them?"

"Well, if I were you," the attendant said, rolling the tire over to Finley, "I'd go out and talk to Hans Gustafson. He's an antique dealer. Lives about eight miles east of here on County Road 6. He's been around here longer'n just about anyone."

"Thanks," Finley said. "What do I owe you?"

"Fifty cents."

Outside of town, he passed a country church and a small country schoolhouse. The windows of both the church and the schoolhouse were boarded up, and the vegetation surrounding them grew almost up to the window ledges. Farther down the road, he passed an abandoned gas station. A tall, thin, old-fashioned gasoline pump protruded above the dead weeds.

Behind Finley's car, swirling clouds of dust rolled out into the prairies and dissipated above the recently harvested wheatfields. Finley glanced down at his odometer and saw that he had traveled precisely eight miles out of Danvers. He checked the next two mail boxes alongside the road. The third mailbox had a thin metal strip on top with the name "Hans Gustafson" painted on it. Finley turned his Studebaker into the narrow dirt road and drove up to the farmyard. Just outside the farmyard, a stately black crow perched on a gray fence post.

Finley parked the car next to a metal fence and walked up to the front door. He knocked twice. When there was no answer, he turned and walked in the direction of a gentle tapping sound that filtered out of a small barn across the farmyard. As he passed a smaller shed, he looked inside and saw an assortment of saddles, bridles, and other restored leather goods hanging from pegs. Pipe organs, trunks, violins, and other unrelated pieces of furniture were neatly arranged along the floor of the shed. Finley resisted the urge to enter and explore.

Inside the larger barn, restored carriages were lined up around the four walls. In the center of the room, an elderly, white-haired man, wearing a beret very much like Finley's, was working industriously on a carriage wheel. The western wall of the small barn contained a huge sliding door that was open. Through the door, the descending sun was clearly visible above the distant prairies.

"Excuse me, are you Hans Gustafson?" Finley said softly, not wanting to startle the old man. When the old man did not respond, Finley spoke again, this time louder. "Are you Hans Gustafson?"

"Huh?" the old man said, looking up from the carriage wheel and cupping his hand to his ear.

Finley realized he was hard of hearing. "Are you Hans Gustafson?" he asked loudly.

"Ya, I'm Hans Gustafson," the old man said in a strong Norwegian accent.

"The service station attendant in town told me you might be able to help me find someone."

"Vait a minute," he said, turning up the volume on his hearing aid. "Der. I turn dis off ven I'm vorking. Now, vat is it you vant?"

"I need some information. On two people who might have lived in Carver County in the 1920s. Can you help me?"

"Da twenties. The vife and I ver back in da old country den. Who are ya lookin' for?" Gustafson placed a large metal chisel on top of the carriage wheel as he spoke.

"Have you ever heard the name Katharine McCarthy?" Finley asked.

"Nope," Gustafson said firmly. "I've never heard dat name."

"What about the name Judd McCarthy?"

"Now I tink I've heard dat name. But I don't know vere."

"He disappeared in the 1920s with the Hanley Brothers Construction Company payroll," Finley said, handing Gustafson the newspaper article he had cut out of the *Danvers Sun*.

Gustafson took a small pair of bifocals out of his pocket, fitted them to his nose, and read the article. Then he handed it back to Finley. "Vell, I've heard about dis before. But dis newspaper article tells you more'n I know 'bout Judd McCarthy."

"Did any other McCarthys live around here in the 1920s?"

"Nope," Gustafson said, turning the carriage wheel over on the work bench. "But dis is a Scandinavian county. Der vas a lotta prejudice 'gainst da Irish in da old days. They settled farther northa here."

Finley pulled the photograph of the old Victorian farm house out of his pocket. "Have you ever seen this farmhouse in Carver County?"

Gustafson studied the photograph carefully. "It looks like von a da farms by da old Sioux Line Railroad. Rich farmers at von time. Made a lotta money. Den vent broke like da rest of us in da 30s."

"But you don't know who might have owned this farm in the 20s or 30s?"

"No. Could've been a couple dozen farms over der dat looked like dis in da old days. Don't look dat good no more, dough. Most of dem are gone or 'bandoned. Corporations keep buyin' up da land." Gustafson turned the photograph over and studied the back side. "This picture vas taken round here, dough. Dat much I can tell you."

"Why do you say that?" Finley asked.

"See dis?" Gustafson pointed to a faded impression of a small gramophone with the initials "PH" printed on the back of the old photograph.

"Yes."

"Means 'Hornsby Studios,'" Gustafson said, handing the photograph back to Finley. "Phillip Hornsby. He had a picture studio in Danvers back in da 20s and 30s. He died in da late 30s. Drank himself to death." Gustafson carefully moved his index finger along the wooden grain of one of the axles of the old carriage wheel. Then he bent over to examine it closely.

"Well, thank you very much," Finley said, placing the photograph back in his pocket and preparing to leave.

"You know, I vas tinking dough," Gustafson said, looking up from the carriage wheel. "Dat name McCarthy. Der vas a Maureen McCarthy lived round here. No one could ever forget her. But dat vas back in da 1890s."

"What can you tell me about her?"

"Vell, she came over from da old country. Round 1895, I tink. Quite a high spirited young woman. Used ta drink with da men in Danvers. Long for dat vas considered proper."

"What happened to her?"

"Vell, let me see now," Gustafson said, carefully pondering the question. "She vurked for a time on da Graham farm. Den der vas a lotta talk about her. You know how women are 'bout someone who's prettier'n da rest a dem."

"Was she married?" Finley asked.

"No. Seems to me der vas some big scandal 'bout her. Vent to prison, I tink. No, vait, I 'member now. She vas committed to an insane asylum."

"Why?"

"Now dat I don't know. But she vas certainly diffrent. Loved a good time. Laughed a lot. But I couldn't tell you vy she vas sent to an insane asylum."

As Gustafson leaned back over the carriage wheel and began working on it industriously, Finley looked out the open doorway at the descending sun.

"You certainly have a beautiful view of the sunset," Finley said.

"Ya," Gustafson said, looking up from his work. "It makes da prairies look so serene an peaceful. But der are a tousand shattered dreams out der. Lying just a few inches under da topsoil. I've buried most of dem in my lifetime."

As the sun descended behind the horizon, the shadows crawled slowly over the brown stubble of the newly harvested wheatfields. With one last burst of energy, the departing sun turned the cloud banks on the western horizon into brilliant shades of purples and oranges and fiery reds. In the distance, two or three clusters of trees protruded out of the wheatfields and slowly darkened as the sun sent its last rays across the prairies and over the carriages that lined the four walls of Hans Gustafson's barn.

VII

The moonlight filtered through the tiny window of Joel Hampton's room on the second floor of the Farmington State Mental Hospital. The pale light fell across the thick iron bars and sent elongated, distorted shadows across the bedspread.

Joel Hampton lay with his arms and legs securely attached to the side of the bed. The growth of beard was spreading rapidly across his face, concealing his once-handsome features and giving him a fierce, menacing look. The moonlight reflected off the few gray hairs in his dark beard.

A steady moaning sound drifted into the room from the other end of the hospital corridor, and an occasional muffled scream filtered through the steel door. Outside the window, the crickets chirped noisily in the dead grass.

A night orderly entered the room and gazed down at the tall, sleeping form of Joel Hampton. The orderly checked the leather restraints and then walked quickly out of the room.

Joel Hampton slept peacefully as the moon slipped slowly across the black sky and the elongated shadows created by the iron bars crawled steadily across the bedspread.

If only he could find the eagle and the tiny streets of the small town. Maybe then he would remember. And maybe he would find Katharine, his lovely Katharine, and she would forgive him. . . .

VIII

Late that evening, Ned Finley sat alone in the lobby of the Danvers Hotel. Behind the counter, the hotel clerk was asleep on his cot. In the front of the room, two radiators hissed next to the window overlooking Main Street.

The lobby was dark except for a small light that glowed behind the back counter and the lights that filtered through the front windows.

Finley sat in one of the padded easy chairs and watched the lights flicker gently over the old photographs.

The street lights fell across a picture of a group of men proudly surrounding a horse-drawn fire wagon. Another photograph depicted the Danvers Hotel much earlier in the century, as a steam-driven automobile chugged down the dirt road while several hotel guests eyed it suspiciously from the upstairs windows overlooking Main Street. The large, framed photograph of John J. Sylvester, occupying its place of honor in the middle of the eastern wall, was in the shadows, though Sylvester's eyes glowed out of the darkness from behind his gray mustache.

After returning from the Gustafson farm, Finley had placed a call to the Farmington State Mental Hospital. He had left a message for Aurther Schlepler. If a Maureen McCarthy had been committed to an insane asylum in the 1890s, Finley reasoned, it would undoubtedly have been Farmington. There was no other such institution within a hundred miles of Danvers.

Finley was hoping that perhaps his earlier conversations with Schlepler had stirred the deep well-springs of compassion that were so much a part of this eccentric genius, and Schlepler would condescend to search the catacombs of Farmington for any record of a Maureen McCarthy who might have been committed in the 1890s. Going through proper channels to get this information would take too long. And he didn't have much time.

As Finley sat in the semi-darkened lobby, he felt the ominous, ghostly presence of the many faces that stared out at him from the photographs displayed around all four walls. He also began to consider the full impact of what he was trying to prove now that he was back in Carver County. He was in search of a man who had lived in the 1920s and who maybe, just maybe, continued to live on inside the subconscious mind of a young attorney some thirty years later. The whole thing suddenly struck Finley as being too far-fetched, too utterly improbable to be taken seriously by anyone—much less by a professional psychologist who had been trained to look for more plausible explanations for his patients' behaviors.

Reincarnation? The supernatural? It was all too preposterous, much too preposterous. For a moment, Finley wished he hadn't grown so fond of Joel and Susan Hampton. Maybe he could have driven up north for two weeks? Done some fishing? Maybe by that time Joel would have regained his senses? Sometimes these conditions were temporary and they just had to work themselves out—with or without the help of a trained psychologist.

Still, at the very least, there was something very strange about this small town. The dead dog, the punctured tire, the feelings of being watched and followed —*something* was amiss in Danvers. But did it necessarily involve Joel Hampton? Or was it something else?

The desk clerk began to snore loudly as Finley rose from his chair and walked up the two flights of stairs to his room. Most of the rooms up and down the hallway were dark. Finley glanced at his watch and noticed that it was 12:30.

As he reached into his pocket for the hotel key, he looked down at the sliver of light that crept under the door and out onto the carpeted hallway. He stepped back quickly, remembering that he had turned the light off when he had walked down to the hotel lobby earlier that evening. He crept back softly to the door, knelt down, and placed his ear within a few inches of the keyhole. He could hear the distinct sound of footsteps and the clatter of vanity drawers opening and closing on the other side of the door. Finley stood up and threw the door open.

A thin man with one arm flopping uselessly by his side stood next to the bed. He whirled around quickly as Finley stepped into the room. The man's eyes darted nervously from side to side as he looked for an avenue of escape.

Finley recognized the man as one of the card players he had seen in the hotel lobby earlier that week. He had dealt cards with his right arm, while his left arm had hung limply in his coat pocket.

"What's going on here?" Finley demanded as his eyes moved slowly over the clothes and personal belongings that were strewn over the floor of the hotel room.

The intruder's eyes continued to dart nervously around the room. He did not answer Finley's question.

"Who are you?" Finley demanded again.

The intruder still did not speak. "Who the hell are you?" Finley repeated angrily.

"Burt," the man whispered nervously as he tucked his useless left arm into his coat pocket.

"What are you doing in my room?" Finley asked, gesturing toward the clothing strewn across the floor.

The intruder still did not speak.

"Listen," Finley said emphatically, "unless you give me some answers, I'm going to grab you by your good arm and haul you over to the sheriff. Maybe he can get you to explain why you've been destroying my things."

"I was told to do this," the thin man replied nervously.

"Who told you to do this?"

"I don't know."

"What the hell do you mean you don't know?" Finley demanded.

"There was a note in my mailbox. Couple days ago. It had a hundred dollars in it," he sputtered.

"And?" Finley demanded again.

"It said I would get another hundred dollars. If I would get you out of town."

"Who sent the note?"

"There was no signature."

"You expect me to believe that?" Finley asked.

"Please, I'm no criminal," he pleaded. "I needed the hundred dollars. I can't work. Not with this." He pulled the useless left arm out of his coat pocket and held it up to Finley. The fingers were curled into a small ball at the end of a thin wrist.

"Are you sure there was no signature?" Finley demanded.

"Yes! Please, don't tell Wally! I can't afford to get thrown out of here! There's nowhere else to go!" he pleaded.

Finley glared at the man standing in front of him. "You didn't have to kill a damn dog to get me out of town," he said finally. "There was no need for that."

The man who had identified himself as Burt looked puzzled. "I don't know what you're talking about," he said slowly.

"The dog you killed and threw across my bed, damn it!" Finley repeated angrily. "You know you did it! Don't play any more games with me!"

Fear and confusion played alternately across the eyes of the man standing across the room. "I didn't kill no dog, mister," he said quietly. "I threw your clothes on the floor and smashed your watch and put an ice pick in your tire, but I don't know nothin' about no dog."

"Don't lie to me!" Finley muttered angrily.

"Look." The man held up his limp arm again. "How could I kill a dog with this?"

Finley paused. His eyes moved back and forth between the paralyzed arm and the man's face. "You didn't kill a dog and spread him across my bed?"

"No!"

"You're not lying to me?"

"No, please, I've never killed anything in my entire life I'm just trying to survive, that's all."

Finley, as a professional, sensed the sincerity in the man's plaintive denial. He studied the intruder's eyes for a few more seconds. Then he stepped back from the open doorway.

The thin man darted swiftly past Finley and disappeared into the darkness at the end of the hallway. Finley stepped quickly back into the hotel room. He locked the door behind him, turned off the light, and walked over to the front window that overlooked Main Street.

His encounter with the intruder had temporarily eliminated the doubts Finley had had earlier while he sat alone in the hotel lobby. Clearly, he was on to something. Something important enough for someone out there in the darkness to try to drive him out of the small town. But did it involve Joel Hampton? Or was it something else? And who was it out there who wanted him out of Carver County? And how far would that person go to see to it that he, Ned Finley, never found what he was looking for?

Finley leaned against the window sill and watched the street lights play across the abandoned stores and shops on the Main Street of Danvers. For a moment he thought he saw someone standing in the shadows on the other side of the street. But then he realized it was only the moonlight catching the silhouette of the stone eagle and projecting it onto the side wall of the store immediately adjacent to the County Building.

Chapter Seven

I

"The record of Maureen McCarthy's confinement at Farmington," Schlepler said as he placed the cardboard box on the floor in front of Ned Finley and began toying with the pieces of the picture puzzle.

Finley sat down and studied the papers. He had hurried from Danvers to the mental hospital, arriving just as darkness fell, in the hope that Schlepler would be able to retrieve this file. "It says here that she escaped from Farmington," he mused.

"Yes," Schlepler agreed as he inserted a small piece of the puzzle into the autumn landscape scene.

Finley ran his index finger slowly across the brown page. "'Maureen McCarthy...committed to Farmington for lewd and immoral conduct.' What kind of 'lewd and immoral conduct'?"

"Someone had her committed," Schlepler said without looking up from the puzzle. "The signatures are at the bottom of the page."

Finley moved his eyes to the bottom of the document. "'Witnesses to the lewd and immoral conduct of Maureen McCarthy...Frank Graham, Helga Graham, Oscar Sumners, Agnes Sumners...dated April 14, 1895.' Four signatures were enough to have her committed?"

"If they were very influential people."

"What do you make of this?" Finley asked. "What kind of 'lewd and immoral conduct' are they talking about?"

Aurther Schlepler reached for the document and laid it flat on the coffee table. "There are several things about this document that raise one's suspicions about the motives of everyone involved. You will note, for example, that Maureen McCarthy was confined to the western wing. In the nineteenth century, Farmington's western wing was reserved for unwed mothers who were considered morally unfit to live in the community."

"So that is the 'lewd and immoral conduct' they accuse her of," Finley said softly.

"Yes, Maureen McCarthy was undoubtedly pregnant when she escaped."

"Was it common practice in the 1890s to put unwed mothers in insane asylums?" Finley asked.

"No, but a young woman with powerful enemies might end up in one. Especially if she had no one to defend her. In this case, as you said earlier, she was a young, rather attractive Irish woman in a Scandinavian county. Undoubtedly, her manner of living tempted some of the husbands of Danvers' finest and she made many enemies in the process. The world back then was not quite so willing to accept a high-spirited, independent woman."

"Why do you suppose these specific individuals signed this?" Finley asked, pointing to the four signatures at the bottom of the page.

"That is difficult to say. It's possible that they were merely appointed to carry out the wishes of the community. Or perhaps they had their own personal reasons for wanting her declared insane."

"Why do you say that?"

"Intuition maybe. Also I found this." Schlepler handed Finley a small piece of writing paper with a note scratched on one side.

"'Dear Maureen', " Finley read. "'I can't believe they are doing this to you. I'm sorry. Love Maynard.'" Finley paused momentarily to contemplate the meaning of the note. "Who do you suppose Maynard is?"

"Now that is one of the great mysteries in this whole affair, Ned," Schlepler said as he toyed with two pieces of the picture puzzle. "Like the vines growing on the granite walls outside that window, the lives you are dealing with here are becoming progressively more intertwined. One can only hope that the death of the flower will reveal the common root from which they all sprang." Schlepler inserted two more tiny pieces of the picture puzzle into the autumn landscape scene. "Tell me, Ned, why are you so involved in the Hampton case? Certainly you have worked with other schizophrenic personalities. Why is this one so special? Is it because of Tony?" Schlepler asked after a short pause.

Finley nodded weakly as he glanced back at the darkened landscape outside the window. "I suppose. At least that's part of it."

"You aren't even sure that he was your son," Schlepler continued.

"He was looking for me when he died," Finley said lamely.

"Those were only rumors, Ned. You can't be sure. Why punish yourself?"

Finley glanced down at the picture puzzle on the coffee table. "Those who were close to his mother told me he was my son and he was looking for me when he died . . . or committed suicide . . ."

"You didn't even know of his existence until it was all over," Schlepler interrupted him. "Shouldn't his mother have told you, if she wanted you to know?"

"I lost all contact with her. Deliberately, I suppose. But I have no idea what she told him about me. Perhaps he assumed the worst. Perhaps he had a right to assume the worst. But he was obviously trying to find out for himself before he died." Finley paused momentarily. "Every son has a right to know his father, Aurther."

Schlepler sighed and began toying again with the picture puzzle. "And you think something like that is happening to Joel Hampton?" he asked.

"I don't know," Finley admitted. "I'll be the first to admit that I'm losing some of my objectivity in this case. I'm sure you noticed the resemblance between Joel Hampton and the picture I have of Tony. But, like I said, that's only part of the reason." As he spoke, Finley stood and walked over to the rear window of Schlepler's room. Outside, the moonlight played gently over the empty fields, and light cloud formations drifted lazily beneath a star-filled sky. "I've been in this profession for almost thirty years, Aurther," Finley said as he leaned against the window sill. "And I'm more aware than anyone of the inadequacies of contemporary psychological theory. Oh, we find convenient labels to attach to various forms of deviant behavior. But we know—all of us, every psychiatrist or psychologist who ever lived—that terms like 'schizophrenia' or 'paranoia' or 'psychopathic tendencies' are only partial explanations for human behavior. But it goes deeper than that, much deeper than that."

Schlepler looked up from the picture puzzle. "And?" he inquired gently.

"I've always felt in my guts," Finley continued, "that there are other explanations for the kind of behavior we see around here." As he spoke, Finley turned away from the window and gestured toward the outside hallway. "I've always sensed that we may live on the edge of a thin, but impenetrable veil between this life and other lives we have lived. For some reason, in Joel Hampton's mind that veil has been pierced and he is slipping over to the other side."

"Do you feel this is a universal phenomenon?" Schlepler asked cryptically as he lit an old pipe lying on the coffee table next to the picture puzzle.

"I don't know what you mean," Finley continued. "But it's possible that many so-called psychological traits are really the results of earlier patterns of behavior and experiences from previous lives. And it's equally possible that unresolved traumas from past lives work their way up through our subconscious minds, frequently manifesting themselves in forms of anti-social behavior. Of course I have no proof for this."

"Your colleagues will never accept such a theory, Ned. Even if there is some truth to it. They will think you have taken temporary leave of your senses," Schlepler said as he puffed contentedly on the pipe. "You may even be excommunicated from the profession."

"Psychology is still an infant," Finley said as he looked back out the window at the clouds moving across the sky. "It has much to learn about itself. What I'm suggesting is no more far-fetched than what Freud was arguing for half-a-century ago. Perhaps in another half-century the theory of past lifetimes and their influence on contemporary behavior will be equally acceptable—or at least plausible."

Schlepler sighed deeply. "And you think Joel Hampton is the key to this breakthrough?" Schlepler asked somewhat sardonically. "Perhaps he is the proof you need?"

"Maybe," Finley said as he rubbed the back of his neck and continued to stare out the window. "At the very least, I've never before worked with a patient who so clearly reflects memories of some previous existence. If that does not qualify as a 'breakthrough,' certainly it must at least give us reason to pause and reflect upon what we are doing here at Farmington. Freud taught us to go back to earliest childhood to find the source of all aberrant behavior. Perhaps he did not teach us to go back far enough. Perhaps we have to go back even beyond the moment of conception."

II

After his conversation with Aurther Schlepler, Ned Finley walked down Farmington's dark corridors. He climbed the stairs to the second floor and entered the room where Joel Hampton was strapped to the frame of his bed. Susan Hampton was sitting in a wooden chair next to her husband. Behind them, the pale moonlight filtered through the small window and reflected off the white blanket that covered Joel Hampton's body. Susan Hampton was gazing indifferently out the window at the darkened landscape.

"Has there been any change?" Finley asked as he walked over to her.

Susan Hampton shook her head.

"I've asked the nurses to keep him tranquilized, at least temporarily," Finley said gently. "They'll be moving him down to the first floor, so it'll be more pleasant for you to visit him. When we get some more answers, we'll cut back on the medication and see what he remembers."

Susan nodded to indicate she understood. Then she reached into her coat pocket and pulled out the notebook she had found at the bottom of Joel's briefcase. "I found this yesterday," she said. "It's Joel's. It was on top of his desk. He must have been doodling in it before Jim Morris sent him down to the vault."

Finley sat down in the other small wooden chair and began paging slowly through the notebook. He paused and ran his fingertips lightly over the last page, which was completely darkened in by bold, sweeping strokes from a lead pencil. Finley felt the perforations where the pencil strokes had left grooves and small tears in the thick legal paper.

"What do you make of it?" Susan asked.

"It looks like some kind of a record of the thoughts that have been tormenting your husband," Finley said. "There is tremendous violence and passion in these drawings. Also great confusion." Finley flipped back through the notebook. He paused at the drawing of the old Victorian home. "Unless I miss my guess," he speculated, "this is the same farmhouse as the one in the photograph."

"Has Joel ever seen the photograph?"

"Yes, but not long enough to remember all this detail. Unless, of course, he has a photographic memory."

"No," Susan shook her head. "Joel's very intelligent but he doesn't have a photographic memory."

Finley glanced over at the hospital bed. "Then he's probably been in Carver County before. Maybe even in the 1920s."

"Why do you say that?" Susan asked.

"An antique dealer told me this house was most likely one of the old Victorian farmhouses out by the Little Sioux River northwest of Danvers. He also knew of a Maureen McCarthy who lived in Carver County in the 1890s. She was eventually committed to Farmington. I don't know if she has any connection to all of this."

Finley pulled the note out of his pocket that Aurther Schlepler had found in the basement of the Farmington State Mental Hospital. He handed it to Susan. "Aurther Schlepler found this. He's a friend of mine."

"I know. He stopped by," Susan said as she read the note. "Who's Maynard?"

"I don't know. But he obviously has some connection to Maureen McCarthy. And maybe to your husband."

Both Finley and Susan looked at the pale full moon floating through the darkness outside the small window. Then Finley glanced over at Susan again. He had noticed a kind of listlessness and weariness creeping into her manner and demeanor, and it worried him. He was altogether too aware that the spouses of the mentally ill were frequently subjected to so much stress that they themselves became psychologically traumatized. Finley had even worked with cases where the patient was eventually cured, but the patient's spouse slipped into deep, suicidal states of depression.

"How are *you* doing?" Finley asked gently. "Are you standing up to the strain of Joel's condition?"

Susan nodded weakly and looked over at Finley. "I'm tired," she said. "But I'll be all right."

"Are you sure?"

"Yes, I'm sure. Don't worry about me, Dr. Finley. Worry about Joel." Susan paused momentarily. Then she looked back at her husband. "Dr. Finley, do you suppose it's possible that Joel is incurably insane?" Susan Hampton asked suddenly.

"I'd like to think that isn't the case," Finley answered gently, putting his arm around her shoulder. "Come on. Let's go downstairs and get a cup of coffee. You look exhausted."

As Ned Finley and Susan Hampton walked out of the room, the moonlight reflected off the white blanket and touched the thick beard on Joel Hampton's face. There was an almost imperceptible movement across his dry lips.

Maynard? He had heard that name before. He was a young boy. Just big enough to walk. He was sitting in the shadows at the bottom of a stairway. Bright light from the next room poured out onto the floor. The light was only a few feet away from where he was sitting. He hadn't been able to sleep and he had walked down the long flight of stairs. But he saw the light and heard the man's voice and he thought maybe he shouldn't go in there. So he sat down on the bottom of the stairs and he listened as a man and a woman talked in hushed tones. That's when he heard the name "Maynard." It was followed by a woman's voice. She was crying. The man said something but the crying didn't stop. He stood and walked back into the darkness at the top of the stairs. Long

*into the night he heard the crying. And he remembered the
name Maynard.*

III

The Danvers library was a small granite structure located alongside a foothill north of Main Street. Two polished
stone pillars were set solidly in granite blocks on both sides of
the front entrance. Above the entrance, large stone letters
spelled out the name, "Andrew Carnegie Library." As Finley
stepped into the small hallway, his footsteps echoed loudly on
the tile floor. The large door creaked slowly shut behind him
and made a long, drawn-out, mournful wail as its wooden
edge slipped tightly past the metal jam.

Finley climbed a short flight of stairs to the main floor of
the library. A small, trim, elderly woman was working behind
a large, pulpit-shaped desk in the middle of the room. She
was busily repairing several old manuscripts and leather-
bound books that were organized neatly across her desk.
Nearby, four homemade display cases were spaced symmetrically
around the room. Other historical artifacts and collections
were arranged along the built-in book shelves that ran the
length of all four walls.

"Yes?" the old woman inquired cheerfully as she looked
up from a leather binding she was carefully gluing to the back
of an old bible.

"Are you Marsha Williams?" Finley asked.

"Yes, I am," she replied again cheerfully.

"The clerk at the County Recorder's Office said you
might be able to help me."

"What is it you need, young man?"

"I'm looking for a 1920s map of Carver County. I need to
know the shortest route between Danvers and Carson in
1926."

Marsha Williams finished running her finger carefully
along the newly glued edge of the leather binding. Then she
set the bible on a table behind the front desk.

"What do you know about the history of Carson?" She asked the question as though eager to begin a lecture on the subject.

"Nothing," Finley answered. "A fellow in the County Building told me it was kind of a boom town. Sprung up quickly and died just as fast."

"Carson was part of the last major period of railroad expansion in this area," she began. "The town just kind of grew up alongside the intersection of the Little Sioux Line Railroad and the Great Northern Railroad. The Great Northern Railroad pulled out of this area almost as soon as the last track was laid. Rerouted its lines through Tyler. The Little Sioux Line Railroad folded a couple of decades later, in the twenties. Carson sprang up and died so fast that no county roads were ever built to connect it to Danvers."

"How did people get from Danvers to Carson?" Finley asked.

"By railroad, when the trains were running. Schedules were kind of irregular in those days. Otherwise on foot or horseback. They just followed the railroad tracks—the Little Sioux Line. Used to be an old Indian trail in the 1800s. People walked it all the time."

"Where can I find this Sioux Line Railroad?"

"Well, they don't use it anymore. Haven't for years. Railroad buffs walk it every once in a while, but there's no traffic on it. Weeds and marshlands have pretty much covered the old ties and railroad tracks. Come over here. I'll show you where it is." Marsha Williams stepped out from behind her pulpit-shaped desk and led Finley over to the western wall of the Carnegie Library. A large white map of Carver County was prominently displayed in the middle of the wall above the book shelves. It was labeled "Carver County-1933."

Marsha Williams unhooked a long wooden pointer hanging on the wall next to the bookshelves. She raised its metal tip and ran it along the white surface of the large county map. "This is Danvers here and this is Carson," she said, pointing at two different sections of the map. "The Sioux Line Railroad ran right alongside the Little Sioux River, just west of here about two miles. Farther north, it veered away from the Little Sioux River and angled off in a northeasterly direction toward Carson."

"How far is it between Carson and Danvers?"

"Oh there are roads that go that way now. Dirt roads. Kind of bumpy but they'll get you there. Probably about thirteen miles."

"No, I mean how far is it from Carson to Danvers along the Sioux Line Railroad."

"Nine miles. It's exactly nine miles. Are you planning to walk it?"

"Yes, I think so," Finley said, carefully studying the map. "Incidentally, have you ever heard of a Katharine McCarthy who might have lived around here in the 1920s?"

"No. No one by that name," Marsha Williams responded, considering the name carefully. "I've known just about every family in Danvers for more than sixty years. I'd remember that name if she'd lived here."

"What about a Judd McCarthy?" Finley asked. "Have you ever heard that name?"

"Oh my, yes, he was a ruffian and a scoundrel. He disappeared with some payroll money. My brother was with the group that went looking for him."

"Did they ever find him?"

"No."

"Did they ever find a body?"

"No. They figure he headed for the Dakotas."

"Didn't he disappear somewhere along the Sioux Line Railroad?" Finley asked, gesturing towards the large map.

"Well, he was in Carson when they last saw him. He could have headed out in any direction from there. Most likely he went west with the money, not south along the Sioux Line Railroad."

Finley continued to study the map carefully. "It seems kind of strange to me," he finally said, "that they would send a man on foot to pick up the payroll. It would seem much safer to have the payroll shipped by railroad car right to the construction site. Didn't the Little Sioux Line run right through the Hanley Brothers Construction site?"

"Yes, it did. My, you do know a lot about the history of Carver County," Marsha Williams said admiringly.

"Only what I read in a newspaper article," Finley replied. "It said something about the construction site for the Little Sioux Water Reclamation Project. I assumed that meant next to the Little Sioux River."

"Yes, it certainly did. And of course you're right. Normally they did ship the payroll by armored car, right to the construction site."

"Why didn't they this time?"

"Well, if I remember correctly, the normal procedure was for the payroll to come via the Great Northern Railroad. Actually, it was another smaller railroad that leased the line from the Great Northern after they rerouted their tracks to Tyler. The payroll would then be transferred to the Little Sioux Line in Carson and accompanied by armed guard to the construction site just outside of Danvers."

"It seems strange that they would normally take so many precautions. Yet this time they sent one man to Carson to pick up the payroll."

"There was some question about that, if I remember correctly," Marsha Williams mused as she looked up at the old map of Carver County. "Fred Hanley said he didn't want the payroll sitting in Carson for two days until the next train came through on the Little Sioux Line Railroad. And I guess the men hadn't been paid for a while and there were some grumblings. So he sent McCarthy."

"Alone?" Finley asked.

"Yes."

"It seems to me they would at least send several armed men."

"McCarthy had a reputation," Marsha Williams said. "Fred Hanley didn't think anyone would try to mess with him."

"Were they certain that someone didn't 'try to mess with him'?" Finley asked.

"Oh my, yes," Marsha Williams said as she and Finley walked back to the front desk. "No body was ever found. And there was no sign of a struggle. My brother told me they were convinced McCarthy had fled into the Dakotas with the money. They put out a reward for him, you know?"

"Yes, I know. Did anyone ever collect on it?"

"Nope."

"Well, thank you very much," Ned Finley said as he walked toward the entrance to the library.

"Are you going out to walk the Little Sioux Line?" she called after him.

"Yes, I am."

"Be careful."

"Why?"

"It's overrun with wildlife. Snakes and skunks all over the place. They probably won't cause you no harm unless you step on them. But you should be careful."

"Thanks," Finley said as he started walking down the small flight of stairs.

Behind him, Marsha Williams looked down at her desk and uttered, "Oh drats. He didn't sign the register."

She turned the register slowly around on top of the front desk. There were only two signatures entered between the neatly lined spaces. Marsha Williams pulled the quill-shaped pen out of its holder next to the registration book and scratched something in one of the empty spaces.

"There," she said, admiring her handiwork. "'Tall man with brown beret.' He can sign beneath that if he ever comes in again."

IV

Ned Finley drove his Studebaker onto the gravel shoulder of a country road some two miles west of Danvers. Small rocks crunched beneath the weight of the automobile as it came to a halt next to the stubble of a corn field. Dust billowed out from beneath the automobile, swirled across the ditch next to the road, and dissipated above the jagged corn stalks.

Finley stepped out of the car and looked across the empty corn field. In the distance, a long, winding embankment protruded out of the prairies, arching out of sight in a northerly direction. The old railroad line curled across the Midwestern landscape like a huge snake slumbering beneath a layer of dead weeds.

Finley had no idea what he hoped to accomplish by walking the old Sioux Line Railroad. Clearly, there were many suspicious events surrounding the disappearance of Judd McCarthy. But did McCarthy's disappearance have anything to do with Joel Hampton? At the very least, Finley rationalized, even if his journey to Carson accomplished nothing else, he would familiarize himself with some of the sights Judd McCarthy had seen prior to his disappearance some thirty years earlier. Maybe something along the way would provide a clue as to the reasons behind McCarthy's disappearance? Or maybe he could find something he could later use to prod Joel Hampton's subconscious mind to determine once and for all if there was a connection between his young patient and Judd McCarthy?

As Finley picked his way through the furrows and jagged corn stalks, he could hear the distant popping sound of the cylinders of a small tractor. In the extreme northern end of the empty corn field, a thin stream of smoke poured steadily out of a small John Deere tractor. As Finley approached the abandoned Sioux Line Railroad, he had to walk across several newly plowed, black furrows. On the other side of the furrows, he climbed the embankment and walked to the top of the Sioux Line Railroad.

Dry, matted vegetation covered most of the wooden cross ties and rusty iron tracks of the Sioux Line Railroad. Dead crab grass, dandelions, and other weeds filled the areas between the rotting railroad ties, and tall sunflowers grew alongside the railroad embankment, their brown and yellow heads tilted upwards at the bright sun that moved lazily across a clear blue sky. Clumps of trees on both sides of the railroad embankment surrounded and concealed old barns and sheds and abandoned homes. To the north, the railroad embankment disappeared into a thick marshland.

As Finley's feet crunched through the dry vegetation, he looked out over the surrounding countryside. The Little Sioux River ran almost parallel to the railroad embankment for the first three miles of the journey to Carson. Finley could hear the gurgling waters as they drifted slowly southwards.

Two miles into his trip, Finley saw several deep trenches that had been dug almost to the very banks of the Little Sioux River. At the bottom of one of these trenches, a concrete culvert had been partially exposed by the constant erosion of rain and flood waters. Piles of discarded lumber and steel molds were also scattered around the bottom of the trench, and an abandoned railroad car rested on two rusty rails several feet above the concrete culvert. Finley studied the general layout of the trenches, the culvert, and the abandoned railroad car. He suddenly realized that he had stumbled upon the remnants of the Little Sioux Water Reclamation Project.

Finley walked down the railroad embankment and sat on a weathered packing crate located next to a pile of discarded lumber at the bottom of the trench. He took a large handkerchief out of his back pocket and slowly wiped the beads of perspiration from his brow. In the distance, a windmill groaned plaintively to the blue sky. The only other sound was that of the breeze blowing gently through the dead weeds and grass that covered the bottom of the long trench.

As he folded his handkerchief and put it in his back pocket, Finley noticed a slight movement underneath one of the piles of lumber. He leaned over to get a closer look, then lifted a rotting wooden pallet and found himself staring into the sleepy eyes of a huge snake. Finley froze momentarily as the snake's eyes glared sinisterly out of the darkness at him. Then he dropped the pallet and scurried quickly back up the side of the railroad embankment. The sound of the groaning windmill accompanied him for several hundred yards as he moved in the direction of the distant marshland.

V

It was mid-afternoon when Finley entered the city limits of Carson. The town was small, much smaller than Danvers. There was no sign of human activity as Finley walked down the narrow main street and entered a building that had a sign over the doorway reading, "Carson Chronicle." A sign inside the doorway directed him to the second floor of the small wooden structure.

At the top of the steep flight of stairs, Finley entered a

stuffy room with two heavy wooden tables located in the middle of the floor. No one else was in the room, but rows of old newspapers cluttered shelves that were located along the four walls. Above each shelf, a hand-lettered sign conveniently indicated the year in which the newspapers had been published. Finley paged through a small pile of newspapers shelved under the year 1926. When he found what he was looking for, he carried the newspaper back to the large tables in the center of the room. He placed the newspaper on one of the tables and slowly paged through it. The paper was dated October 14, 1926.

On the second page he found a small article under the headline, "Local Wrestler Defeated."

Local residents were treated Saturday afternoon to an old-fashioned dogfight between Judd McCarthy, a wrestler of some repute from the Danvers area, and Farmer John Tobin, said to be the biggest and strongest man in Carson. When the smoke had cleared, Judd McCarthy was the victor, and also the winner, rumor has it, of a considerable amount in wagers. A picture of the exhausted combatants appears elsewhere in this week's edition of the *Chronicle*.

Ned Finley paged eagerly through the newspaper until he found the caption, "Exhausted Participants in Wrestling Match Shake Hands." There was a hole in the newspaper, just above the caption, where someone had carefully run a pocket knife or razor blade over the boundaries of the photograph, neatly extracting it from the yellowish-brown page.

Finley stared for several seconds at the hole in the newspaper. Then he placed it back on the shelf, descended the narrow stairway, and walked out into the Main Street of Carson. Overhead, the sky was still clear and blue, but the sun was beginning to dip toward the western horizon, and Finley knew he would have to start back to Danvers immediately or risk walking the last few miles of the railroad line in total darkness.

Outside of Carson, Finley again climbed the railroad embankment and began the nine-mile journey back to Danvers.

He listened to his feet crunch through the dry vegetation. Occasionally, pheasants ran through the brush on both sides of the railroad embankment.

Finley wondered about the meaning of the missing newspaper photograph. Everything Finley knew about Judd McCarthy now made him suspicious. Nothing about McCarthy's life and disappearance was normal. His life had many layers of meaning, or so it seemed. Even if it turned out that there was no connection between Judd McCarthy and Joel Hampton, Finley felt himself becoming increasingly obsessed with the man.

Off to the side of the railroad embankment, the gray gable of an abandoned barn protruded above a small cluster of trees. The barn was surrounded by shattered corn stalks that had been destroyed by an earlier hail storm. The corn stalks bent toward the ground at awkward angles, and the tassels and small ears of corn hung limply a few feet above the black, leaf-strewn furrows. A weather vane in the shape of a rooster adorned the top peak of the ancient structure. The front door of the barn hung precariously from one hinge.

Ned Finley stepped off the railroad embankment and walked over to the barn. Inside, sunlight streamed through the many holes in the roof and walls, illuminating the dust that hung suspended in the air, and casting long shadows across the dirty, straw-covered floor. A green tractor was rusting against one wall and plowshares were lined up in neat rows along another wall. In the middle of the room, a stone grinding wheel was leaning heavily against a wheelbarrow. Several burlap sacks containing seed corn were stacked behind the grinding wheel.

Suddenly, as Finley moved towards the center of the barn, there was a loud rustling sound overhead. It was followed by the frantic noise of flapping wings as three sparrows flew out of the rafters and darted quickly across the rays of sunlight, causing the particles of dust to swirl wildly in the still air. Two of the sparrows flew out of the barn through large holes in the roof. The third sparrow smashed into one of the dust-covered window panes. It beat its wings frantically against the glass, then it too darted through a hole in the roof and disappeared.

Finley's curiosity was aroused by a wooden cabinet

which was secured by a huge, rusty padlock. He pried at the padlock half-heartedly, then lost interest and wandered back in the direction of the wheelbarrow and stone grinding wheel in the center of the barn. The wheelbarrow contained an assortment of junk. Pieces of leather harnesses and bridles, twine, old stoneware jars, rusty nails, and several horseshoes were intertwined at the bottom of the wheelbarrow. Finley placed several of the smaller items in his pockets, then turned and walked toward the front door.

As he was about to step out into the sunlight, he heard it—the distant popping sound of a .22-rifle. Within seconds, the small window shattered and pieces of glass exploded onto the straw-covered floor. Other bullets splintered the rotting panels of the barn.

Finley dropped to the floor of the barn as the popping sounds built in intensity and the broken glass and splinters of wood splattered on the straw and dirt all around him. The popping sounds built to a crescendo pitch, then grew more distant and finally faded away altogether.

VI

"Get those patients out of there," one of the muscular orderlies yelled from the top of the staircase leading down to the main floor of the Farmington State Mental Hospital. "We're bringing Hampton down."

Joel Hampton stood at the top of the staircase. He was dressed in a faded green hospital uniform, and his arms were strapped to a large leather belt that circled his waist. The thick, black beard now covered his face and neck, and he stared straight ahead, unblinking, almost catatonic.

Two large hospital orderlies each grabbed an arm and led him down the flight of stairs towards the main floor. Another hospital orderly and a young nurse scattered the patients at the bottom of the staircase. The patients slowly shuffled off.

"Where are you taking him?" the nurse asked.

"Room 111," the orderly replied as he stepped off the stone staircase.

"Who authorized the transfer?"

"Finley."

"Is he safe?" she asked.

"He hasn't caused us any problems. Just sleeps or lies there staring at the ceiling. He'll be under sedation as long as he's down here."

The nurse shook her head in disgust. "I don't know what they expect us to do. We've already got more patients than we can possibly handle. Now they give us one who has psychopathic tendencies."

"Only following orders," the orderly shrugged.

The nurse shook her head again. "Bring him this way."

As the nurse turned to leave, the old woman with a paralyzed face suddenly stepped out of an adjacent room. She curled her index finger and whispered, "Come see, please, come see..."

"Sophie, get back in that room!" the young nurse admonished the old woman.

"Please, come see," the old woman pleaded.

"Sophie!" the nurse scolded the old woman. "Get back in there, right now!"

Joel Hampton's head turned slowly towards the old woman. He stared into the paralyzed mass of flesh....

Something had happened to him shortly after he stepped off the small hill. No, it was not a hill. It was...it was a railroad embankment. A long, narrow railroad embankment winding across the prairies. He remembered it now. He had stepped out of the marshland and...

"Christ, I can't budge him," one of the orderlies muttered angrily as he tugged at Joel Hampton's arm.

He was beginning to remember why he was walking on the railroad embankment. But what had happened to him in the thicket? Why had he forgotten everything from the moment he had entered the thicket until he found himself in this strange room, surrounded by these even stranger people?...

"Do you need some help?" the young nurse asked the two orderlies as they tugged on Joel's arms.

"Christ, he's stiff as a board," the other orderly muttered. "I can't even bend his elbow."

"Wait!" the first orderly said.

"What is it?"

"He's starting to relax. Give him a couple seconds."

The muscles in Joel's arms and shoulders began to relax noticeably. He stared straight ahead as the two orderlies led him toward the darkened hallway to the right of the staircase. *He was beginning to remember it all....*

VII

It was almost dusk when Ned Finley entered the marshland just outside of Danvers. Dead leaves, propelled by gentle autumn breezes, hopped and skipped across the countryside, and an occasional pheasant clucked contentedly in the nearby brush. Overhead, a flock of Canada geese flew southwards in V-formation, the lead goose bellowing a challenge to the departing sun as his flock disappeared from sight. Reeds on the edge of the marshland swayed gently in the early evening breezes. And, in the nearby sloughs and ponds, the crickets began to chirp contentedly; and frogs, startled by the crunching sound of human footsteps, leaped off fallen logs and splashed into shallow pools of water.

The marshland covered less than two acres, and Finley soon stepped out of the tall reeds and stood on the edge of an empty wheatfield. In the west, the sun was touching the horizon and casting long shadows across the wheat stubble. Ahead of him, the Little Sioux River flowed parallel to the railroad embankment, disappearing into the small foothills just outside of Danvers. In the distance, the church steeple and water tower protruded above the rolling prairies. And, in the silence of early evening, the mournful lament of an old windmill filtered distinctly across the countryside, mingling with the sound of the crickets chirping in the marshland behind Finley.

Suddenly he saw something concealed in the shadows of a large clump of trees to the east of the railroad embankment. In the departing sunlight, it looked like a human figure standing among the colorful autumn leaves and the tall, dead grass and weeds.

He walked across the empty field and paused at the edge

of the cluster of trees to peer into the shadows. What he had taken to be a human figure concealing itself in the shadows of the thicket was instead a large birdhouse suspended at the top of four long wooden poles. An old bicycle with one wheel missing was propped up against the wooden supports of the birdhouse, and, nearby, a rusty children's swing set tilted awkwardly toward the ground. An old plow and disc harrow rusted among the dead weeds beneath a tree to the east of the swing set.

In the middle of the clump of trees, the concrete foundation and basement of an old farmhouse yawned out of the dark black soil. Dead weeds and grass grew out of the cracks in the concrete walls, and the floor of the basement was littered with broken mason jars and puddles of water. A small shed, seemingly untouched by the devastation that had vented its rage on the farmyard, stood nearby.

"Tornado," Finley whispered to himself as he wandered around the abandoned farmyard.

On the northern side of the basement's foundation, Finley reached down into the weeds and grass and extracted the shattered face of a child's doll. At that moment, he felt the ground beneath his feet shift ever-so-gently. The slight movement was followed by a loud groan and then the sound of rotting lumber as boards cracked and splintered all around him.

Finley tried to step back but the rotting boards gave way beneath his feet and he plunged down into the darkness.

Chapter Eight

I

As the sun climbed the eastern horizon, it cast a pale gray light over the empty fields outside of Danvers. The dead autumn leaves hung motionlessly in the nearby trees.

Overnight, a light dew had settled on the trees, and as the sunlight entered the groves, the tiny beads of moisture glistened and sparkled, accentuating the colors and veins of the dead autumn leaves. As the sun rose higher in the eastern sky, the tiny beads of moisture evaporated, and the drooping leaves began to flicker ever-so-gently in the early morning breezes. Within an hour, the leaves were dancing in the trees and rustling their wrinkled bodies against one another.

In the tornado-ravaged farmyard, the sunlight fell across the splintered boards and entered the deep hole. Under Finley's weight, the rotting boards that covered the opening of an old cistern had collapsed, and he had fallen through the splintered lumber into the darkness. Several of the old boards had fallen into the cistern behind him, splashing into the dirty water that covered the bottom of the concrete chamber. One of the pieces of lumber had hit Finley on top of the head as he fell, momentarily stunning him.

When he came to, he found himself collapsed across a pile of rocks and lumber, with only his head and shoulders above water. In the darkness, he decided to wait until daybreak before making an attempt to get out. He constructed a small platform out of rocks and pieces of lumber, and, leaning against the concrete wall and dangling his feet in the dirty black water, he sat on the rotting boards throughout the night. He dozed off occasionally, but for most of the evening he stayed awake, listening to the sounds of the crickets in the darkness above him.

In the morning, as the sunlight entered the cluster of trees and filtered into the darkness of the cistern, Finley studied his predicament. He was at the bottom of an old well, the mouth of which was perhaps ten feet above where he sat. Even by standing and stretching, he could only reach to within five or six feet of the concrete rim of the cistern. Perhaps by piling the rocks and boards and other debris against the walls of the cistern, he reasoned, he might be able to stretch that final five or six feet and climb out.

Two frogs and a large garter snake lay in the shallows of the water on the other side of the cistern. In the darkness, Finley had sensed a slight, undulating movement across the surface of the water. As the moonlight filtered into the deep hole, he decided it was nothing more than the black, striped body of a harmless garter snake. In the morning, as he looked across the well, he was relieved to find that his original guess was correct; he had nothing to fear from his fellow prisoner.

Finley reached into the water at the bottom of the well and began stacking rocks, lumber and other debris against one of the concrete walls. Several of the objects he threw aside as unusable. Most of the objects, however, he patiently piled on top of the boards and rocks alongside the concrete wall.

Several times, as he plunged his hands into the bottom of the dirty water, the frogs and the garter snake scurried to different sides of the circular, concrete walls. Once he grabbed the neck of a broken bottle and cut his index finger. He wrapped his handkerchief around the wound and continued.

When he had extracted everything usable from the bottom of the well, he stepped gingerly up onto the rock pile, balancing himself carefully against the concrete walls with his long arms. At the top of the pile of rocks and boards, he stretched mightily toward the sunlight and the concrete rim of the cistern. Still, he was at least three feet short of the opening to the well, and there was no way he could leap off the pile of rocks to gain the extra distance he needed to climb out.

Finley reached for one of the thicker pieces of lumber that dangled above his head. He pulled on it and found that it was firmly attached to something outside the mouth of the well. He reached high on the piece of lumber, grasped it firmly with both hands, and then stepped off the pile of rocks.

He pulled himself up slowly toward the open mouth of the cistern and then reached out with one hand for the concrete rim. As his hand almost grasped the edge of the concrete rim, there was a loud groaning sound overhead, then a sharp crack like a tree limb breaking off, and he tumbled back into the water, still clutching the rotting piece of lumber with one hand.

He fell hard into the black scummy water and, for a few seconds, he was completely submerged. When he surfaced, the frogs and garter snake were swimming frantically. One of the frogs croaked a belligerent note of defiance as Finley retrieved his brown beret. Then Finley stepped out of the water and crawled back to the top of the pile of rocks and boards.

He rested for several minutes, then studied the walls of the cistern, looking for any holes in the concrete surface that might provide footholds. But there were none. Finley looked up at the blue sky and the small clouds that were drifting serenely past the circular opening at the top of the cistern. The clouds seemed almost close enough to touch. In the distance, he heard the distinct popping sound of the small cylinders of a tractor. As Finley rested at the bottom of the well, the sound came closer and closer to where he was sitting. When the tractor seemed only a few hundred feet away, it suddenly backfired, then coughed and sputtered and was silent.

"Help! I'm in here!" Finley yelled. He felt both foolish and relieved at the same time. "Help! I'm trapped in here!" he yelled again.

As he yelled, he could hear his own voice echo across the deep cistern, and he was afraid the sound might be muffled between the concrete walls. Then he heard what sounded like a metal door slamming shut.

"Help!" he yelled again, this time even louder.

The sound of his voice was interrupted by the put-put-put of the cylinders of the tractor. The sound grew louder, then faded and disappeared across the prairies.

II

For the next few hours, Finley examined the walls of the cistern. He ran his fingers carefully over the concrete surface to make certain that he hadn't overlooked any metal rungs that he knew were cemented into some cisterns. He even went so far as to pound against the concrete walls with a large rock, hoping that perhaps he could chip out two or three small footholds to help him climb out of the cistern. But nothing worked and he sat back down on the pile of rocks.

The irony of his situation did not escape him. He had gone to Carson in search of a man who had disappeared mysteriously in 1926, and now, unless he could figure something out, he too would vanish and would probably never be heard from again. What would happen to Joel? Would he grow old? Die in that same catatonic state? And Susan? And Aggy? It was too ironic, too coincidental, almost amusing in an insane way. Perhaps Aurther Schlepler's fates were trying to tell him something? Perhaps they did not want him to find out what had really happened to McCarthy? The thought made Finley angry and he stood up to consider new ways of escaping from his prison.

Finley reached into his pocket and extracted three of the old nails he had pulled out of the rusty wheelbarrow back in the abandoned barn a few miles outside of Carson. He put two of the nails in his mouth. Then he reached high on the concrete wall with the third nail and began pounding on it with a large rock. The rusty nail snapped almost immediately.

He was able to drive the second nail about half an inch into a small crack in the concrete wall before it too snapped. The third nail sunk about two inches into the small crack and held firm. Finley grasped the head of the large nail with his right hand. As the metal dug deeply and painfully into his palm, he raised himself slowly off the rock pile, using his feet to provide leverage against the concrete wall. As he reached out for the concrete rim several inches above his hand, the nail suddenly broke loose from the small crack, and again Finley went tumbling down the pile of rocks and into the black water.

This time, as he surfaced out of the dirty water, he found himself looking up at a puzzled face poised at the top of the cistern. The man's battered straw hat and gray bib-overalls were clearly outlined against a blue sky.

As the frogs and the garter snake swirled around him and the dirty water ran out of his hair and down his cheeks, Finley stared in disbelief at the farmer.

"What the hell you doing down there?" the farmer finally asked.

"I'm taking a bath," Finley replied, not quite knowing why he said it.

"Do you need any help gettin' outta there?"

"Yes, for Christ's sake, I've been stuck here all night."

"I'll be right back," the farmer said as his face disappeared from the opening.

Within a few minutes, the farmer returned and slid an aluminum ladder into the cistern. The metal scraped against the concrete lip of the well as it slid deeply into the dirty water. Once more Finley retrieved his beret. Then he quickly scrambled up the ladder toward the blue sky.

"How'd ya get down there?" the farmer asked as Finley crawled past the broken pieces of lumber and sat down just outside the opening to the well.

"I was looking around the farmyard when those boards collapsed under my feet."

"You're mighty lucky."

"Why do you say that?"

"Tractor broke down out there," the farmer replied, pointing out at a small John Deere tractor that stood at the end of several long black furrows. "I came over to the shed to get some tools to fix it. Heard ya poundin' on the walls of the cistern."

"Is this your land?" Finley asked.

"Well, it's on my land," the farmer answered. "But I didn't even know that well was there. Weeds covered it so much over the years. I'll bring over the grader and fill it with rocks so no one else'll fall in."

"Before you do that," Finley said, "I want to get something out of the bottom of the cistern."

"What's down there?"

"Do you have a burlap bag?" Finley asked as he started climbing back down the ladder into the depths of the well.

"Why?" the farmer yelled after him.

"I want to take something back to town with me." Finley's muffled voice filtered out of the darkness at the bottom of the cistern.

"What is it ya want to take back with you?"

"This," Finley said as he crawled back up the ladder and rolled a human skull over the lip of the well and out onto the dead grass.

"Jesus Christ!" the farmer said slowly as his eyes grew wide and he stared at the skull that rolled past his feet. Then he ran quickly toward the small shed as Finley again descended into the darkness of the cistern.

III

Joel Hampton sat in a wheel chair next to a window on the first floor of the Farmington State Mental Hospital. Behind him, several patients wandered around the hallway jabbering incoherently to one another. Other patients, completely lost in thought, shuffled across the tile floor as music from an overhead intercom system filtered through the halls and corridors.

Joel's arms and legs were strapped to the metal frame of the wheel chair, and he stared out the window at the strange, bizarre world just beyond the red granite walls of the mental hospital. . . .

He knew where he was. He had passed it several times during his wanderings in the early 1920s. He remembered the red granite walls rising out of the prairies and the strange stories and legends about the people imprisoned inside. But why was he now a patient? What had he done that he should

*be committed to an insane asylum? And what was that
strange world unfolding just beyond the window where he
sat? He had seen cars, of course. But not like the ones that
cruised past the huge open gate on the edge of the hospital
grounds. And he had seen airplanes. But not airplanes that
streaked through the blue sky, leaving long white tails streaming out behind them. He watched the white vapor disintegrate
in the blue sky, and he knew he had entered a world stranger
than anything he had ever dreamed possible. More terrifying
in its own way than any nightmare. Still, he knew he must
escape and enter that world if he was to change what had been
left undone. And he must get back to his Lady Kate. He needed
her now, even more than before. Now that he was alone—in
this strangest of worlds—how his soul cried out for Kate. . . ."*

"Come on Hampton, let's get you back to your room,"
one of the hospital orderlies said as he reached down to
unlock the wheel chair.

*He would escape and somehow he would get back to
Carver County . . . And to Kate . . . And he would find those
who had done this to him . . . And why he, Judd McCarthy,
now found himself staring out the window at the strange
world just beyond the red granite walls . . . Now that he
remembered his name, it was time for him to go back. . . .*

IV

"Where'd you find these?" the County Coroner asked
Finley as he studied the skull and the other human bones
spread out across an examining table in the basement of the
County Building.

"In an old cistern, about three or four miles west of
here," Finley answered as he too peered closely at the
human skeleton that was slowly taking shape beneath the
bright lights that illuminated the examining table.

"You don't know which farm?" the Coroner asked.

"Nope, but I can take you out there," Finley replied.
"Looks like a tornado destroyed it many years ago."

"About three miles west of here?"

"Ya."

"Must be the old Johnson place," the Coroner said as he poked a small light into the mouth cavity of the skull and examined the brown teeth. "What were you doing out there?"

"Looking for worms," Finley lied. "I was going fishing."

"Fish don't bite that well this late in the year," the Coroner said as he switched off the light and stepped back from the table.

"Tell me," Finley said. "How long has that skeleton been there?"

"Hard to say," the Coroner said as he wiped off his hands. "Probably thirty, forty years judging from the decomposition of the bones and teeth. But it could be much longer. Hard to say, really."

"It looks like the skull was fractured in three places. Arm was broken too," Finley said, pointing at the bones just above the right wrist.

"Yup, sure are," the Coroner agreed.

"Think the fall would have done that?"

"Not very likely," the Coroner answered, pointing to the three cracks in the skull. "Fall probably would have caused one of these. No way it would've done this much damage to his head. No, he was hit repeatedly over the head with something. Probably a large rock."

"Murder?"

"Most likely. A fall wouldn't have done that to his head," the Coroner repeated emphatically.

"How tall do you suppose he was?" Finley asked.

The Coroner picked up a note pad he had been writing in earlier. "Well, these are only my preliminary observations, based solely on what we have in front of us. But he's probably a male Caucasian . . . cause of death, a blow to the head . . . age, probably fifty or sixty . . . and he's, oh, couldn't be no more than five feet seven inches."

"Are you sure?" Finley asked.

"Give or take an inch or two."

"Are you positive he wasn't a much younger man? Probably well over six feet?"

"How much younger?"

"Probably thirties. Forties at the most."

"Nope. Frame and bone structure don't match that at all. He's closer to sixty and much less than six foot tall. Why do you ask?"

"I was reading about someone who disappeared around here in 1926. He was probably in his thirties, well over six foot tall."

"Well, this isn't him," the Coroner said as he picked up the dirty burlap bag and dropped it into a nearby wastepaper basket, then began packing the bones in an aluminum storage crate. "Most likely just some old hobo who was killed and his body dumped in a convenient spot."

V

Finley was feeling tired and disappointed as he walked up the flight of stairs into the hotel lobby. Behind him, the dark clouds spread across the sky, sending ominous shadows out over Main Street. Maybe, he thought, this *was* just a wild goose chase? He knew he couldn't devote his whole life to solving McCarthy's disappearance. First he had to prove that there was *definitely* a connection between McCarthy and Joel.

Inside the hotel lobby, the lights were turned on and two card games were in progress next to the western wall. Gus was sitting quietly in one of the padded easy chairs. He was staring out the window at the shadows that were moving across the storefronts on the other side of Main Street. Finley sat down beside him, and the two men looked out onto the street as the wind whipped against the huge windows causing them to creak and groan in their ancient casings.

"Feeling better, Gus?" Finley finally asked.

"Yup," Gus answered as he chewed on a wad of tobacco.

"Do you remember who I am?" Finley asked politely.

"Yup. You're the fella who was askin' 'bout Judd McCarthy the other day. Day before they took me to the hospital."

"Can I ask you some more questions about McCarthy?"

"What is it you want to know?"

"You said you worked with him."

"No, I said I worked for the Hanley Brothers Construction Company," Gus corrected Finley. "But I didn't work with McCarthy. We were assigned to different parts of the county."

"But you do remember when he disappeared?"

"Oh, yes, that I remember," Gus laughed softly to himself. "He took the payroll and left town. Cost me three months' wages."

"Are you certain there was no other explanation for his disappearance?"

"Nope. He picked up the payroll in Carson and took off into the Dakotas."

Outside, the rains began to beat heavily against the large glass windows of the hotel.

"Do you think it's possible that McCarthy ran into foul play on the way back from Carson?" Finley asked.

"Nah, he was too big. Too tough," Gus said as he spit a dark stream of tobacco juice into a spittoon next to Finley's feet. "Nobody'd mess with him."

"You don't think there was any other explanation?"

"Nope. He left with the money," Gus said emphatically. "Judd McCarthy wasn't vicious or mean. He just didn't have any sense, that's all. Probably just took the payroll over to the Dakotas and spent it."

Large hail stones began to beat against the windows overlooking Main Street. On the asphalt road, the white hail stones bounced up and down like tiny pieces of popcorn.

"What did this Judd McCarthy look like?" Finley asked after both men had watched the hail stones for several seconds.

"Oh, he was big. Very big."

"Over six foot?" Finley asked.

"Oh my, yes. Closer to six-and-a-half feet."

"How old was he?"

"Must have been in his early thirties . . . You know, if you want to see what he looks like, there's a picture of him over there on the wall."

"Where?" Finley asked.

"Here, I'll show you," Gus said, struggling to get up from his chair. Gus shuffled slowly across the room and paused to peer closely at several of the gold-leaf framed photographs. Then he pointed emphatically at one of them.

"That's McCarthy right there. The big fella in the middle ... with the shovel in his hand."

Finley leaned closer to the photograph and carefully studied the eyes and face of a huge, grinning, dark-haired laborer. Judd McCarthy was staring back at him from the middle of a group of workers who were lined up in front of a newly constructed building on Main Street. McCarthy's large dark eyes glowed with intensity and good humor in the middle of the old photograph, and his huge right forearm leaned rakishly on the handle of the large spade he had thrust several inches into the dirt on Main Street.

"Like I told ya," Gus said as he turned to leave. "He's well over six foot tall."

Finley studied the photograph for several more minutes. Then he walked back and sat down in the easy chair. Outside, the hail had stopped falling, but the rains continued to pour heavily onto Main Street. The cloud cover had blocked out the sun completely, making it seem more like late evening than mid-afternoon.

"Does it always rain this hard around here?" Finley asked.

"Get the heaviest rains in the state," Gus said as he reached into his tin of chewing tobacco and extracted a pinch with his index finger and thumb. He packed the small wad firmly in the area between his lower lip and his front teeth. "Good thing most of the crops are in. Hail'd do 'em in for sure."

"Any problem with flooding around here?"

"Only around the Little Sioux River. Farms out there get flooded most every spring."

"I noticed an unfinished culvert out that way ... about three miles outside of town. Looked like someone started to build it a long time ago and then just gave up. I assumed it was the Little Sioux Water Reclamation Project I read about in the newspapers."

"You 'assumed' right," Gus said.

"How come they didn't complete the project?"

"Ran out of money. John Sylvester started it with the Community Development League in the 20s. Hanley Brothers were called in later to help out. Always ran on a pretty tight budget. When McCarthy disappeared with the last payroll, that wiped it out for good. . . ."

In the dark skies hovering over Main Street, thunder and lightning flashed across the cloud layer and clapped loudly overhead, causing the lights in the hotel lobby to dim momentarily.

"Seems kind of strange that they would lay so much of the culvert and then stop a few hundred yards short of the Little Sioux River," Finley speculated as he watched the lights dim and then glow brightly again overhead.

"Just ran out of funds, I guess. Later there was the Depression and people had other things to worry about," Gus said.

Suddenly the lights went out in the lobby of the Danvers Hotel. "Dammit," Gus sputtered in the darkness. "Just when I had a good mouthful." Gus spit anyhow, in the general direction of the brass spittoon sitting on the floor next to Finley's feet.

"Gus?" Finley said softly.

"Huh?"

"You just hit my leg."

VI

That same afternoon, shortly after the rain stopped falling, Finley drove the 45 miles back to Farmington. A large rainbow arched across the prairies as Finley parked his Studebaker outside the gates of the Farmington State Mental Hospital. The dark black clouds had disappeared, along with the thunderstorm and hail, and puffy white clouds floated overhead in a pale blue sky.

Susan Hampton was waiting for Finley in her husband's room. The shades were pulled tight and the curtains closed to shut out the rays of the afternoon sun. Joel Hampton was sleeping peacefully on the narrow hospital bed. As before, his arms and legs were restrained by thick leather straps attached to the metal frame.

Finley sensed immediately that Susan Hampton was

feeling the deep strain of her husband's condition. In fact, he sensed that she was probably in the early stages of depression. The sullen, listless demeanor, the sense of resignation, the slow, weary movements and glazed eyes—Finley had seen those symptoms before, both in himself and in his patients. The product of two alcoholic parents, Finley had slipped into periodic depressions until he left home at the age of sixteen. Those early experiences created in him an aversion to marriage, at the same time that they made him deeply sensitive to the early signs of depression in other people.

Finley sat down next to Susan and placed a hand on her shoulder. "How are you doing?" he asked gently, paternally.

"I'm fine," Susan said without looking in his direction.

"Maybe you shouldn't spend so much time up here? Maybe you should relax more—at home?"

"I'll be fine," Susan repeated. The tone in her voice was weak and unconvincing.

Finley studied Susan's face for several seconds. Then he decided not to pressure her any further. "How's Joel?" he asked.

"They've taken him off the sedatives."

"Has he talked to you at all?"

"No."

Ned Finley and Susan Hampton sat silently for a few seconds looking at the sleeping form of Joel Hampton.

"Aurther Schlepler came by earlier," Susan said softly. "He asked how you were doing. He seemed very concerned about both you and Joel. It almost seemed like he was going to cry when he saw Joel lying here like this."

"Did he come by for any specific reason?"

"No, he was just concerned. He couldn't sleep two nights ago. He said he sensed that you were in trouble. Before he left, I called the hotel and the clerk said he had seen you just this morning. I told Aurther and he seemed reassured, but he's terrified of a picture you showed him earlier."

"The picture of the old farmhouse you found in Joel's baby clothes. Aurther said it was 'a place of madness.' He warned me not to go there."

"Have you found it yet?"

"No."

Outside the door of Joel's room, an old man in a white hospital gown shuffled past. He paused momentarily to raise his index finger in the air as he babbled something incoherently at the ceiling. Then a nurse grasped him gently by the elbow and led him down the hallway.

"Susan," Finley said. "I'm going to try something with Joel this afternoon, if it's all right with you."

"What do you have in mind?"

"I want to find out once and for all if there is a connection between him and Judd McCarthy."

"You plan to hypnotize him again?" Susan asked nervously.

"There's no need to hypnotize him. Joel is in his own hypnotic state. I just want to ask him some questions."

"Do you think it's wise?" Susan asked. "He seems to be improving."

"He's not getting any better, Susan," Finley said gently. "He's only slipping deeper and deeper into a catatonic state. If he regresses any deeper, we may never be able to bring him back."

"What if he becomes violent again?"

"We can handle the violence. In one respect the violence is a good sign. It means he's fighting the forces that are pulling him deeper and deeper into the past."

Susan stared at her husband's sleeping form. "What do you have in mind?"

"I'm going to ask him what he knows about Judd McCarthy? I'm going to take him back from Carson to Danvers along the Sioux Line Railroad. I'm convinced if I can figure out how McCarthy disappeared, I'll know why his memory still lives on inside your husband, if that is in fact the case."

"Haven't you done that before?" Susan asked.

"I have more of the details now. Maybe one of them will trigger something in Joel's subconscious mind."

Susan Hampton looked in the direction of the open doorway where the old man was again wandering down the hallway babbling at the ceiling. Then she looked back at Finley. "What do you want from me?"

"Nothing. Just your permission."

"If you think it'll help Joel, yes, of course."

Finley walked over to the side of the hospital bed. He looked closely into the face of Joel Hampton.

"Judd McCarthy," Finley began boldly. "You are in a whirlpool of color that has stopped at October 12, 1926. What happened to you on October 12, 1926?"

Joel Hampton continued to sleep peacefully on the hospital bed.

"Judd McCarthy, it's Saturday, October 12, 1926. You are in Carson to pick up the Hanley Brothers Construction Company payroll. Do you remember what happened to you on the way back from Carson on October 12, 1926?"

A short sigh escaped from Joel Hampton's lips and his chin quivered slightly.

"Judd McCarthy," Finley said, leaning over the hospital bed. "You wrestled someone in Carson. Do you remember who it was?"

"Tobin," Joel whispered under his breath.

Tobin reached out for him with both huge arms. But he knew enough to keep moving. Tobin was too big, too overweight. He knew if he kept moving Tobin would tire out. Tobin lunged at him and fell and rolled through the dust and dirt. The dust and dirt mixed with Tobin's sweat and clung to his body. When he got back up from the ground he looked like a brown bear. A huge, dirty brown bear reaching out with both arms as though to maul someone. He heard the ticking of a clock in the background as Tobin lunged and again rolled through the dirt and the dust and the rocks.

"Do you remember a Farmer Tobin?" Finley asked.

"It's a good day for a war, lad," Joel whispered in an Irish accent. "'Tween Norway and Ireland."

"Did Tobin have anything to do with your disappearance, Judd?"

"Tobin, your mama musta been a grizzly bear," Joel laughed softly.

Tobin lay face down on the dirt street, unable to move. Then he rolled slowly over onto his back, his huge chest heaving and gasping for air. His long arms were sprawled out on each side of his body. His face and chest were smeared with dirt. The Farmer Tobin was beaten and he was the champion of Carver County. Then he heard the laughter. It grew louder and louder, thundering off the dirt street and echoing against the railroad depot. It was his own laughter. He had pinned Tobin almost without having touched him. Tobin had worn himself out by rolling in the dirt. The laughter grew louder and louder as he reached down to help Tobin stand up. Tobin glared at him from the ground. His nostrils opened and closed with fierce strength and his chest heaved as he gasped for air.

"I whipped him, Kate," Joel whispered. "Make 'em kiss the Blarney stone too if I could throw 'em that far."

"Who is Kate, Judd?"

Kate was waiting for him down by the river. Kate with her white bonnet and the cotton dress that lifted gently in the breeze. She was down by the river. And he was walking. Walking beneath a clear blue sky . . .

"Who is Kate?" Finley repeated.

"There's the farm. Kate's down by the river," Joel whispered softly, cheerfully.

"What happened to you just outside of Danvers?" Finley pleaded.

The leaves whipped off the small trees in the thick grove and flew out into the prairies. He knew he shouldn't go in there. Someone was waiting for him. Someone he knew. He didn't trust that face. No, it was the eyes that he didn't trust. He remembered those eyes. But it didn't end in the grove. Not yet . . .

"Judd McCarthy," Finley asked boldly. "Who killed you that Saturday when you were on your way back from Carson to meet Kate?"

It's . . . Oh, Jesus, God, it's dark . . . There's just no way . . . Oh, Jesus, let me out . . . Kate . . . Kate . . .

"Kate! Kate! Kate!" Joel Hampton screamed as he struggled against the leather restraints and tried to sit up in the hospital bed. The veins in his powerful forearms bulged mightily and his fists clenched and unclenched with fierce strength as he fought against the leather straps.

"Judd, you're all right! You're all right!" Finley yelled as he pushed hard on Joel's chest, trying to force him back down onto the bed.

"Jesus, God, it's dark!" Joel screamed as his right arm suddenly tore free from the leather restraints.

"Susan, get the nurse! Quick!" Finley yelled as he tried to control Joel's huge, thrashing right arm. Finley fought against the powerful arm with all of his strength, but Joel Hampton lifted him bodily off the floor.

As Finley was struggling to hold onto Joel's right arm, a nurse rushed quickly into the room. She tore back the sheet and plunged a syringe into Joel Hampton's exposed right thigh. Joel fought for several more seconds against the other leather restraints. Then his eyes slowly closed and he fell back onto the mattress.

Finley quickly strapped the right arm back into the leather restraints, and Joel's forearms and clenched fists soon relaxed. He began to sleep peacefully under the influence of the strong sedative.

"Are you all right, Dr. Finley?" the nurse asked.

"Yes, I'm fine," Finley responded as he caught his breath.

"Do you need anything else?" the nurse asked.

"No," Finley panted. "Just keep him under sedatives for three more days. You know how to get in touch with me if anything happens."

"Yes, Doctor," the nurse said as she walked out of the room.

Finley turned towards Susan Hampton who was standing at the foot of the bed. Her eyes reflected a strange, confused mixture of love and fear as she stared at her husband. "I'm sorry, Susan," Finley said softly. "But it was necessary."

"What did it prove?" she stammered.

"It proves that it's definitely Judd McCarthy whose memory lives on inside of your husband. There's no question about it now."

"Why do you say that?"

"McCarthy wrestled a Farmer Tobin the day he disappeared. Apparently he won a lot of money on the wrestling match. Your husband just mentioned Tobin's name. Joel would never have known that—unless he's the reincarnation of Judd McCarthy."

Susan Hampton slumped down in the chair beside her husband's bed. "What kind of a man was this McCarthy?"

"I don't know," Finley said. "I only know him from what I have read and from what some of the old-timers in Danvers have told me."

"What did they tell you?"

Finley considered evading the question, but thought better of it. "They say he was a violent man with a strong temper. Some accuse him of disappearing into the Dakotas with a company payroll. Others speak more kindly of him."

"What do they say?"

"An old man in the hotel told me McCarthy wasn't vicious or mean. He said he just didn't have any sense."

Susan Hampton shuddered. "The man inside my husband acts more like a madman."

Finley thought the statement over carefully. "Susan, it's hard to really know a man when you only meet him through old photographs, stories, and newspaper articles. But I like Judd McCarthy. I don't know why, but I like him. And I think something horrible happened to him, something so horrible that he refused to die in his own lifetime. Instead, he continues to live on inside your husband."

"Why?"

"That I don't know. Maybe Joel is his son?"

Susan stood and walked over to the bed where her husband was apparently sleeping peacefully under the influence of the sedative. She gazed sadly into Joel's face, then looked back at Finley. "I'd almost rather he died than live like this. What does all of this mean for Joel?" she asked, trying to pull herself together. "You said once that this could be permanent—unless we get some answers soon. Does this mean it's too late?"

Finley stood slowly and leaned against the rail at the end of the bed. "Susan, your husband is caught between two worlds—the world of Judd McCarthy and the world of Joel Hampton. Right now, I don't think he knows who he is, or whether he's living in the 1920s or the 1950s. . . ."

"But he's definitely drifting more and more toward that other world, the world of Judd McCarthy, isn't he?" Susan asked, interrupting Finley.

"Yes, he is," Finley admitted.

"Does that mean it's too late?" Susan asked again.

"No, I think we still have some time. But I don't know how much."

Susan looked down at her husband. "So where do we go from here?" she asked.

"Back to Carver County," Finley said firmly as he strode toward the doorway. "Maybe you can join me later?"

Susan glanced up at Ned Finley as he left. Then she looked down again at her husband. "Joel?" she asked softly as she rubbed his muscular forearm. "Joel, do you know who I am?"

Joel Hampton's eyes blinked sleepily, then remained open.

"Joel, it's me, Susan. Do you remember?"

Joel turned slightly. For a moment, he stared into his wife's eyes. "Kate?" he asked sleepily.

"No, I'm Susan Hampton," she replied gently, the tears welling up in her eyes. "Joel, I'm your wife."

"Wife?" Joel whispered. The word seemed to confuse him. His eyes opened and closed sleepily. "Wife?" He repeated the word three more times. .

"Yes, I'm your wife," Susan repeated as she stroked his hand.

"Kate, Kate," Joel sighed dreamily. Then from deep in his chest Susan heard a sound like an enraged bull bellowing out in defiance. The sound grew louder and louder, until it filled the room and echoed out into the nearby hallway.

Susan Hampton stepped back in horror as the nurse again rushed into the room and thrust a syringe into Joel's exposed thigh.

Chapter Nine

I

As he drove back to Carver County, Finley thought about the earlier scene in Joel's room in the mental hospital. Clearly, the name "Tobin" was somehow locked in Joel Hampton's subconscious mind. And, unless Joel had somehow stumbled across some obscure newspaper account of the wrestling match between Tobin and McCarthy—and that seemed unlikely—the name "Tobin" could only have come from some previous life that had been lived in Carver County. The theory of reincarnation was obviously not that far-fetched. Indeed, the strong connection between Joel Hampton and Judd McCarthy, as evident in the single word "Tobin," created a renewed excitement in Ned Finley. Now he was convinced that he was on to something.

Finley's excitement was tempered only by his knowledge that the final revelations might come too late—long after Joel Hampton had slipped into a permanent catatonic state of mind from which there would be no escape. Finley's feelings for both Joel and Susan made that possibility much more agonizing and personal than he wanted it to be. Always before, Ned Finley had tried to maintain an objective, professional relationship with his patients. Such walls and defenses were necessary when one confronted insanity and other lesser psychological problems on a daily basis. But those walls had long since fallen in the Hampton case, and Finley found himself caring deeply, personally, for both Susan and Joel. Such feelings might impair his professional judgment, Finley decided, but they would also give him the motivation and determination he needed to pursue this matter through to the end. And Finley decided to do just that, no matter what the consequences might be to himself and his professional career.

Marsha Williams was standing on the top rung of a small step ladder when Finley entered the main floor of the Andrew Carnegie Library. She was busily adjusting several large photographs that hung crooked on the eastern wall. Stern-faced married couples from the late 1800s and early 1900s stared out of the photographs, their faces reflecting a grim, humorless, puritanical resolve. Beneath each framed photograph, a small white label described the contributions of each couple to the history of Carver County. The largest label was reserved for the portrait of John J. Sylvester, which hung alone in the middle of the wall, as it had in both the County Recorder's Office and the lobby of the Danvers Hotel.

Marsha Williams was preoccupied with the task of straightening the large photographs, and she was oblivious to the stepladder that was swaying and lurching beneath her feet. Finley walked over to the stepladder and steadied it.

"Oh, thank you," Marsha Williams said as she looked down at Finley's brown beret. She continued to move the large picture frames back and forth until she was satisfied with the way they were hanging on the wall. Then she stood erect on the top rung of the stepladder. She put her index finger to her lips and studied her handiwork. "There, they look so much better, don't they?" she said. Then she scrambled quickly down the ladder.

"Yes, they certainly do," Finley agreed as he folded the small stepladder.

"Bring it right over here," Marsha Williams said as she led Finley to a small closet behind the pulpit-shaped desk. "Just put it in there."

Finley placed the small stepladder inside the closet and shut the door behind him.

"My," Marsha Williams sighed, "it would be so much easier if I had a man to help me around here." She pondered the idea for a few seconds, then reconsidered. "No, he would just be getting in my way, I'm afraid." She turned briskly and walked back behind the pulpit-shaped desk.

"Miss Williams..."

"Now you come over here, whoever you are," Marsha Williams said from behind the desk. "Before you do anything at all, you come over here and sign the registration book. We're applying for a state grant and they want to know *exactly* how many people visit our library each year."

"Where do I sign?" Finley asked as he stepped up to the desk.

"Right here," Marsha Williams said as she pointed at the space where she had earlier written "tall man in brown beret."

"Here?" Finley asked.

"Yes, right there. And sign again in the space below it."

Finley quickly scribbled his name in the two adjacent spaces on the registration book. Before he was able to put the quill-shaped pen back in its holder, Marsha Williams had spun the book around on the desk and was studying the signature. "Ned Finley?" she asked.

"Yes."

"Well, Mr. Finley," she said cheerfully, extending her tiny hand and smiling at him, "I'm Marsha Williams and I'm pleased to meet you. What can we do for you today?"

"I was wondering if you could tell me more about that map over there," Finley said as he pointed at the large county map hanging on the western wall. "I would like to know more about the people who lived along the Sioux Line Railroad in the 1920s. I don't think I showed you this the first time I was here," he added as he handed the photograph of the old farmhouse to Marsha Williams. "Do you know if this farm was located anywhere in Carver County in the 1920s?"

Marsha Williams studied the photograph carefully. "I don't know," she said thoughtfully. "Picture looks like it was taken from across a field. Farm is almost too far away to tell." She turned the photograph over and looked at the picture of the gramophone and the initials "PH" on the back side. "The picture was developed in Danvers. That much you can be sure of. That's the mark of the Hornsby Studios. Phillip Hornsby."

"Yes, I know," Finley responded. "But do you have any idea who might have owned this farm?"

"Well, it was most likely a farm out along the Sioux Line Railroad. They all looked pretty much the same. Big Victorian homes. It could have been any one of them."

"Could you show me where some of those farms are located?" Finley asked, pointing at the map.

"Yes, of course." Marsha Williams took the long pointer down from the wall and raised the metal tip toward the map. "All of these darker areas are the old farms and homesteads from the 20s and early 30s."

"Looks like there were at least sixty or seventy farms between Danvers and Carson in the 20s," Finley said.

"At least."

"How many of them can you identify?"

"Probably ten or twelve."

"Tell me about the ones that were located closest to Danvers."

"Well, this is the old Johnson farm. . . ."

"The one destroyed by a tornado?" Finley asked.

"Yes, how did you know that?"

"I was out there the other day."

"Oh, I see," Marsha Williams said as she turned her attentions again to the map. "This is the Bentley farm and . . . I don't know who owned this one right here, but this one is the Graham farm. Son still lives there, I think. And right across the river here is the Mosley farm."

"What was this Graham's first name?" Finley asked.

"Fred, I think. No, that's not it. It was, let me see." Marsha Williams paused, trying to remember the name. "It was Frank. That's it. Frank and Helga Graham."

"Did they live out there in the 20s?"

"Oh my, yes, they certainly did," Marsha Williams said as she continued to run the marker along the white surface of the map. "And this is the Helgeson farm. Now this one I don't remember. No, I do too. This is the Sumners' farm and this . . ."

"Wait," Finley said, interrupting her. "That farm there. You said it was the Sumners' farm."

"Yes, I believe that's the old Sumners' place. Wealthy people. All dead now."

"What were their first names?" Finley asked.

"Oh, I'd have to look that up."

"Miss Williams, do you remember anything at all about a Maureen McCarthy who lived around Danvers in the 1890s?" Finley suddenly blurted out.

"I think I've heard that name. Why do you ask?"

"A Maureen McCarthy was committed to the Farmington Mental Hospital in the 1890s. If I'm correct, she was committed by two families, the Sumners and the Grahams."

"I'd have to look that up, Mr. Finley. Would you want me to call you if I find anything?"

"Yes, please do. I'm staying in the hotel . . ."

Suddenly, the fire siren began wailing and screaming outside the library and the notes of "Amazing Grace" filtered in through the thick windows.

"Oh my, that's too bad," Marsha Williams said as she glanced out the window.

"What's too bad?" Finley asked.

"There must have been a funeral. Harmon gets drunk and kind of sentimental whenever someone dies in Danvers. Takes him almost a week to get over it. He'll be playing 'Amazing Grace' for a couple of days now. I wonder who died?" Marsha Williams scratched the back of her neck and a sad, distant look crept into her blue eyes. Then she looked quickly up at the map and began enthusiastically pointing at the remaining farms. "That's the Jenstad farm there and . . . there's only one more that I remember. Oh yes, one of the earliest homesteads in Carver County. Jerry Tobin lived right there for many years."

"Farmer Tobin?" Finley asked excitedly.

"No, a brother, Jerry Tobin. Kind of a strange man. Kept to himself the last fifteen or twenty years of his life. I don't know much about him except by reputation. Seems to me people said he was kind of crazy."

II

Gus was sitting alone at a large oak table when Finley entered the old saloon adjacent to the lobby of the Danvers Hotel. Gus was sipping quietly on a beer as he studied a nearby mural painted across one entire wall of the barroom. In the mural, Buffalo Bill sat on a huge, golden stallion that stood on its hind legs and pawed at the air as its magnificent white mane flowed in the wind. On the other end of the mural, an Indian chief was mounted on a smaller, black and white pony. The Indian chief was sadly watching a long train that raced through the middle of the mural scattering a herd of buffalo across the prairies. Dead and dying buffalo littered the areas on both sides of the railroad tracks.

"Gus, I need your help again," Finley said as he sat down.

"Do you see that?" Gus said, pointing at the mural.

"See what?" Finley asked.

"Buffalo Bill."

"Yes."

"He had blue eyes."

"So?"

"Whoever painted that mural painted his eyes brown," Gus answered as he sipped slowly on his beer.

"Gus, what do you know about a Farmer Tobin?" Finley asked, changing the subject.

"The wrestler?"

"Yes. What kind of man was he?"

"Oh he was big, tough, but gentle as a newborn calf."

"Do you think he might have had it in for Judd McCarthy?"

"In what way?"

"Do you think he might have been involved in McCarthy's disappearance?"

"You mean, was he in cahoots with McCarthy?"

"No. Do you think he might have killed McCarthy when he was coming back from Carson with the payroll?"

Gus coughed and spit into a red handkerchief he held in

his left hand. "Judd McCarthy and Farmer Tobin were like brothers outside the ring," he said, clearing his throat. "They boasted about killin' one another. But there was nothin' to it. They were a lot alike. Kind of big and dumb. Neither one of them really fit into town life. Preferred the country."

"Didn't Farmer Tobin have a brother?"

"Yup. Jerry Tobin. Lived a few miles outside of town."

"Do you suppose he had it in for Judd McCarthy?"

"Might have. He was a little crazy. But you shouldn't jump to any conclusions."

"Why's that?"

"Jerry Tobin fell from a barn in the early 20s. Lay flat on his back for the next twelve years of his life before he died. Couldn't even get outta bed. Just lay there with a broken neck askin' anyone who came through the room to kill him. That's how he was crazy. He wanted someone to kill him. He wasn't capable of killin' anyone himself."

"Are you . . ."

"You'd better go over to the counter," Gus said, interrupting Finley and pointing at the doorway leading into the hotel lobby. "Wally's wavin' for you to come over there."

Finley turned around and looked in the direction of the hotel lobby. The desk clerk was holding up a black telephone and pointing at Finley. "For you," the desk clerk yelled across the lobby.

"Just a minute," Finley yelled back as he stood up from the table. He walked quickly across the lobby and took the telephone from the extended hand of the desk clerk. "Hello, this is Ned Finley."

"Mr. Finley," a cheerful female voice said at the other end of the line. "Land sakes, it's a good thing you signed the register this time. Otherwise I'd never have known your name."

"Miss Williams?" Finley asked.

"Yes, this is Marsha Williams, up in the library. I found something just after you left this morning."

"Did you find any information on Maureen McCarthy?" Finley asked eagerly.

"No, I couldn't find anything on her. But you asked if I knew the first names of the people who owned the Sumners' farm. Remember?"

"Yes."

"Well, their names are Oscar and Agnes Sumners. I really should have known that," Marsha Williams said, admonishing herself. "My memory just isn't what it used to be."

"They're the ones who had Maureen McCarthy committed," Finley said, remembering. "What kind of people were they?"

"Oh, they were very wealthy. Very influential people in this area. Then they went broke. Agnes Sumners hung herself in the 30s."

"But you don't know what their relationship might have been to Maureen McCarthy?"

"No, I haven't found anything about that. But I did find something else you might be interested in."

"What's that?"

"Well, remember the first day you came into the library?"

"Yes."

"You asked about a Katharine McCarthy."

"What did you find out about her?" Finley asked eagerly.

"I couldn't find anything about a Katharine McCarthy. But when I was looking up this information on Oscar and Agnes Sumners, I found something else that you might be interested in. They had a daughter. Her name was Katharine too. Katharine Sumners."

"What do you know about her?"

"Nothing really. I should know, but I just can't seem to remember anything about her. I'll see what I can find out for you."

"Thanks very much, Miss Williams," Finley said as he handed the receiver back to the desk clerk. He walked back into the saloon and joined Gus next to the large Western mural.

"Important?" Gus asked.

"I don't know," Finley said. "Gus, did you ever hear of a Katharine Sumners who lived in Danvers?"

"Yup. Lived on a farm just northwest of here."

"Whatever happened to her?"

"Went East, I think. Never returned so far as I know. Couldn't get along with her mother."

"Who lives out there now?"

"Someone by the name of Walker. I don't know her first name. Never seen her downtown."

"How do I get out there?"

"Just drive northwest of here about three miles. It's not too far from the old Sioux Line Railroad. It's a shame, isn't it?" Gus said softly.

"What's that?"

"Buffalo Bill," Gus said as he sipped again on his beer. "They shoulda painted his eyes blue."

III

Ned Finley drove his Studebaker onto the gravel shoulder of a country road some three miles northwest of Danvers. In the distance, on a slightly elevated foothill, a ghostly gray, Victorian farmhouse was clearly visible in the middle of a cluster of trees. A damaged windmill and a silo with the dome missing were located on opposite sides of the old farmhouse. Finley recognized the windmill as the one he had heard groaning across the empty fields on the day he had walked the Sioux Line Railroad to Carson.

Finley stepped out of the car and pulled the old photograph out of his pocket. He held it up to the horizon and moved his eyes slowly back and forth between the photograph and the distant farmhouse.

"It's the same house!" he said emphatically. "The picture must have been taken from this road! Perhaps I'm finally on the right track."

Finley climbed back quickly into the car and drove toward the entrance to the Sumners' farmyard. He had to turn sharply to enter the narrow dirt road that led up to the farmhouse. The tires of the Studebaker fit tightly into two ancient ruts that were covered with weeds and dead grass. Finley parked the car next to an old wooden fence that surrounded the farmyard. He waited for the dust to settle around the car and then he stepped out the side door.

There was a sense of lost grandeur and dignity in everything about the old Victorian home. Shingles were missing from the roof, paint was peeling off in large scabs on the exposed walls, and the windows were caked with dirt. From somewhere, perhaps from the interior of the house or maybe carried on the wind, Finley thought he heard the distant sound of music, a lilting romantic melody played on an ancient gramophone. He glanced up at the gables of the Victorian farmhouse and what appeared to be a human face moved quickly across one of the dirt-caked windows and disappeared.

Several large trees surrounded the farmhouse. A steady autumn breeze stripped away the leaves and sent them skipping out into the nearby prairies. A swing, hanging by one rope from the huge branch of one of the oak trees, swayed ever-so-gently in the breeze. And a gray wagon, shorn of one wheel, stood weathering among dying, waist-high vegetation a few feet away from the oak tree.

To the west of the house, the rusty windmill groaned high overhead. Two of its metal blades had broken off and fallen to the ground, where they lay next to an old water pump. On the other side of the house, clinging vines grew almost to the very top of the damaged silo. A few feet to the east of the silo, a partially exposed concrete wall and a heavy wooden door protruded out of a hillside.

Finley listened carefully to the sounds of the wind rustling the leaves across the farmyard and in the nearby trees. Then he looked up at the gables one more time to determine if he had indeed seen a human face move across the dirty windows, but the windows were empty. Above the gables, several wood shingles flapped steadily against the roof.

Finley walked up the jagged stone pathway to the front porch of the farmhouse. A courting swing hung from two rusty chains bolted into the ceiling of the front porch. The swing creaked on its rusty hinges as it swayed slowly back and forth in the breeze.

Finley knocked once on the front door, waited several seconds, then knocked again. A thin, elderly woman opened the door a few inches and squinted out into the sunlight. There was a distant, almost senile look in her eyes, Finley thought, as she peered out at him.

"Yes?" she asked in a meek voice.

"Are you Miss Walker?" Finley asked.

"Yes, I'm Gina Walker."

"Miss Walker," Finley blurted out, "I need some information on the family that lived in this house before you moved in. Can you tell me anything at all about the Sumners family?"

"I'm sorry. That was long before my time."

"Anything you can tell me about the Sumners family would be greatly appreciated," Finley said. "Anything at all."

"I'm sorry. I know nothing about them," the elderly woman said as she started to shut the door.

"Please..."

"You'll have to excuse me now. I'm busy," the old woman said as the door scraped past the wood jamb and a bolt lock clicked shut on the other side of the doorway.

Finley stood on the porch and stared at the heavy wooden door. Then he turned and walked back down the narrow stone pathway.

Before climbing into the Studebaker, he looked back at the farmyard. As he did so, a sudden gust of wind caught the old swing that hung from the oak tree, causing it to glide forward a few feet. As the windmill groaned high overhead and the breezes played across the ancient shingles and whistled through the weathered siding, Finley thought he again heard a lilting, romantic melody played on a gramophone from somewhere in the interior of the old farmhouse.

IV

"Christ, he looks mean with that beard," one of the hospital orderlies said as he looked down at Joel Hampton.

Joel's eyes were open and he was lying on his back staring at the ceiling.

"Maybe you should shave him?" the young nurse said as she adjusted the straps around Joel's forearms.

"Not on your life. I read his chart. I don't want him biting off my fingers."

"Then you shouldn't complain about the way he looks," the nurse admonished him. "You never know what these people can hear."

"Well, I only know that I don't intend to shave him. But he sure as hell looks mean with those eyes staring out of that beard. It looks like the devil himself staring back at you."

As the nurse and orderly walked out of the room, Joel continued to stare at the ceiling. He unclenched his fist and slowly twisted his right forearm in the leather straps. . . .

He had learned that by clenching his fists as they tightened the straps, he could move his arms more freely once they had left the room. It was only a matter of time now before he would slip out of the leather restraints and escape. He would slip down the empty corridor, scale the red granite fence outside the hospital, and disappear into the night. They would come looking for him. But he would keep to the riverbank. And he would work his way up the Little Sioux River to Carver County. He would look for the thicket and the old farmhouse. And he would find those who had done this to him and to Kate. . . . He would make them pay. . . . And then he would be with Kate, forever. . . .

V

After leaving the Sumners' farm, Finley drove immediately back to the library. Marsha Williams was studying an old newspaper behind her pulpit-shaped desk on the main floor. She looked up as Finley approached the desk.

"Mr. Finley, did you get my message?" she asked cheerfully.

"What message?"

"The message I left for you in the hotel."

"No," Finley said. "I haven't been back there yet. I just got back from the Sumners' farm."

"Well, I remembered something unusual about that family," Marsha Williams said as she held up the old newspaper. "I hope you won't be disappointed, but Katharine Sumners died in 1927. In a boarding house fire back East. This article describes the funeral."

Finley took the newspaper from Marsha Williams and

quickly read through the article. "Where is this Peace Lutheran Cemetery?" he asked.

"Three miles south of here, on the Mill Dam Road."

"Thank you," Finley said, setting the newspaper back down on the desk.

"I have something else to show you too," Marsha Williams said as she stood up from the desk and led Finley over to the many photographs that hung on the eastern wall of the main floor. "That's them, right there," she said, pointing to the stern visages of a married couple who stared out of a black and white photograph.

"Who are they?" Finley asked.

"Oscar and Agnes Sumners. This photograph was taken in 1914, on their thirtieth wedding anniversary."

Finley studied the grim, humourless faces. "They don't look any too happy about it, do they?"

"Those were conventional poses in the early part of the century. It wasn't considered proper to smile."

"You don't have a photograph of Katharine Sumners here, do you?" Finley asked.

"No, in fact I can't find anything at all on her, except for the newspaper article you just read. She must have kept to herself a lot. I can't even remember what she looked like."

Finley drove his car along a narrow dirt road that curved gradually up to the top of a small foothill. On each side of the road, recently harvested fields of hay lay in neat rows awaiting the balers. The Peace Lutheran Cemetery was located in the middle of a cluster of trees at the very top of the foothill.

Finley parked his car and walked through the metal gateway into the cemetery. A bronze statue of a Union soldier stood on a large granite block in the middle of the rows of tombstones and footstones. The soldier held his rifle and bayonet in a horizontal position as he ran into battle. The small twigs of a bird's nest protruded over the top of his cap.

Finley began walking among the many tombstones, looking carefully at the various names and dates inscribed on the granite surfaces. Most of the tombstones were extremely old, dating back to the middle of the nineteenth century. In a distant corner of the cemetery, he located the Sumners' family plot. There were three tombstones, all level with the ground and partially concealed by weeds and dead leaves. Finley knelt down to clear away the accumulated debris from the graves of Oscar, Agnes, and Katharine Sumners. As a lone bird chirped in a nearby tree, Finley's eyes moved slowly back and forth over the inscriptions on the three tombstones. The inscriptions read: Oscar Sumners (October 2, 1860–December 12, 1920), Agnes Sumners (May 2, 1862–July 14, 1933), and Katharine Sumners (January 16, 1899–April 30, 1927).

Finley stood beside the graves for several minutes. He stared at the weathered inscriptions and pondered the significance of the dates. When he looked up, he could see the Danvers water tower and church steeple rising out of the distant prairies. A peacefulness and quietude lingered over the cemetery, reminding Finley of an old proverb he had heard as a small boy. He couldn't remember the exact words, but he knew it was something to the effect that "No matter what good or evil men have done, the silence of the grave claims them each and every one."

Finley glanced back down at the three tombstones. Already the wind had redeposited several dead leaves and pine needles over the inscriptions on the tombstones. Then he noticed something else in the center of Katharine Sumners' grave. A circular-shaped object protruded above the dead autumn leaves. He reached into the leaves and extracted the wire-meshing from a small wreath. Several dead flowers still clung to the thin strands of wire.

Finley turned the wire meshing over several times before placing it back on the grave. Then he walked toward the gate of the old cemetery and climbed into his car. He drove back through Danvers, turned left on a gravel road about two miles northwest of the small town, and parked his car next to an empty field.

Susan Hampton was waiting for him by the banks of the Little Sioux River as planned. She was sitting in the dead autumn leaves. Below her, the Little Sioux River flowed slowly, gently southwards.

At the river's edge, Aggy was playfully throwing small stones and pebbles into the water. She laughed gleefully as the cold water lapped gently against her bare feet and her toes sunk deeply into the sandy river bottom.

"Why did you ask me to meet you here?" Susan Hampton asked as she looked up at Finley.

"I wanted to see if you had been able to find out anything on Maureen McCarthy," Finley lied. He had actually wanted to get Susan away from Farmington, if only for a few hours. "Aurther Schlepler told me you were helping him go through some more of the old files in the basement of Farmington."

"We found nothing," Susan said softly. "Maureen McCarthy just seems to have disappeared."

"On purpose, no doubt," Finley said. "She was probably afraid they would take her back to Farmington."

"How about you? Have you found out anything else about Judd McCarthy?"

"No, but I found out where the picture of the old farmhouse comes from."

"Where?" Susan asked eagerly.

"It's a farm located just west of here, not too far from the Sioux Line Railroad. It was owned by Oscar and Agnes Sumners."

"Weren't they the ones who signed to have Maureen McCarthy committed?"

"Yes. They also, perhaps more importantly, had a daughter, Katharine Sumners. I just came from the Peace Lutheran Cemetery where they are all buried."

"Is this the 'Katharine' Joel was talking about?"

"I don't know, but McCarthy was definitely planning to meet someone named Katharine when he got back from Carson," Finley said as he looked out at the river flowing a few feet below where they were sitting. "He was going to meet her right about here, on the banks of the Little Sioux River."

"And you think it was Katharine Sumners?"

"I don't know. Susan, what was the birthdate on the back of Joel's adoption certificate?"

"May 4, 1927."

"Are you sure?"

"Yes, why?"

"Katharine Sumners died on April 30, 1927."

"Then she couldn't possibly be the Katharine McCarthy who signed the adoption papers," Susan said.

"Doesn't seem that way, unless there was a mix-up in the dates. I suppose there could be one other explanation."

"What's that?" Susan asked.

"Maybe this is just another dead end."

"Then why would the picture of the Sumners' farmhouse be hidden in an old box of Joel's baby clothes?"

"I don't know," Finley admitted.

For a time Ned Finley and Susan Hampton sat and quietly watched the waters of the Little Sioux River flow steadily southwards.

"Dr. Finley," Susan said abruptly, "you once said that you had your own reasons for taking an interest in Joel. I know it's none of my business, but do you want to talk about those reasons?"

Finley shifted nervously in the dead leaves as he glanced out at Aggy who was still playing by the edge of the river.

"I'm sorry. I shouldn't have asked," Susan said, admonishing herself.

"No, it's okay," Finley said thoughtfully as he picked up a twig and began breaking it into tiny pieces. "I don't talk about it often. But I guess we're friends now. . . ."

"You really don't have to . . ." Susan interrupted him.

"No, it's okay," Finley repeated. "I don't mind." He reached down into the dead leaves and extracted another twig. "I've never been married. I guess you know that. Part of it has to do with my childhood, I'm sure, which was an unhappy one. I've always preferred the bachelor life—no ties, nothing to stop me from wandering when I want to. But I have known women. One of them bore me a son, or so it was rumored. He was a young man when he died. He was looking for me. I didn't even know of his existence until years later. Apparently he was having emotional problems. I always wished I would have known . . . maybe I could have helped."

"Do you see something of your son in Joel?" Susan asked gently.

Finley sighed. "I never knew my son, but after I found out about his existence, I always wondered what he must have thought of me. Somehow I feel that Judd McCarthy was also a better man than the people in Carver County say he was. And if Joel is his son, well . . ."

"You seem to be convinced that McCarthy was Joel's father."

"No, but the possibility exists. And if I can be of any help in clearing McCarthy's name. Well... maybe it helps me deal with some of my own guilt."

"I'm sorry about your son," Susan said softly.

Finley smiled gently. "It's kind of hard to think of him as my son. He's more... like a patient I couldn't help. . . . I send flowers up north sometimes—for the grave. . . ." Finley paused and contemplated something deeply. "Which reminds me, there's something else that's very strange about this business with Katharine Sumners," he said finally.

"What's that?" Susan asked.

"There was a wreath on Katharine Sumners' grave. Although she died in 1927, someone is still putting flowers on her grave in 1959."

"Who?"

"I don't have the slightest idea," Finley admitted. "But there must be someone around here who still cares about Katharine Sumners."

VI

It was late afternoon when Finley drove back to the hotel. Inside the hotel lobby, Finley paused beside the old photograph of the construction crew. He studied the rugged, smiling face of Judd McCarthy for several minutes. Then he walked over to Gus who was dozing in one of the large easy chairs overlooking Main Street.

"Gus?" Finley said as he sat down.

"Huh?" Gus said as he opened his eyes sleepily.

"Gus, would there be a photograph of Katharine Sumners somewhere in the lobby?"

"Very doubtful," Gus said as he struggled to keep his eyes open.

"Why?"

"Katharine Sumners' mother was a society type. But the girl was kind of peculiar. Very shy... kept to herself a lot."

"Tell me, is there any chance that she would have been seeing or dating Judd McCarthy?"

"Never," Gus said emphatically. "McCarthy was a low-level drifter. Had no goals in life. The Sumners? They were wealthy. There were other reasons too."

"What reasons?" Finley asked.

"Judd McCarthy was interested in a different kind of woman," Gus laughed softly to himself. "If you know what I mean?"

As Gus fell asleep in the easy chair, Finley looked out at the dark shadows that were beginning to fall across Main Street. Then he stood and walked out of the hotel lobby.

He walked up the small foothill to the high school, opened the huge glass door, and stepped into an empty hallway. He heard the huge door groan slowly shut behind him as he entered the dark corridor. His heels echoed on the tile floor as he walked past the dark green metal lockers and turned left into the adjacent hallway.

Finley walked to the very end of the hallway where the graduation pictures hung above the glass trophy cases. In a black and white photograph, labeled "Graduating Class of 1918," he found Katharine Sumners in the middle of a group of twenty or thirty graduating seniors. Katharine Sumners was not a beautiful girl, but there was something about her that was gentle, attractive, and mysterious. In the middle of the more somber faces that surrounded her, she smiled shyly out at Finley. Something in that shy smile told Ned Finley he would have liked Katharine Sumners. It was the same feeling he got when he looked at the rugged, smiling face of Judd McCarthy. In fact there was something about the two smiles that was very similar, Finley thought, as he studied the eyes of Katharine Sumners.

VII

The night orderly checked the leather restraints. Then he pulled the bedspread up over Joel's stomach and chest.

After he had finished adjusting the bedspread, the orderly

glanced out the window at the thick cloud formations that were drifting lazily beneath a star-filled sky. As the cloud formations covered the sky, they blocked out the light of the moon and stars and sent large shadows creeping slowly across the hospital grounds. In the distance, a single light glowed weakly above a cluster of trees that surrounded a small farmyard.

The orderly turned away from the window and walked softly out of the hospital room. The adjacent hallway was empty except for several small, green lights that glowed weakly along both walls. The orderly glanced down the hallway toward the night station. A nurse sat behind the large circular desk at the other end of the hallway. Her back was turned to the orderly as he walked in the opposite direction and entered another of the hospital rooms.

In the second room, a frail old man was lying asleep on the floor next to a hospital bed. The old man was curled up in the fetal position.

The orderly paused beside the bed and looked down at the old man. He shook his head in mock disgust. "Jason," he said, chuckling softly to himself, "when are you going to learn to sleep in your bed?"

The orderly lifted the old man off the floor and laid him down gently on the bed. Almost immediately, the old man curled up into a tight ball. He clutched a soft blanket to his cheek and began snoring softly.

"Jason, I wish they were all as docile as you," the orderly chuckled. Then he looked behind him for the hospital chart. "Damn," he rebuked himself, "I left it in Hampton's room."

The orderly walked quickly over to the adjacent hallway. The night nurse was still sitting with her back turned to the long, dimly lit corridor.

In Joel's room, the moonlight had broken through the heavy cloud formations and was shining brightly through the barred window. The bedspread was lying on the floor next to the bed.

The orderly paused and looked down at the wrinkled sheets and the long leather straps that curled out over the empty bed.

"Jesus Christ!" the orderly muttered as he rushed quickly out of the room. "Hampton's not in his room!" he yelled to the nurse at the other end of the hallway.

Chapter Ten

1

Early the next morning, Finley drove out to the abandoned Sioux Line Railroad. He had developed some hunches about the Little Sioux Water Reclamation Project, and he wanted to determine whether or not his suspicions were correct. He walked a few feet into the yawning black hole of the main culvert and chipped several pieces of concrete off the inside wall. Then he drove back to Danvers and deposited the small fragments of concrete in the County Engineer's Office. Afterwards, he walked up the small foothill to the library. He collected everything he could find on John J. Sylvester, the Hanley brothers, and the Little Sioux Water Reclamation Project. He made himself comfortable at a large table in the basement of the library and spent the better part of the morning reading through the materials he had collected.

It was almost noon when he walked up the short flight of stairs to the main floor of the library. Marsha Williams was sitting behind her desk when he entered the room.

"I was just reading through this book on Carver County history," Finley said as he placed a small, hardbound volume on the desk. "Do you know anything about the author?"

Marsha Williams picked up the book and quickly glanced at the front cover. "Oh my, yes. This was written by my neighbor, Myra Stevenson."

"Well, there's something curious about this book. . . ."

"Poor Myra," Marsha Williams said, interrupting Finley.

"Why do you say that?"

"Myra always wanted to be a poet," Marsha Williams said sadly. "Sent her poems in for years but never had one accepted. Then the week after she died *Harpers* sent her a letter saying one of her poems had finally been accepted for publication."

"That's too bad."

"Not really," Marsha Williams exclaimed cheerfully. "They were *ghastly* poems. Now, what is the problem with this book?"

"Well, the section on John J. Sylvester says almost nothing about the ten years of his life before he became governor."

"I suppose Myra just decided to concentrate more on the years when he was a state celebrity. Mr. Sylvester had a short, but illustrious career in state politics," Marsha Williams said proudly. "He was the only man to ever get out of Danvers and really make something of himself. He even thought of running for president, you know?"

"No, I wasn't aware of that," Finley admitted.

"It's a shame. Such an honorable man. He would have made a fine president," she said dreamily. "And what it would have meant for this town."

"Well, what I really need is some information on the public works projects in Carver County in the 20s," Finley said.

"Myra doesn't mention that in her book?" Marsha Williams asked, somewhat perplexed, as she quickly flipped through the pages of the small volume.

"No."

"That is strange," she said, setting the book back down on the desk and looking up again at Finley. "The Community Development League under Mr. Sylvester almost built this town."

"Wasn't that organization involved with the Little Sioux Water Reclamation Project?"

"Yes, it certainly was."

"What was that project supposed to accomplish?" Finley asked.

"Oh, that was one of Mr. Sylvester's many dreams for Danvers. Come over here and I'll show you what he had in

mind." Marsha Williams led Finley over to the large white
map of Carver County. "Now, you must remember that Mr.
Sylvester was a dreamer, a visionary. He hoped to make
Danvers the most prosperous little town in all of Carver
County. Since the big railroads were already abandoning us,
he came up with another plan, a very expensive plan. But
one that he hoped would mean economic prosperity for the
people of Danvers for years to come."

"What was the plan?" Finley asked as Marsha Williams
unhooked the long wooden pointer from the wall.

"The plan was to divert the flood waters of the Little
Sioux River, both to alleviate the flooding problem and also to
get the overflow to other parts of the township where it was
desperately needed." Marsha Williams began running the
long wooden pointer over the map. "Now, you must remember that the farmers along the Little Sioux River were flooded
out almost every spring. It cost the farmers and the people of
this area a fortune in lost crops and damaged farmland. Mr.
Sylvester's plan was to build a huge culvert under the prairies. Its purpose was to collect the flood waters and divert
them to two different parts of the township."

"Is that what those lines represent?" Finley asked, pointing
at two broken black lines that branched off from the point
where the main culvert joined the Little Sioux River.

"Yes, this one here was to take the waters farther east
where they would be stored in a reservoir to be drained off
by the farmers during the dry years. Curiously, although we
get all kinds of rain along the Little Sioux River, there have
been years when the farmers east of here haven't had enough
water to grow a thing."

"What about the other culvert?"

"Well, now here is where you see that John J. Sylvester
was a dreamer and not at all a practical man. This culvert was
to use the floodwaters to power a large electrical plant
southeast of Danvers. The power plant was never built,
incidentally. It was much too impractical."

"Why?"

"A power plant could only have been used in the spring
when the floodwaters came pouring off the Little Sioux River.
The rest of the year there wouldn't be enough water to power
its turbines. And the problem with the other culvert, of

course, is that even if you got the flood waters over to the farmers east of here, there was still the problem of digging irrigation ditches so they could get the water to their crops. it was all highly impractical and much too expensive."

"If there were so many obvious problems with the project," Finley asked, "how come the people in Danvers went along with it?"

"You must remember," Marsha Williams said, "that John J. Sylvester was a dreamer. And the people in this town got caught up in his dreams and went along with them, even when they were impractical. They knew that John J. Sylvester had their best interests at heart. And his dreams were better than most of the realities they were accustomed to."

Finley paused for a time to study the thin black lines that wandered in two directions away from the Little Sioux River. "You wouldn't have anything on the financial dealings of that organization, would you?" he finally asked.

"What organization?"

"The Community Development League and the Little Sioux Water Reclamation Project."

"Yes, I think so. Just a minute." Marsha Williams disappeared into one of the small side rooms behind the front desk. She returned shortly with a large, leather-bound volume. "This is Volume II of *The Public Works Projects in Carver County (1920-1930)*. It's the original copy. Now, what exactly is it that you need?"

"The cost breakdown of the Little Sioux Water Reclamation Project. Also, anything on its financial dealings with the Community Development League."

Marsha Williams flopped the book open on a large table and carefully paged through the handwritten volume. "There should be a section here on the financial records of that project. Yes, here it is. Oh my!"

"What's wrong?" Finley asked.

"Those pages have been torn out!"

II

After leaving the library, Finley walked back to the County Building on Main Street. He walked down a short flight of stairs into the basement and approached the front desk of the County Engineer's Office.

"Do you have the results on the concrete samples I brought in?" Finley asked the County Engineer who was sitting at a desk in the back of the room.

"Yes, I have them right here," the County Engineer said as he slowly stood up and walked over to the front desk. He laid a small piece of paper on the front counter. The paper had a series of handwritten formulas and notations scribbled down the middle of the page. "Now, what is it you need to know?"

"Would that concrete stand up under stress?" Finley asked.

"Depends on what you were planning to use it for," the County Engineer said as he adjusted his glasses.

"The sample was taken from a culvert, a flood control project."

"No, it would never last. It's well below minimal engineering requirements. Water pressure would blow it out in a few years."

"Does that mean the entire culvert was of inferior quality?"

"Not necessarily. It means that this one section is inferior. You would have to take samples from several sections to determine if the entire system is defective."

"Thanks," Finley said as he turned to leave.

Finley walked back out to Main Street and got into his car. Immediately, he drove west toward the Little Sioux Water Reclamation Project. He parked on the gravel shoulder of a country road, took a large flashlight and a burlap sack out of the trunk of his car, and walked across the empty fields to the Sioux Line Railroad.

Finley walked along the old railroad line until he came to the abandoned railroad car resting on an embankment overlooking the deep, weed-filled trench. The reddish-gray siding on the railroad car was warping and buckling beneath the bright sunlight, and the iron wheels were set firmly on two rusty tracks that disappeared in the nearby weeds and foliage. The name "Sioux Line Railroad" was painted in faded white letters that were turning gray and blending into the color of the wood siding as the railroad car weathered beneath the October sky.

Finley walked down the embankment toward the scattered piles of old lumber and iron molds that littered the bottom of the trench. He was careful to leave considerable room between himself and the rotting wooden pallet where he had earlier seen the huge snake coiled sinisterly in the darkness.

A gust of wind suddenly whistled through the warped siding on the railroad car as Finley paused next to the huge, yawning mouth of the culvert. He peered into the darkness of the old flood control system. There was an ominous silence from the dark interior of the culvert as it stretched for miles beneath the prairie topsoil. Dead weeds and grass clung to wide cracks in the sides and floor of the concrete tunnel. Small puddles of water were scattered around the floor next to dead leaves that had drifted into the tunnel opening.

Finley switched on the flashlight and stepped into the mouth of the huge culvert. As he walked deeper and deeper into the interior of the flood control system, he chipped tiny pieces of concrete out of the tunnel walls and deposited them into the burlap sack he carried with him. The concrete fragments came out easily, looking more like sand and gravel pouring out of the huge cracks in the concrete walls.

In some sections of the culvert, boulder-sized segments of the concrete walls had broken free and fallen to the tunnel floor. Occasionally, a frog or lizard darted quickly across the puddles of water as Finley moved deeper into the flood control system, following the narrow beam of his flashlight into the darkness.

Almost without warning, the huge culvert suddenly angled off sharply in two directions. Finley realized immediately that this was the point he had seen on the map in the library where the two tunnels separated, one moving off in an easterly direction towards the reservoir, and the other bending in a southeasterly direction towards the power plant.

Finley directed the beam of the flashlight as deeply as he could into the two tunnel openings. In the second tunnel, his flashlight illuminated the white, gleaming teeth of several rats as they scurried across the concrete floor and glared back at him defiantly. The high-pitched squeal of the rats echoed across the concrete walls as they scurried into the depths of the tunnel and disappeared. Finley focused his flashlight on their retreating tails. Then he took one last sample of concrete from the culvert wall and walked back in the direction of the tunnel entrance.

As he walked back toward the mouth of the huge culvert, he heard another sound mingling with the high-pitched squeal of the rats. Ahead of him, in the darkness, there was the distinct rumbling sound of heavy machinery and equipment moving around just outside the large tunnel entrance. The rumble of the heavy machinery grew progressively louder, then became strangely muffled as Finley rounded the last curve in the tunnel wall.

Where the bright sunlight should have greeted him at the mouth of the tunnel opening, there was instead a huge wall of black dirt filling the culvert from floor to ceiling. Beyond the wall of dirt, the muffled sound of heavy machinery faded and gradually disappeared altogether as Finley ran the beam of his flashlight across the glistening, black topsoil.

Behind him, the high-pitched squeal of the rats echoed throughout the entrails of the old flood control system.

III

Joel climbed the red granite wall surrounding Farmington and fled into the nearby countryside. The thick cloud formations covered the moonlight as he ran through the plowed and harvested fields. Occasionally, he stepped on corn and wheat stubble, and the pain shot up into his ankles and calves. But still he ran, following an instinct that kept his legs moving long after he was exhausted.

When the moonlight broke through the thick cloud cover, he sought refuge in the sparse brush and clusters of trees that dotted the wide expanse of the prairies. As the thick clouds moved across the moon, blocking out the light, he stumbled to his feet and ran, moving always, or so he thought, in the direction of the Little Sioux River.

He was disoriented from lying so long in the hospital bed and from the strangeness of the world that surrounded him. The prairies he remembered had been covered with brush and trees and large unplowed areas of open land.

Finally he collapsed on the edge of a thicket of trees. His hands and knees sank into the damp grass and weeds as he gasped for breath. Then, slowly and laboriously, he rolled to a sitting position and fell back against a tree. He stared up at the clouds and the stars. . . .

How far had he come? Unless he had completely lost his sense of direction, surely he could not be that far from the Little Sioux River. He would have to be there before morning. They would be looking for him, and the brush and trees along the banks of the Little Sioux River would be the best place to hide. When he was safe, then he would find Kate. He remembered her golden hair and he could almost feel her breathing gently against his strong chest as he held her close.

Suddenly, he heard the barking of a dog and the sound of crunching weeds and brush. In a few seconds, a small golden Labrador retriever shot out of the underbrush and came to a sudden halt a few feet away from where he was sitting. The dog barked again, then snarled menacingly and backed away.

"Ah, so ya be a tough guy, huh?" Joel laughed softly as he reached a hand out to the dog. "Come on over here. Ah ain't gonna hurt ya."

The Labrador backed away a few more feet, then crouched down in one of the furrows of the plowed field that surrounded the thicket. A soft, almost imperceptible noise rumbled deeply in the dog's throat as it studied Joel.

"Come over here, old buddy," Joel whispered gently, still holding his hand out. "Ain't nuthin' here gonna hurt ya. Ah just wanta say hello, that's all."

As the saliva dripped off its tongue and glistened in the moonlight, the dog slowly raised itself to a sitting position. The Labrador glanced out into the open fields, then slowly and cautiously crept over to where Joel was sitting.

"Ya sure make a lotta noise for a little fella," Joel said gently as he scratched the top of the dog's head. "Sounded like a grizzly bear poundin' through those trees. 'Most scared me to death."

The dog laid its head on Joel's lap and the saliva quickly soaked through the thin fabric of the hospital uniform. It felt good to have company out in the darkness of the prairies.

"Strange sky up there tonight..." Joel paused as he heard another noise in the thicket behind him. He turned quickly to see a light flash on in a farmhouse buried deep in the trees. A woman, her nightgown silhouetted against the bright light behind her, stepped up to the screen door.

"Charlie, you comin' in tonight?" she yelled into the darkness. "Do I have to come out and get you, Charlie?"

Fearful of being discovered, Joel reached down and picked up the young dog. He held it under one arm while he grasped the dog's snout so it could not bark. The dog's legs and body thrashed frantically beneath Joel's strong grip. A frightened whine filtered out of its throat.

"Charlie, what you got out there?" the woman yelled from the porch.

Suddenly, a male voice from inside the house interrupted her. "Ah, he's probably just chasin' some damn rabbit. Let em be."

"But it looks like rain."

The dog struggled even more frantically in Joel's arms, and he increased the pressure on its chest and snout.

"He's been out in the rain before," the man's voice yelled disgustedly from the farmhouse. "Ain't gonna hurt him one damn bit."

"But..."

"Get back in here!" the man bellowed loudly.

Joel heard the screen door creak slowly shut. Then the light went out in the farmhouse. He heard the steady drone of voices for several seconds, and then there was again silence.

He bent over to place the dog on the ground. "Now, old

buddy, don't ya make no noise as I be leavin'. Ah don't want ya gettin' me in trouble."

The Labrador collapsed in a heap as he set it on the ground. "What be the matter with ya?" Joel inquired as he turned the dog over gently. He felt the dog's chest. There was no movement beneath his hand. "Ya be all right?" he asked with deep concern as he lifted the dog and tried to look into its glazed eyes. The dog's body was limp and its head flopped to one side.

"Ah, no, I didn't mean to..." Joel whispered sadly. He placed his ear to the dog's chest, but there was no heartbeat. "Ah only meant ta keep ya quiet, lad. Ah didn't mean ta kill ya."

He placed the dog on the ground and covered it quickly with dead weeds and grass. Then he shook his head and patted the lifeless mound. "I didn't mean ta kill ya, lad. I'm mighty sorry."

As he gazed at the dead animal he had accidentally suffocated, the light suddenly flashed on again in the farmhouse and the screen door burst open. A huge man in pajamas stomped out onto the back step.

"Goddamnit, Charlie, get in here!" the man yelled into the darkness. "She ain't gonna let me get no sleep until you quit chasin' that rabbit an' get in here!"

Joel stood and crept slowly along the edge of the thicket, moving toward the other side of the house. Behind him, he heard footsteps crunching through the underbrush. He looked all around and ran once more out into the open fields.

Was he that strong? So strong he had killed something when all he had wanted to do was hold it and keep it quiet? Maybe that's why he was at Farmington? Maybe there had been others....

IV

Susan Hampton heard the telephone ringing almost as soon as she stepped out of the car. Aggy was sitting in the back seat, clutching two large Halloween pumpkins.

"Honey," Susan said as she fumbled with her purse and rushed toward the front door, "you go over and play with Robin for a while. I'll answer the phone and get everything out of the car. Then I'll come over and get you."

"Can we carve the pumpkins tonight, Mommy?"

"I don't know. It's kind of early. We'll have to see." Susan inserted the key into the lock and turned it quickly counter-clockwise. The phone was still ringing loudly in the kitchen as she stepped through the front door.

Susan rushed across the living room floor and yanked the telephone receiver off the kitchen wall. "Hello," she asked, almost out of breath.

"Mrs. Hampton?" a male voice inquired at the other end of the line. "Mrs. Hampton, this is the Security Division at the Farmington State Mental Hospital."

"Yes?"

"Mrs. Hampton, I'm calling to tell you your husband escaped last night. . . ."

"What?" she gasped. She felt the fear rise in her throat.

"He was missing around midnight. Right after the last bed check. We're checking the hospital now. It's quite possible he's still inside. But we thought we should let you know. For your own safety."

Susan could not speak for a moment. "Have you contacted Dr. Finley?" she asked finally, her voice still rising with fear.

"We've called the Danvers Hotel several times but they haven't seen him since early morning. We left a message for him to call us as soon as he returns."

"What do you want me to do?" Susan asked weakly.

"Just stay home. Keep your doors locked. The police are looking for your husband. If he should be coming in your direction, we'll get him. But keep your doors locked. Just in case."

"What . . . why . . ." Susan stammered.

"Your husband is considered to be a dangerous man, Mrs. Hampton. We don't know if he would try to hurt anyone. But we don't want to give him the chance."

Susan Hampton composed herself and spoke softly into the telephone. "Do me a favor, please?"

"Yes, Mrs. Hampton."

"If you get in touch with Dr. Finley, have him call me."

"Yes ma'am."

"Thanks."

Susan placed the telephone back on the wall and sat by the kitchen table for a time staring blankly out the window. Then she picked up the telephone again.

She gave the operator the number and waited for a response.

"Hello."

"Alice, would you please send Aggy home?" Susan whispered into the telephone receiver.

There was a pause at the other end of the line. "Aggy?"

"Yes. Please send Aggy home. We've got some things to do."

"Susan, Aggy's not over here with Robin. I haven't seen her all day."

"I just sent her over."

"Susan, have you checked outside?"

"No, just a minute." Susan rushed toward the front door and stepped out onto the porch. She walked quickly down to the sidewalk and looked as far as she could down both ends of the street. "Aggy!" she yelled the name loudly three times.

"Did you find her?" Alice poked her blond head over the top of the hedge and yelled across the street at Susan.

"No." Susan felt herself starting to panic. Joel loved Aggy. He would never do anything to hurt her. She took a deep breath and tried to control her fear. But all she could think of was the knife blade slashing through the attic door. He'd wanted to kill them then.

"You look over there," Alice said, pointing down one end of the street. "I'll check the other end."

Susan felt almost immobilized with fear as she started down the long street. Suddenly she heard a weak voice behind her.

"Mommy, were you calling me?" Aggy asked as she stepped through the screen door and walked out onto the porch of the brownstone house.

Susan turned slowly and looked in that direction.

"I was getting some toys to bring over to Robin's," the little girl said meekly. "I was upstairs."

Susan Hampton suddenly felt the full weight of the terrible pressure she had been laboring under for the past few weeks, and her shoulders and arms began to shake uncontrollably. *Why? Why us? My God, what have we done?* For the moment, at least, the tears seemed trapped inside of her—unable to overflow the protective walls she had built around herself. There was only the terrible shuddering sensation that she could not control and the horrible feeling of being completely alone. . . .

"Susan, my God, what's wrong with you?" Alice asked, walking up and placing a consoling hand on Susan's quivering shoulder.

Susan tried to say something, but her head was aching and the words would not come. She reached a hand up to her throbbing forehead, but the hand was shaking so uncontrollably that she quickly thrust it back into her coat pocket.

"Susan, are you all right? What is it? Should I call a doctor?" A strong note of panic crept into Alice's voice. "Susan, should I call someone?"

Susan shook her head vigorously.

"Are you sure?"

"Yes . . . Please . . ." Susan blurted out. She breathed deeply several times and her shoulders and arms began to shake less noticeably.

"Look, come over to my place for a few hours. Until you pull yourself together," Alice pleaded with her.

"No!" Susan said firmly, struggling to control herself. She took another deep breath. "I'll be all right."

"Susan, maybe you should come over and talk about this?" Alice insisted. "What is it? Is it Joel?"

Susan nodded her head weakly.

"What's wrong with him?" Alice implored.

"He tried to . . . And now . . ." Susan could not find the right words.

"Are you two having *problems?*"

"Joel had a nervous breakdown. He's hospitalized at Farmington. He's . . ." Susan bit the words off carefully. Then she paused, unable to explain to Alice what was happening to Joel and her.

"I knew something was wrong," Alice said gently. "Frank and I heard strange noises over there in the middle of the night, and we knew something was wrong. What is it? His job? Are you two fighting?"

"No, he's... I mean, yes. Joel's been under tremendous pressure. He thinks he's..." Susan wanted to explain to Alice that Joel was undergoing some strange transition in which he was taking on the personality of someone who had lived back in the 1920s. But she knew Alice would not understand. "It's nothing serious... He just needs a rest...."

"Are you sure?" Alice asked again.

"Yes."

"I can't talk you into coming over for coffee?"

"No." Susan glanced down at Aggy who had crept up silently to the sidewalk. Aggy placed one hand gently on her mother's coat. "I have to make supper for Aggy," Susan insisted.

"You can eat over at our place...."

"No, thanks Alice, but we have quite a bit to get done tonight."

"Susan," Alice said reassuringly. "These things happen. Frank and I almost split up three times. People get over these things. It just takes time."

Susan nodded weakly. She knew there was no way to make Alice understand what was happening to Joel and her.

"Let me know if you need anything. Okay?"

"Thanks, Alice." Susan smiled lamely as Alice turned and walked away.

"Are you sure it's nothing else?" Alice asked again, turning around.

"No."

Susan watched as Alice walked across the street and disappeared behind the hedge that ran the length of the sidewalk. Then she looked down at Aggy.

"Mommy, what's wrong with Daddy?" the little girl asked. Her eyes were filled with fear and confusion.

For a moment, Susan thought that perhaps she should divert her daughter's attention to some other subject. But then she realized there were some things even a four-year-old girl should know.

"Honey," Susan began slowly. "There's something wrong ... with your Daddy... He's..."

"Is Daddy dead?" Aggy asked sadly, interrupting her mother.

Susan dropped to one knee and held her daughter close

to her. "No, honey, your Daddy is not dead. But he's . . . very sick. And you and I are going to be alone for awhile . . . until he gets better."

"Did Daddy hurt you?"

"No, honey, why do you ask?"

"Because you're crying." Aggy pushed herself gently away from her mother as she spoke. "The last time you cried was when Daddy chased us into the attic."

"That was an accident, honey. Daddy didn't mean to scare us." Susan paused and looked into her daughter's eyes. "Honey, you have to do one thing for me."

"What?"

"If you see Daddy at any time," Susan said slowly, "you mustn't talk to him or go near him. Come to me or go over to Robin's . . ."

"Why?"

"Because your Daddy is sick. And . . ." Again Susan found herself searching for the right words to explain Joel's actions.

"Will he hurt us?" Aggy asked blandly.

"He might," Susan admitted. "He doesn't want to, Aggy. But your Daddy's sick and he could hurt us."

"Will he hurt my dolls again?"

"No, but you must remember what I told you. Don't talk to your Daddy or go near him if you see him. Then he won't hurt any of us."

"Okay, Mommy."

Susan picked up Aggy and carried her toward the front porch of the brownstone house. "When Daddy's well, honey, then you can talk to him again." Susan set Aggy down on the porch and together the two of them walked through the front door. "Now, honey, you go upstairs and play for a few minutes while I make something for us to eat."

"Okay, Mommy," Aggy said somewhat sadly. She trudged slowly up the stairs and disappeared at the top of the staircase.

Susan quickly locked the door behind them. The telephone receiver was hanging limply from the wall when she walked back into the kitchen. She placed the receiver back on the hook and walked over to the cupboards next to the sink. She indifferently selected a can of tuna fish and placed it on the counter. Then she idly rummaged through a nearby drawer, looking for a can opener.

Suddenly, behind her, she heard a noise and she whirled quickly in that direction. She held her hand to her pounding heart as the basement door swung slowly open a few inches, then groaned to a slow halt. Susan stared into the darkness, gulped, and sighed deeply as she realized the lock had apparently not caught and the door had creaked slowly open by itself.

Susan walked quickly across the linoleum floor and reached for the metal knob on the door. As she did so, she suddenly remembered that Joel had come out of the basement after he had carried Aggy downstairs. And he had disappeared again into the basement after threatening them in the attic. Just what was down there that so intrigued him?

Susan peered into the darkness. Then, hesitantly, she walked down the flight of wooden stairs. At the bottom of the stairway, she groped into the darkness overhead. After moving her hand in a circular motion for several seconds, she finally managed to grasp the thin cord. She pulled hard on it and the harsh glare of a lone lightbulb flooded the room.

Susan found herself standing on the edge of a concrete floor that was littered with the wreckage of glass jars, boxes, and pieces of furniture they had been keeping in storage. Even the water heater and gas meter had been bludgeoned and slashed repeatedly with some sharp object. In the middle of the wreckage, Susan noticed the shattered remains of several of her best steak knives.

As she reached down to examine one of the knife handles, she again heard the basement door creak slowly open behind her. As she turned quickly in that direction, she found herself looking up at Aggy who was silhouetted against the lights from the kitchen windows.

"What are you doing down there, Mommy?" she asked innocently. "Is Daddy down there?"

V

Ned Finley ran the beam of his flashlight over the huge, moist pile of topsoil that covered the entrance leading into the old culvert. Then he turned and walked into the depths of the flood control system.

At the point where the two tunnels branched off in different directions, he paused and focused the beam of the flashlight into the darkness. He decided the tunnel to his left was probably the main culvert system and the one that had most likely been completed before the Little Sioux Water Reclamation Project was abandoned. The high-pitched squeal of the rats drifted out of the other culvert. Reason would suggest that he take the main culvert and not the one the rats had turned into their private sanctuary. But if the rats were this deep into the flood control system, Finley reasoned, then they must have come in from the other end of the culvert and not from the end where he had entered it. If that was the case, then there must be another opening in the flood control system somewhere southeast of Danvers.

Finley threw the burlap sack over his shoulder and stepped into the second tunnel opening as the rats squealed and scurried into the darkness ahead of him. As he walked deeper and deeper into the culvert, he played the flashlight beam over the circular concrete walls. In some sections, large concrete chunks had broken free and crumbled to the tunnel floor. Finley walked rapidly, holding firmly onto the burlap sack, his sole weapon should the rats lose their fear of him and leap out of the crumbling walls.

A veteran of many combat experiences, Ned Finley was not a man to panic easily, but the thought of being trapped underground with thousands of rats staring out at him from the darkness chilled him to the bone. As he walked deeper into the old flood control system, he played his flashlight over the crumbling concrete walls. He fought to control the fear and the panic as the flashlight reflected off the tiny, gleaming white teeth of the rats that stared down at him from the holes and cracks in the walls along both sides of the culvert.

Long, drooping networks of cobwebs hung down from the ceiling in several sections of the old culvert, and overhead the flashlight beam occasionally fell on small black bats, their sharp claws embedded in the pitted concrete ceiling. The disturbed bats would chortle in unison and the sound would echo up and down the walls and ceiling of the old tunnel.

Finley walked for what seemed like several miles, constantly playing the flashlight beam over the concrete walls and floors of the culvert. Then, ahead of him, he saw a mound of dirt that had tumbled into the tunnel, closing it off completely.

Finley ran the flashlight beam over the pile of debris. Then he turned the flashlight off and walked back and forth across the concrete floor of the tunnel. In the darkness, he peered into the huge mound of dirt, looking for any small rays of light that might reveal an avenue of escape out of the old culvert.

Suddenly, behind him, he heard the soft padding of tiny feet on the concrete floor. He switched on the flashlight and quickly pivoted in that direction. As he aimed the beam of the flashlight at the floor, several large rats hissed at him defiantly before retreating back into the darkness.

Then Finley sat down on one of the larger chunks of concrete. He ran the beam of the flashlight back and forth in the direction where the rats had disappeared. Just beyond the beam of light, the rats continued to hiss defiantly in the darkness.

Finley was annoyed at himself for having chosen this branch of the old flood control system. Obviously, there was no avenue of escape through the large pile of rock and debris. And the real question was whether or not he could go back to try the other branch of the culvert. The batteries in the flashlight were weakening and it was obvious that the flashlight was his only real defense against the hordes of rats. Once the batteries died, the rats would lose all fear. Then it was only a matter of time.

Suddenly, he heard a soft rustling sound to his left and he quickly directed the flashlight beam toward the floor of the culvert. The beam of the flashlight fell on two large rats that were scurrying up the pile of dirt and rocks. At the top of the pile of debris, the rats burrowed into the black soil and quickly disappeared.

Finley watched the rats disappear. Then he too climbed up the rocks and debris towards the ceiling of the culvert. He tore aside several small chunks of concrete and thrust his arm into the moist black soil.

Somehow a portion of the ceiling had remained intact on the other side of the mound of dirt. Finley tore at the remaining rocks and chunks of concrete until he had created a small opening just below the ceiling. He grabbed the burlap bag and squeezed slowly through to the other side of the culvert, where he directed the beam of the flashlight into the darkness. The tunnel curved gradually out of sight, just beyond the narrow flashlight beam.

Finley scrambled down the other side of the mound of dirt and stood once again on the concrete floor of the culvert. Large puddles of water had accumulated on the floor and a rusty pile of steel reinforcement rods were stacked up next to one wall. Finley walked past the rusty pile of metal and moved deeper into the old culvert.

He had walked another mile or two when he saw a glimmer of light in the darkness ahead of him. As he moved closer, the light began to glow brightly on the tunnel floor. Almost immediately, he stepped through a weed-strewn opening and out into the bright sunlight.

He found himself standing on the side of a small hill. To his left, the church steeple and water tower rose out of the small foothills. In front of him, the long black furrows of a newly plowed field stretched across the prairies from north to south.

Finley breathed a sigh of relief as he turned to look back into the darkness of the ancient culvert. As he did so, a lone rat scurried out of the tunnel opening and disappeared into the nearby brush and weeds. Finley watched the rat disappear. Then he turned and walked toward the water tower and church steeple.

VI

Finley caught a ride with a farmer who was driving to Danvers on a small Ford tractor. The farmer dropped him off on the northwestern edge of town, about two miles from where his Studebaker was parked alongside the gravel road. Finley crossed the empty fields and climbed up onto the old railroad embankment. He followed the railroad tracks to the Little Sioux Water Reclamation Project.

When he arrived at the site of the flood control project, the mouth of the huge culvert was covered with fresh black dirt. Huge tire tracks crisscrossed over the top of the freshly turned black soil, then angled southwards across the stubble field that separated the railroad embankment from the Little Sioux River.

Finley walked down the railroad embankment and followed the large tire tracks to where they intersected with a gravel road farther south. Large clumps of black dirt had fallen off the huge rubber wheels and were scattered over the gravel road. There were no tire tracks in the field on the other side of the gravel road. Finley looked down both ends of the road as far as he could see. Then he walked back toward the Studebaker.

Finley immediately drove back to Danvers. He pulled the burlap sack out of the trunk of the car where he had stowed it and carried it into the basement of the County Building. The County Engineer was sitting at a desk in the back of the room.

"I've got the samples for you," Finley said, setting the burlap bag on the front counter.

"Be with you in a minute," the County Engineer said as he scribbled some notations on a large chart in front of him. Then he joined Finley at the front counter. "What do you have here?"

"More concrete samples from the flood control project I told you about earlier. You said I would have to collect samples from several sections to determine if the entire system was defective. Here they are," Finley said, dumping the contents of the burlap bag on the front counter.

The County Engineer picked up several of the small concrete fragments and crumbled them between his thumb and index finger. "You don't have to run these through analysis," he said as the small fragments of concrete and sand fell onto the counter. "It's obvious that whoever mixed this didn't know what he was doing. See—it falls apart in your hand."

"So a flood control project constructed from this concrete would definitely be defective?" Finley asked.

"No question about it. Much of it would wash away and collapse in a couple of years. Certainly within a decade or two."

"Thanks," Finley said as he started to put the concrete samples back into the burlap bag. "Incidentally, who was responsible for burying that culvert three miles west of here?"

"What culvert?"

"The Little Sioux Water Reclamation Project."

"They buried it?" the County Engineer asked, seemingly surprised.

"Just this morning," Finley answered.

"I don't know nothin' about that," the County Engineer said, scratching his chin. "State's been meanin' to do it for some time now. But I sure didn't know they were planning to do it today."

"How come they let it sit for over thirty years? Then all of a sudden they decide to bury it?"

"It's a health problem." The County Engineer glanced over at an older woman who had stepped up to the other end of the counter. "Be right with you, ma'am."

"No hurry," the woman said as she set her purse on top of the counter and walked across the hall to a nearby water fountain.

"What kind of a health problem?" Finley asked.

"Rats. Rats all over that system. Get out into the fields and into the towns. 'Bout time they do something to get rid of those rats."

"Who had the authority to bury it?"

"State health authorities, most likely. They been after

the County to do it for years. Probably just decided to do it themselves since we've been kind of slow about it. Haven't had the money."

As the County Engineer walked over to help the woman at the other end of the counter, Finley swept the concrete samples into the burlap bag. Then he walked back up the short flight of stairs to Main Street.

It was late afternoon when Finley stepped out into the Main Street of Danvers. A slight chill was in the air and the blue skies of Indian summer were yielding gradually to the grayer tints of late autumn. The few trees that grew between the buildings on Main Street had been stripped almost bare by the steady autumn breezes. Their naked branches clutched at the sky like bony arms and fingers.

Finley threw the burlap sack into the trunk of his Studebaker and slid into the front seat behind the driver's wheel. As he reached up to adjust the rear-view mirror, he heard a sinister rattling sound from somewhere in the backseat of the Studebaker. Without moving his body, he turned the rear-view mirror downwards ever so slowly, carefully focusing it on the back seat. A huge rattlesnake slowly appeared in the mirror. It was coiled on the back seat, shaking its rattles as it prepared to strike.

Finley threw his body down suddenly across the front seat of the car, and the snake lashed out at the movement and missed. Finley quickly opened the passenger door and crawled out of the car. He slammed the door tightly shut behind him.

Outside the car, he looked through the rear window at the rattlesnake as it slithered and recoiled on the back seat of the Studebaker.

VII

"Someone sure meant to scare the hell out of you," the policeman said to Finley as they stood together in a small cubicle in the basement of the County Building. The dead rattlesnake was stretched out across a long wooden bench next to them. "But they sure weren't out to hurt you."

"Why do you say that?" Finley asked.

The policeman took a pen out of his shirt pocket and pried the snake's mouth open. "Snake has no fangs. Someone pulled them out with a pliers."

"What the hell?" Finley blurted out as he looked at the two bloody holes at the top of the snake's mouth.

"Some people'll go a long ways for a joke," the policeman said as he took the pen out of the rattlesnake's mouth.

The jaws of the huge snake slowly closed as Finley glanced suspiciously in the direction of the County Engineer's Office.

"Tell me something," Finley said, looking back in the direction of the policeman who was writing up his report on the pages of a black book. "Whatever happened to John J. Sylvester?"

"The Governor?"

"Yes. A book I was reading didn't give the date of his death. In fact it didn't say anything about his later years."

"Probably a good reason for that," the policeman said as he closed the black book and put it back on his desk.

"What do you mean?" Finley asked.

"He ain't dead yet. Owns the bank right across the street. Has for years."

"How old is he?" Finley asked, surprised.

"Probably late sixties. Early seventies. He was the youngest governor the state ever had. That's probably why he's still around."

"What about those pictures of him hanging all over town? When were they taken?" Finley asked.

"Probably ten, fifteen years ago. Hasn't changed that much. Maybe a little heavier."

"That explains a lot of things," Finley said more to himself than to the policeman.

"Explains what?" the policeman asked.

"Nothing," Finley said. "Listen, the next time you talk to the County Engineer, tell him they buried the Little Sioux Water Reclamation Project much too early."

"Why?" the policeman asked, perplexed.

"Because all the rats aren't in there yet!"

VIII

He had made it safely to the banks of the Little Sioux River long before daybreak. From there, he had followed the river upstream for perhaps eight or ten miles. As the sun came over the horizon, he took refuge beneath the exposed roots of a large tree that grew alongside the river embankment. Then he had fallen asleep.

He awoke to the gentle sound of the sluggish water as it lapped against a dead log at the river's edge. For the rest of the day, he sat there.

And he remembered how very much he had always liked to sit on the banks of the Little Sioux River, watching the gentle waters flow toward the Mississippi and the Great Sea beyond. That thought had always brought out the wanderlust in him. That is, until he met Kate. She was the first woman he'd ever loved. There had been others—but not the kind a man would ask to marry. He had to find her again. But first he would have his revenge.

It was late afternoon when he heard the loud honking sounds overhead. He peered through the roots at a flock of Canada geese weaving gracefully across the sky. The geese seemed to be following the course of the Little Sioux River as they disappeared from sight.

For a moment, his spirit responded to the majestic freedom of the geese flying gracefully southwards, and he wished that he could join them.

The light green hospital uniform was covered with dirt and his feet were bloody from the sharp wheat and corn stubble he had run through the previous evening. He laid his head back on the damp riverbank and fell asleep.

And he dreamt of the geese and the river—the river that opened up onto the largest body of water he had ever seen, a body of water that stretched beyond the horizon and seemingly into the sky itself. And he felt himself being pulled away into that river. . . .

But then he saw the girl in the swing. Always before, she

was sitting with her back turned toward him. But now she was looking in his direction. It had been so long, but he remembered those soft eyes and the shy, gentle smile....

And he knew, although the river beckoned, that it was not yet time for him to go....

Chapter Eleven

I

Finley left the County Building and walked immediately across the street to the Danvers State Bank. The bank building was the oldest structure on Main Street. High above the brick portico, the date "1880" had been inscribed.

Fake pillars and columns climbed the granite walls on both sides of the front door, and tiny stone nymphs sported and skipped across the top of the front wall, just below the roofline. A small green light bulb glowed feebly above the front entrance.

A middle-aged woman in a black and white business suit was pulling the shade down over the front window as Finley climbed the flight of stairs to the front door of the bank building.

"I'm sorry, we're closed," the woman said politely.

"I have an appointment with Mr. Sylvester," Finley said as he opened the door and stepped into the lobby.

"You must be mistaken," the woman said as she tried to stop Finley from walking any farther into the bank building.

"Mr. Sylvester is expecting me," Finley said firmly as the door closed slowly shut behind him.

"But, you can't!" the woman blurted out.

"Let Mr. Finley in, Miss Phillips!" a deep baritone voice suddenly boomed out across the bank lobby.

As Finley looked in that direction, a tall, heavy-set man stepped into an open doorway in the rear of the bank lobby. He stood with one hand in his coat pocket while the other hand held a long cigar. As the swirling smoke dissipated, John J. Sylvester posed in the open doorway like a Shakespearean actor about to step out onto the stage.

Sylvester's snowy white hair and bushy mustache were accentuated by deep blue eyes that gleamed across the bank lobby. He wore a dark blue business suit and his large frame was illuminated by the light from a window behind him. An aura of power and nobility clung naturally to the majestic presence of John J. Sylvester.

"Let Mr. Finley come in to see me, Miss Phillips," Sylvester's deep baritone voice boomed out again as he raised the cigar slowly to his mouth. "He is right. We have an appointment."

As Sylvester disappeared behind the cloud of smoke, Miss Phillips stepped aside. A look of disdain crept into her eyes as she watched Finley shuffle past in his dirty tan pants and rumpled sweater. His dirt-caked shoes left muddy tracks across the tile floor.

Sylvester was sitting behind a large desk when Finley stepped into his private office. Sylvester's left arm was cocked confidently at his side as he sat motionlessly in a black swivel chair. "Sit down," he instructed Finley politely but firmly.

As he sat down, Finley's eyes swept across the many photographs that lined the walls of the office. Sylvester himself stared out of most of the old photographs.

"I understand you have a keen interest in local history," Sylvester said as his bright blue eyes stared across the desk at Finley. "What is it you want from me?"

"I think you know what I've been looking for," Finley said, trying to avoid Sylvester's sharp, intimidating stare.

"Why don't you tell me, then, so we may both be enlightened?" Sylvester said as he placed the cigar in a large metal ashtray and sat back in his chair.

"I think you know I've been investigating the disappearance of Judd McCarthy. I know you had something to do with his disappearance and death. But I'm not exactly sure how you were involved."

"If my memory serves me correctly," Sylvester said, seemingly unperturbed, "McCarthy disappeared with a company payroll."

"That was a smokescreen, as you very well know," Finley

said. "Some powerful people had him put away. You were one of them."

"Why don't you tell me what you *think* you know, Mr. Finley? Then I'll see if I can help you."

"I know you inherited this bank in the 1920s," Finley began. "You were a young man, full of ambition, but the bank was only marginally successful as a business. Then you became President of the Community Development League which controlled city funds for growth and expansion. You were also involved with the Hanley Brothers Construction Company and the Little Sioux Water Reclamation Project. It was a perfect opportunity for you to filter city funds and construction funds into your bank, and you did so with the help of Fred and Ben Hanley."

"And how did we succeed in this venture?" Sylvester asked somewhat sarcastically as he picked up his cigar from the ashtray and relit it with a silver lighter.

"By inflating labor costs and contract costs, at the same time that you used inferior materials in the construction of the Little Sioux Water Reclamation Project. It gave the Hanley brothers a wider profit margin and it gave you the necessary capital to expand your bank's investment capabilities. The people in this town believed in you and you took them for a ride through the Community Development League."

"Can you prove this?" Sylvester asked coldly.

"There is no need to prove it," Finley said. "You would never be prosecuted for a crime that took place thirty-three years ago."

"Then what is it you want from me?"

"Undoubtedly the metropolitan papers would love to get their hands on a scandal involving a former governor. Especially one who was so popular and who was held in such high esteem by his constituency."

"Money? Is that what you want?" Sylvester asked, leaning forward. "Is this blackmail, Mr. Finley?"

"I only want the truth. What happened to Judd McCarthy on October 12, 1926? If you tell me that, I'll leave you alone."

"I don't know what happened to him," Sylvester said, sitting back in his chair.

"Then I'll just have to go to the newspapers," Finley said as he stood to leave.

"No, wait, Mr. Finley. Much of what you have said is true, but I don't know what happened to Judd McCarthy. I'm busy now," Sylvester said, gesturing toward the outer lobby. "I must help Miss Phillips. If you will come back this evening, I will tell you everything I know. Then you can decide for yourself whether or not it will be worth pursuing this affair."

Finley studied the sharp blue eyes of John J. Sylvester. "What time?"

"Make it eight o'clock, Mr. Finley," Sylvester said as he smiled strangely and squashed his cigar in the metal ashtray. "I promise to have some answers for you."

II

That evening Finley paced nervously outside the Danvers State Bank Building. Main Street was dark except for the oblong street lights that glowed feebly on the corners and in the middle of the blocks. Overhead, a light cloud cover moved slowly beneath a black, star-filled sky. The smell of hay and straw drifted in from the surrounding countryside.

After he had paced back and forth for almost half an hour, Finley walked up the short flight of stairs to the front door of the bank building. The small green light was glowing feebly above the brick and stone portico. Through the window, Finley could see a thin sliver of light glowing above the open doorway of John J. Sylvester's private office. Finley tested the front door, found it open, and walked into the dark lobby of the bank building.

Sylvester was seated at his desk when Finley entered his private office. He had just finished sealing a letter and was running his closed palm across the back side of the envelope.

"You're late, Mr. Finley," Sylvester said, looking up. "This is for you." Sylvester handed Finley the letter, then leaned back in his desk chair and lit another cigar.

Finley examined both sides of the white envelope. "What is it?"

"Just some things you might want to know. I have

another letter here too," Sylvester said, patting the smaller
envelope that lay flat on his desk. "You will know what to do
with it after our conversation."

Finley sat down and looked suspiciously around the
room.

"You have nothing to fear, except of course your own
imagination, Mr. Finley. I am the last survivor of those who
were involved in the events you described this afternoon.
There is no one else."

"Are you ready to tell me what I need to know?" Finley
asked.

"Yes, but first I want to apologize for what happened to
you this afternoon. I understand you found a rattlesnake in
the back seat of your car? I did not order that. It happened
without my approval."

"And I suppose you didn't order the flood control system
to be buried with me inside?" Finley asked sarcastically.

"You were inside the culvert?" Sylvester asked, seemingly
surprised.

"You know I was," Finley said firmly.

"No, I did not," Sylvester said nervously as he stood and
began pacing back and forth between his desk and a small
window that looked out onto an adjacent alley. "I am glad you
managed to get out. I know you don't believe that, but I
didn't know you were inside the culvert."

Finley watched Sylvester suspiciously, not knowing whether
he was witnessing a sincere confession or a carefully rehearsed
role played by a skilled actor and master politician. "Did you
have anything to do with the dead dog that was spread out
across my bed?" Finley asked.

"The panther has four paws, Mr. Finley. Burt was one of
them, but there were others. It should not concern you. I
tried many ways to get you out of town," Sylvester continued,
"so that we would not need to have this conversation. I could
have killed you many times, but I chose not to. You are a
most stubborn detective. I commend you for that."

"What happened to Judd McCarthy on October 12,
1926?" Finley asked. "That's all I want to know. Then I will
leave and you will never hear from me again."

"Yes, *Mr. McCarthy*," Sylvester mused as he puffed on
his cigar and looked out the side window. "You know, you can

only see a tiny part of Main Street from this window. Not enough really. But I have sat in that outer lobby many times, late at night, looking at the abandoned stores and shops along Main Street. You have no idea, Mr. Finley, of the dreams I had for this small town. . . ."

"Those dreams didn't seem to stop you from embezzling money through the Community Development League," Finley said, interrupting Sylvester.

"No, you are wrong," Sylvester said, returning to his desk. "The Community Development League was a sincere effort on my part to help this town. It all went sour when the Hanleys came into it."

"What happened?"

"The Little Sioux Water Reclamation Project could have turned this entire town around. It could have meant economic prosperity for the rest of this century. But Ben and Fred Hanley turned it into a boondoggle. Their greed is what destroyed it."

"And you went along with them?" Finley asked.

"Only much later, after there was no turning back. I was inadvertently sucked into their schemes. By the time I knew what was going on, full disclosure of what they were up to would have meant the end of my career, the end of my dreams for this town. I only went into politics for one reason, you must understand that."

"What was that reason?"

"To filter money back into Carver County through the state government. It was my way of paying these people back for what they had lost on the Little Sioux Water Reclamation Project. I know you think of me as an evil and vicious man," Sylvester said, turning to face Finley. "But I can assure you it was Ben and Fred Hanley who pulled the strings. They made it possible for me to get into politics. And then they made it necessary for me to get out."

"How?" Finley asked.

Sylvester started pacing between his desk and the rear window. "Without my knowledge and with me as an ignorant participant in their schemes, they bilked everything out of the Community Development League. By October of 1926 there was nothing left to embezzle except for the final payroll, which involved a great deal of money. They came to me with a plan. When I refused to go along with them, they threatened to plant incriminating evidence against me, then leave town. I had no choice. I went along with them."

"Was McCarthy sent for a phony payroll?" Finley asked.

"Yes, how did you know?" Sylvester asked.

"I was only speculating."

"The payroll McCarthy carried back with him from Carson was worthless paper cut to the size of currency. They set him up," Sylvester continued.

"And then they had him killed?" Finley asked.

"No, there was someone else involved. . . ."

"Who?" Finley demanded.

"Let me finish what I was telling you about my political aspirations, Mr. Finley. Then we will return to your interests in Judd McCarthy." Sylvester paused to light another cigar. "We split the payroll—Ben Hanley, Fred Hanley, and myself. I used the money to finance my first political campaign for the state senate. With his share, Fred Hanley moved to the East Coast and retired. Ben Hanley moved to Florida. I wasn't to see either of them for years. Then, in the 30s, Ben Hanley approached me when I was thinking of making a bid for the presidency. He wanted a political favor. It would have involved another scheme in which thousands of innocent people would have lost their money and their dreams. I refused. Ben Hanley then said he would go to the press with the story of my involvement in the Community Development League and the Little Sioux Water Reclamation Project. That's when I decided against running for the presidency. I told him I was through with politics and there was nothing I could do to help him, even if I wanted to. He gave up and went back to Florida. I had carried the heavy burden of those sins for too long. I had no desire to add to them. You must remember that these people believe in John J. Sylvester," Sylvester said loudly and dramatically, gesturing toward Main Street. "Mr. Finley, if you take those dreams away from these people, they will have nothing left!"

"I have no desire to take anything away from these people," Finley said firmly. "I only want the truth."

"Did you see that green light outside the front door of the bank?" Sylvester asked.

"Yes," Finley said.

"I keep it burning day and night for these people. It is the last bit of hope I have to give them. You have seen them, wandering the streets half insane, drinking themselves to death, trying to live with shattered dreams. That small light above the bank of John J. Sylvester is the last bit of hope they have. You must not take it away from them!"

"I only want to know what happened to Judd McCarthy," Finley said softly. "Then I will leave you and your town and I will never say a word to anyone."

"But can we really count on that, Mr. Finley?" Sylvester asked as he sat back down behind his desk. "Human nature is a devious thing. You may leave this office with the best of intentions and yet someday find it expedient or financially attractive to tell the true story of John J. Sylvester. I'm not sure we can afford to let that happen."

"You have my word. Just tell me what happened to Judd McCarthy."

"No, I cannot trust you, Mr. Finley," Sylvester said as he pulled a small revolver out of the top drawer of his desk. "I have been too trusting of men in the past and I have paid dearly for it. I do not intend to make that mistake again."

"What do you plan to do?" Finley asked, startled.

"As you can see," Sylvester said, holding the pistol up in the air dramatically, "I have just taken a pistol out of my desk drawer."

"Do you plan to save your reputation by killing me?" Finley asked calmly as Sylvester pointed the pistol at him.

"It was very foolish of you, Mr. Finley, to come into a bank after closing hours," Sylvester said, ignoring Finley's question. "It will be very easy for me to explain to the authorities that I was working late and you surprised me. Thinking you were a bank robber, I shot you. It's a perfect alibi."

"Before you fire that gun, would you at least tell me who killed Judd McCarthy?"

"Mr. Finley, someone else despised Judd McCarthy for reasons even I don't know or understand."

"Does it have something to do with Katharine Sumners?" Finley asked boldly.

"That's enough, Mr. Finley. Our conversation has come

to an end. It is time for you to take leave of us now. Please turn around and walk slowly toward the front door."

"But . . ."

"No more talk, Mr. Finley. Please stand and turn toward the doorway."

Finley stood up slowly and turned around.

"Now, walk slowly toward the front door," Sylvester commanded from behind the desk. "I have a heavy conscience, Mr. Finley, and you are about to help me relieve it."

"Do you really think this will relieve the burden on your conscience?" Finley asked as he moved slowly across the office toward the open doorway.

"Yes, I'm sure it will do it a great deal of good," Sylvester said firmly. "Stop right there, Mr. Finley. That's far enough. You must remember that I tried in every way to discourage you. I did not mean to hurt you in any way. And I certainly never meant to kill you."

"Then why are you doing this?" Finley asked as he stared at the dim street lights glowing outside the bank building.

"Because there is always a chance you will leak something to the newspapers," Sylvester said from behind him. "I am an honorable man, Mr. Finley. I have made only one major mistake in my entire life and you have discovered it. My honor is important to me. It is even more important to those people out there. I would not want for them or for me to live without it."

"So you are going to kill me to protect your honor?"

"No, Mr. Finley, you are wrong again. Just look at that street out there so you will know why I am doing this."

As Finley stared at the dim lights outside the abandoned shops and stores on the Main Street of Danvers, a gunshot echoed across the private office of John J. Sylvester. Finley shuddered, stiffened, and then turned slowly around. John J. Sylvester was slumped across his desk, the small revolver clasped in his right hand and a bullet hole in his temple.

III

"You're free to go, Mr. Finley," the policeman said as he and Finley stood together in the office of John J. Sylvester. Sylvester's body had been removed earlier by ambulance, but a dark pool of blood still glistened on top of the desk.

"What does the note say?" Finley asked, trying not to appear too curious.

The policeman folded the note carefully and placed it in his shirt pocket. "Governor Sylvester said he had cancer. He said he met you this afternoon. Found out you were a clinical psychologist and asked you to come back this evening to help him deal with his depression. Later this afternoon he decided instead to take his life. He said he was leaving the note so we wouldn't think you were involved. It's really a shame, isn't it?"

"Yes, it is," Finley agreed.

"He meant so much to this town and yet no one knew he had cancer. Maybe we could have helped him?"

"Maybe he had it for a long time and just didn't want to tell anyone," Finley said.

"I suppose—but it's a shame," the policeman said. "Will you be around for a few days in case we need anything from you?"

"Yes, I'm staying in the hotel," Finley said.

Finley and the policeman walked through the outer lobby and stepped out into the Main Street of Danvers.

"You know, there just aren't too many men like John J. Sylvester," the policeman said sadly as he locked the door behind them and turned off the light above the portico. "He was a most honorable gentleman."

"Yes, indeed he was," Finley agreed.

When Finley walked back to the hotel, there was no one in the lobby except for the desk clerk who was snoring peacefully on his cot behind the counter.

Finley slipped quietly past the hotel desk and walked up

the stairs to his room on the third floor. Then he sat down on the bed and pulled out Sylvester's letter.

As he read and reread the letter, Finley tried to place Sylvester's story in the context of the other information he had managed to gather. But still he was puzzled. It was early morning before he finally fell asleep.

In the street below Finley's room, Benny folded his awning pole and stepped into the old poolhall. He fell asleep on one of the dusty slate tables, one arm draped over the awning pole like a man cuddling up to his wife. Farther down the street, Harmon lay dead drunk across the front counter of his newspaper office. He snored face up and dreamed of the novel he was going to write someday. Elsewhere, Marsha Williams stepped out from behind the DX Station and looked out at the dark prairies on both ends of Main Street. It was her birthday and she had been unable to sleep because old memories kept haunting her dreams. So she got up and walked out into the darkness.

As a young girl, she had often gotten up at night to walk down to Main Street. She liked to stand in the middle of the street and look up at the stars that hovered high in the sky above the sleeping town. And she liked to smell the freshly cut hay and straw as it drifted in from the prairies. But most of all, she liked to sit on the curb and dream about the fake Greek pillars and arches that adorned the front walls of John J. Sylvester's bank. They made her think of far away places and wild exotic loves and romances she had never experienced.

But sometimes they too were not enough. Sometimes, no matter how hard she tried, her dreams were not strong enough to take her away from the small prairie town and the smell of hay and straw and the sight of the abandoned buildings on Main Street. This was one of those nights. She sat for a long time, until she felt the cold breeze against her cheeks. Then she pulled her shawl tightly around her shoulders and walked home.

She would have to tell John Sylvester the next time she saw him, she thought as she walked across Main Street, that the light above his doorway had burned out and would have to be replaced.

IV

As Martha Williams disappeared behind the corner of the DX Service Station, someone else stepped out of the shadows across the street from the bank building. He had been standing there for hours, watching the stars overhead and waiting for the street to clear so he could step out and see if the buildings were as he had remembered them.

He had watched the ambulance pull up to the bank building and he had seen the attendants carry the sheet-draped stretcher down the short flight of stairs to Main Street. Later, from his hiding place, he had overheard bits and pieces of the conversation between the policeman and the tall man in the brown beret. From their conversation, he knew that John J. Sylvester had died earlier that evening. He was disappointed because he knew that Sylvester was involved in some way in what had happened to him in the thicket on October 12, 1926. Now Sylvester would not be able to tell him what had happened. He would still find out, but it would be more difficult.

He padded slowly out into the center of Main Street. His bare feet were bloody from walking through the wheat and corn stubble, and the pain shot up into his ankles and calves as he walked across the granular, asphalt surface. But he ignored the pain. He had known greater pain before— much greater pain. It was not going to stop him from doing what he knew had to be done.

The Main Street of the small town was almost as he had remembered it. Some of the buildings were older and he did not recognize the names on many of the signs. Still, the brick and stone structures looked very much as they had on the day that they had completed construction on the County Building.

He felt the cool evening breezes penetrate the thin green hospital uniform as he walked down the street to the County Building and stood beneath the shadow of the huge eagle.

Everything had been so right then. It had felt so good to be alive as he stood on a ledge beneath a clear blue sky and guided the eagle to the top of the County Building. After the eagle was secured to the side of the building, he had waved his cap to the cheering mob of construction workers in the street below. And the mob had laughed and roared back its approval. Even John J. Sylvester had stepped out of his bank building to participate in the celebration. Sylvester had smiled up at him, but he had never trusted Sylvester. And he refused to smile back.

As he looked up at the eagle, the cool breeze continued to penetrate the thin hospital uniform. He needed different clothes. And he needed a shave.

He could not search for Kate looking like this. Even if he should find her, she would never recognize him. It was important that their reunion be right. It had been so long since he'd seen his beautiful Lady Kate.

He padded softly back toward the bank building, peering into the shadows of the small shops along the way. In the back of one of the stores, he saw piles of men's work clothing folded neatly on top of several small tables. He put his shoulder to the door and pushed hard. The lock snapped easily.

He shut the door slowly behind him and peered back out into the street to make certain no one had seen him. Then he retreated into the shadows in the rear of the building.

Boots, shirts, hats, pants—everything he needed was arranged across several display tables. He tore off the hospital uniform and quickly put on a new shirt, pants, and a pair of boots. Then he slid a wood panel off a glass display case and pulled out a long hunting knife. He began hacking at the thick beard with the sharp blade.

He would reset the lock on the door and he would bury the hospital uniform in the empty fields outside of town. Then he would find someplace out in the country and he would sleep during the day....

Suddenly he heard a sound outside the window, and he quickly lowered the hunting knife and retreated farther into the shadows.

As he looked in that direction, a bearded face appeared above the display case. Slowly, the eyes in the middle of the beard glanced upwards at the tattered canvas awning that ran the length of the store front. Then the figure raised a long pole, and slowly the awning groaned out over the concrete sidewalk.

Benny? Of course. He had seen him walk into the poolroom earlier that evening. But he did not recognize him. He had forgotten Benny. Benny was only a teenager, walking the streets with his awning pole when he had last seen him. He remembered that some of the locals had teased Benny mercilessly. They fed him rotten fruit and taught him to make grotesque faces at strangers. But it was Fred Hanley who had played the cruelest joke of all on Benny. When Benny did what Fred Hanley told him to do, the girl screamed hysterically. Then she went home to tell her brothers. They came back and beat Benny until he was unconscious. After that they laid him out on the road, pulled down his trousers, and stomped on him with their heavy boots until the blood poured out onto the dirt alley.

He remembered how he had found Benny that way, moaning incoherently and clutching with both hands to stop the blood from pouring out of his wounds. And he had carried Benny up the hill, but the doctor just shook his head and sewed what was left of him back together. Benny never spoke to anyone ever again. He just patrolled the streets of Danvers, cranking the awnings out over the sidewalks and then cranking them back up again. But his mind was gone, and with it went the laughter and the trust.

He remembered how he had confronted the Farwell brothers several days later. He had planned to make them pay for what they had done to Benny, but they begged and pleaded with him and told him they knew now that it was Fred Hanley's fault, and he let them go because he knew that what they were telling him was the truth.

As he thought about Fred Hanley, he was filled with rage. At what Hanley had done to Benny. And what Hanley had done to him as well. It had to have been Hanley. Who else? Hanley had hated him ever since Benny had been nearly killed in the streets of Danvers, and he, Judd McCarthy, had stormed into the company offices and threatened to do to Hanley what the Farwell brothers had done to Benny.

"You touch me, Mac, and I'll have your job or your life,"

Hanley had said as he backed against the wall and hissed at him like a rat fighting for its life.

"Ain't no threat ya can make'll keep me from callin' ya a son of a bitch," *he had fired back at Hanley.*

"I been called worst," *Hanley blurted out.* "Besides, weren't my fault the Farwells thought so highly of their sister's honor. It got outta hand, Mac, I admit, but it weren't my fault."

He had glared at Hanley as he fought the urge to throw him against the wall until he was battered into submission.

"Look, Mac, I know ya got a sweetheart. And I know ya got plans. But ya ain't goin' nowhere unless ya got a job. An I'll see that ya never work again, leastways not anywhere along the Sioux Line River. Not unless you get out of this office right now."

The thought of Kate caused him to lower his hands. He had promised her he would never fight again. He glared at Fred Hanley, then turned and walked quickly out of the company office. He heard the laughter behind him as he walked back to town. Months later, he thought he heard the laughter again, from somewhere in the darkness. . . .

It was years ago. But the name Fred Hanley brought back the rage that had burned in his soul. . . .

Joel tucked the hunting knife into the top of his boots. Then he chose a floppy black hat from the back counter, placed it on his head, and walked quickly toward the front door of the store. His new clothes and boots fit him poorly, but at least they were warmer than the hospital uniform and offered some disguise. He closed the door behind him and reset the lock. Across the street, he heard the rusty metal awnings creaking in the night air. He glanced over at Benny, then slipped into the shadows of the adjacent alley and walked to the edge of town.

He remembered that Fred Hanley owned a home two blocks away from the library, next to a small apple orchard. Hanley hated to sleep in the construction tents, and he had bought a home in town—which he planned to sell after the Little Sioux Water Reclamation Project was completed.

The home was pretty much as he remembered it, although the apple trees were much taller. He crept up to a side window and peered into the living room. A single light glowed in the darkness of the small house. Next to the light, someone was sitting with his back turned toward the window.

He felt the anger build inside of him as he walked around to the back of the house. He stepped up into a screen-enclosed porch and gently turned the metal doorknob. When the door would not open, he stepped back, planted the sole of his boot against it, and pushed hard. The door exploded into an adjacent kitchen. As he stomped across the linoleum floor, a figure rose quickly out of a chair in the living room.

"So, Fred Hanley, ya still be alive," Joel muttered as he paused in the doorway leading into the living room.

"Who . . ." a voice whispered sheepishly from the shadows in the living room.

"You know who I be, Fred Hanley," Joel bellowed as he stormed into the living room.

He grabbed the man by the throat and lifted him into the air. "Take a good look, Fred Hanley. Ya thought ya were through with me, now didn't ya?"

An incomprehensible gurgle escaped from the throat of the man as he dangled in the air and fought to breathe. Nearby, a grandfather clock chimed merrily in the darkness.

Joel held the man closer to the light.

What had Fred Hanley looked like? He couldn't remember.

He set the man back down on the living room floor.

"Who . . ." the man could only whisper weakly as he massaged his throat and struggled to speak.

"I be the man whose life you took, Fred Hanley," Joel muttered angrily as he grasped the shirt of the quivering figure in front of him.

"I'm not Fred Hanley," the man finally blurted out.

"Who be ya, then?" Joel twisted the man's shirt and bent him closer to the light.

"I'm . . . his son."

Joel studied the man's face.

He was beginning to remember. No, it was not Fred Hanley. This man was taller, and the lines on his face were softer, gentler.

"Where's your father?" Joel asked, letting go of the man's shirt.

"Dead . . ."

"Dead!" Joel exploded, grabbing the shirt again.

"My father died over twenty years ago," the man whispered weakly as he continued to massage his throat.

Joel studied the terrified face in front of him. Fear and panic gleamed in the man's eyes and he was breathing heavily.

"How did he die?"

"Old age . . . He moved to the East Coast . . . Died in the 1930s."

Joel let go of the shirt and stepped back. "Dead?"

It was incomprehensible. He had come this far only to find that Fred Hanley was already dead.

"Dead?" he repeated weakly.

"Who are you?" the man asked as he stepped back. His eyes glanced nervously around the room. "I've seen you before."

Dead? There was no revenge to be gained on a dead man.

"You're Judd McCarthy, aren't you?" the man asked from the shadows. "But how can you be?"

"How do you know who I am?" Joel demanded.

"My father showed me a picture of you. . . . When I was a boy."

"Did he tell you what happened to me?" Joel demanded.

"No," the man admitted. "But I know he had something to do with your disappearance."

"What did he tell you?"

"Nothing. My father could be a very evil man. But it can't be you. You would have to be . . . seventy years old. . . ."

He had made a mistake. The answer was not to be found in this house. He would have to go elsewhere.

"Sorry," Joel whispered, "I made a mistake. I thought you were . . ."

"What happened to you? Where have you been?" the man inquired.

"I'm not Judd McCarthy . . . I don't know who . . . I'm . . ."

Joel turned and walked toward the kitchen door. He saw a paring knife gleaming on the drainboard and he deftly picked it up and slipped it into his jacket pocket. The hunting knife was still tucked into the top of his boot. He was now ready. The stars were glowing brightly in space as he stomped back out into the night air. . . .

He would follow the Little Sioux River north to Carson. And he would walk the old Sioux Line until he found the thicket where it had all begun . . . Then he would know . . . And he would be free of the nightmare . . . And he would find his Lady Kate again.

At the edge of town, he broke into a brisk trot and he ran across the plowed fields toward the Little Sioux River. The boots rubbed painfully against his feet as he tried to outrun the stars that were chasing him across the darkness of space. . . .

Inside the house, Fred Hanley's son lifted the telephone receiver with shaking fingers.

"Get me the police!" he stammered.

Chapter Twelve

I

Sylvester's letter was long, puzzling, provocative, and it raised almost as many questions as it answered. But more than anything else, it reinforced what Sylvester himself had said before he committed suicide. If he was telling the truth, John J. Sylvester was indeed ignorant of much that was going on behind the scenes of the Hanley Brothers Construction Company and the Little Sioux Water Reclamation Project. Either that, Finley concluded, or else Sylvester was making one last desperate attempt to protect his honor and his reputation. Finley chose to accept the former explanation, for, like the townspeople, Finley had come to believe that John J. Sylvester was essentially an honest man.

In the morning, Ned Finley read the letter one last time. He laid it flat on the small table next to the front window of his hotel room. As he read Sylvester's highly ornate prose style, Ned Finley paused periodically to look out onto the many abandoned shops and stores on the Main Street of Danvers, and he came to understand the agony and torment of John J. Sylvester:

My Dear Mr. Finley,

No doubt, now that you have had the opportunity to savor the significance of our last conversation, you will have arrived at some interesting conclusions concerning the life and career of John J. Sylvester. I trust that your instinct will enable you to winnow away the chaff to find the grain of truth hidden therein. I then trust in your compassion to decide whether the truth or the lie would be the more appropriate way of presenting John J. Sylvester to his small constituency. I myself have expended enough effort in search of human acceptance. I now seek a higher stamp of approval, if such be possible.

No doubt, you will also think I am still hiding some of the facts to protect my tarnished reputation. I can only give you my word that I am telling you everything I know about the disappearance of Judd McCarthy. If I have not your trust, please at least grant me your indulgence and your patience. Very few souls find it expedient to tell lies on the deathbed—which, as one philosopher has written, "is the only truly reliable confessional."

I hear from some of those in our fair town that you suspect there is a connection between Judd McCarthy and Katharine Sumners. I think that not too likely. McCarthy was a semi-literate, itinerant laborer. Katharine Sumners was a young woman of class and social distinction, albeit she was somewhat reluctant to accept the obvious advantages of her birthright. All of which is to say that Katharine Sumners had no designs on greatness, but rather was shy and timid and undemanding of life. I knew Katharine Sumners closely, but not intimately, for almost one year, though it would be fair to say it was more her mother's design than anything Katharine Sumners herself felt for me. Agnes Sumners wanted her daughter to be the wife of a wealthy banker, but Katharine Sumners was not charmed, certainly not in awe of the mystique that surrounded John J. Sylvester. So we parted, if "parting" is an appropriate term for two people who were never truly together. After the spring of 1926, I was never to see Katharine Sumners again. As you know, she died in a fire in Chicago and her remains were returned to our small town for burial.

So you see, I think you must search elsewhere for the clue to the disappearance of Judd McCarthy.

I would suggest you begin with a scene that I am about to describe to you. I do not understand its significance myself, but it has weighed heavily on my conscience and has been the source of many sleepless nights and many long evening walks.

I knew of the plot to get rid of Judd McCarthy, of course, but I knew nothing of its implementation. The Hanley brothers never trusted me with the details of their many schemes, for I was "unreliable." Perhaps they recognized an ethical dimension in John J. Sylvester that was surpassed only by his ambition. I suppose it could be said that my ambition placed a crown on its head and proclaimed my shackled virtues slaves to the throne. Nonetheless, I had it in my power to terminate their schemes at any time, simply by telling McCarthy of the designs on his life. The fact that I failed to act in this manner was my own undoing.

What little I know of the *details* of McCarthy's disappearance I learned during a late evening conversation with Fred Hanley. I was alone in my office on the evening of October 12, 1926, when there was a loud knock on the front door of the bank lobby. When I walked out into the lobby and opened the door, Fred Hanley stepped into the room. The smell of liquor was heavy on his breath and he carried a large bottle of whiskey with him. He was breathing heavily, like a man who had just run a long distance. There was a maniacal grin on his face as he reeled past me into my private office. When I joined him, he was raising the bottle to his lips like a man toasting a victory.

"We did it!" he said loudly, thumping the bottle down hard on my desk and laughing like an insane man.

"Did what?" I asked.

Fred Hanley looked at me with the fierce glow of hatred and revenge in his eyes. "We got rid of that bastard!"

"McCarthy?" I asked.

"Yes, we got rid of McCarthy for good," Fred

Hanley said as he drank deeply of the bottle of whiskey. "He knew too much, that no-good Irish bastard. He suspected what we were doing with the Community Development League, did you realize that? Can you imagine? It was only a matter of time before he went to the authorities. But he won't be going anywhere now." Hanley laughed hysterically, almost bending over in his chair.

"What did you do to him?" I asked.

"Nothing. I didn't have to do nothing! Oh, maybe I lent a little assistance, but I didn't have to do nothing except move a little dirt around." He laughed again hysterically. Then he grew deathly serious. "There was someone who despised Judd McCarthy even more than we did, John J. Sylvester. Someone who wanted him dead a long time ago."

"Who?" I asked.

"*John J. Sylvester,*" he said sarcastically, "the great tin God of this dumpy town, there are some things you should never know. And that is one of them. Let us just say McCarthy is out of our way for good and we can now split the real payroll and leave this Godforsaken bump on the prairie."

Fred Hanley was obviously pleased with himself that evening. He sat in my office and drank the bottle of whiskey while he ridiculed my reputation and spoke of McCarthy in the most vindictive terms imaginable. Then he said something strange. I do not know what credence to place on it. Perhaps it was merely the ramblings of a drunken mind.

"Mr. *John J. Sylvester,*" he said sarcastically. "Do you remember that Irish woman who came through here in the 1890s?"

"What Irish woman?" I asked. "I was a boy then."

"She spit in my face, that slut," he growled. "But tonight I got even with her through her bastard son." He laughed loudly again and drank to his revenge. "No one would ever guess who was his father," Hanley said, looking up at me with the eyes of a madman. He would not say anything more.

Before he left that evening, Fred Hanley unwrapped a large money belt from around his waist. He placed several large stacks of currency on top of my desk. It was my share of the real payroll. He laughed as my fingers trembled above the stacks of paper currency. Then he lurched toward the front door of the bank. Still laughing, he disappeared in the darkness outside the bank building.

Mr. Finley, I looked at that money for a long time before I finally picked it up and put it in the safe. To this day, I wish I had had the courage to leave the money on the desk and go directly to the authorities with what I knew about the disappearance of Judd McCarthy. The next thirty years of my life would have been infinitely less agonizing if I would have had the courage to do that one simple thing. But I did not, and so you have found me today, an old man carrying the burden of his guilt in a town that worships his image but knows nothing of his true character. It is an intolerable contradiction, a charade of virtue that conceals the most hideous of crimes.

Mr. Finley, I take my leave of you now. I wish you success in your pursuit of Judd McCarthy and those who took his life. I think if you find the "Irish woman" Fred Hanley talked about that night in my office, you will have the piece you need to complete your puzzle.

As for the reputation of John J. Sylvester, you will have to decide for yourself whether justice would be better served by printing this letter or by having it destroyed.

Sincerely yours,
John J. Sylvester

Ned Finley glanced out the window of his hotel room at the two or three people who were shuffling across the Main Street of Danvers. Then he placed the letter in his shirt pocket and walked downstairs.

The desk clerk spotted Ned Finley as soon as he stepped off the flight of stairs and entered the lobby.

"Dr. Finley," the desk clerk yelled. "I have something for you." The desk clerk held out a small piece of note paper. "A message. It came for you yesterday morning. I must have been asleep and didn't hear you come in last night."

Finley read the note quickly. "Are you sure it was the Security Division that called?"

"That's what I wrote down, now didn't I? 'Security Division of the Farmington State Mental Hospital.' That's who called. Said it was about one of your patients and it was important."

"Thanks."

"You're welcome . . . Oh, and someone else called too. Name of Susan. I forgot all about that one until just now. Must've been my turn to deal and I just forgot to write it down."

"Thanks," Finley said again.

Finley stepped into the phone booth and quickly called the Security Division of the Farmington State Mental Hospital.

"Security Division, Farmington," a husky male voice responded at the other end of the line.

"Yes, this is Dr. Ned Finley. I have a message here to call you."

"Yes, Dr. Finley," the voice continued. "There's a problem with a patient of yours. Joel Hampton. He's been missing for almost two days now."

"He escaped?" Finley asked excitedly.

"We think so. At first we thought he was hiding somewhere on the hospital grounds, but we've checked everywhere. Now we're pretty sure he's escaped."

"How'd he get out? Wasn't he in restraints?" Finley was almost yelling into the telephone.

"Yup. Somehow he worked himself loose. We still don't know how he got out of the building. Course Security's pretty lax on the first floor. Shouldn't have had him there in the first place. By the way, who authorized that transfer?"

"I did," Finley admitted, trying to calm down.

"There's gonna be an investigation, I'm sure. Police in five counties are looking for him. Several newspapers have published descriptions. Guess you know he tried to kill a couple of people before he was committed and that's got people around here plenty frightened."

"Look, if they find him, get ahold of me right away. I don't want someone shooting him just because of inflammatory newspaper articles."

There was a short pause at the other end of the line. "Dr. Finley," the male voice continued, "they will, of course, try to take him alive. But if he offers resistance or if lives are endangered, they'll do what has to be done."

"Even if that means killing him?" Finley asked somewhat bitterly.

"Yes, but we don't think it'll come to that. We think we know which direction he's headed. Probably try to do something to his wife and child. Guess he tried it before. But we've got the roads to Kenyon under surveillance, so they're safe. Which reminds me, his wife wants you to call her."

Finley hung up the phone and immediately called Susan Hampton.

"Susan, this is Dr. Finley..."

"Dr. Finley," she interrupted him excitedly. "Joel..."

"Yes, I know. He escaped." Finley tried to sound as calm as possible. "Are you and Aggy okay?"

"Yes, but they think he might be coming this way."

"I don't think so. I don't want the two of you to take any chances, but I don't think Joel's coming back that way."

"Why do you say that?"

"Because I'm convinced the transformation is complete. Your husband is now Judd McCarthy. And if he's going anywhere, it'll be back to Carver County."

"Why?"

"To find out what happened to him in 1926."

There was a pause at the other end of the line. "What do we do in the meantime?" Susan asked.

"Could you join me up here? I need to talk to you in person about some things. And I also need the photograph of the farmhouse and the old envelope it came in. I think I left them with you the last time we met."

There was another pause at the other end of the line. "Shouldn't we be out looking for him?" Susan asked.

"No, the best thing we can do is to try to unravel the

puzzle that is the life and disappearance of Judd McCarthy. If we can do that we'll find your husband, because I'm convinced he'll be looking for the same thing. We just don't want him to beat us there. We want to be there first, waiting for him."

"What if the police find him first?"

"I honestly don't think they're looking in the right direction. They're looking for Joel Hampton. They should be looking for Judd McCarthy. Judd McCarthy will be here in Carver County very shortly—if he isn't already."

"Dr. Finley?" Susan said, a strange tone creeping into her voice.

"Yes, Susan?"

"I love Joel. I want you to know that. If anything happens to him, my life won't be worth living. I'm trying to harden myself for the inevitable—if it comes to that. But, please, just do everything you can to bring him back to me—as Joel Hampton, not Judd McCarthy."

There was a momentary pause at the other end of the line. "I'll do my best, Susan," Finley whispered gently.

II

Finley parked outside the Peace Lutheran Cemetery and walked through the wrought-iron gateway. A large green tent had been set up near the statue of the Union soldier in the middle of the cemetery. Next to the tent, a small pile of glistening black soil was spread out across the dead leaves and grass. As Finley passed the front entrance, he could see that numerous metal chairs had been arranged in neat rows inside the tent, and a green tarp had been stretched across a newly dug grave.

Finley passed the tent and walked toward the Sumners' family plot in a distant corner of the cemetery. Dead autumn leaves had already accumulated over the three tombstones of Oscar, Agnes, and Katharine Sumners. Finley brushed away the leaves with his foot and moved his eyes back and forth across the inscriptions on the three tombstones. Then he looked up at the distant water tower and shook his head dejectedly.

Finley turned to leave, but as he stepped back from the Sumners' family plot, his foot came down hard on something buried below the leaves and dead vegetation next to the grave of Oscar Sumners. Finley tapped at it gently with the toe of his shoe. Then he dropped to his knees and scraped away the damp, matted vegetation, uncovering another tombstone that had sunk deeply into the black soil. Finley had to scrape away the fungus and mold that covered the ancient letters on the dark-brown granite block. The stone, obviously forgotten by the caretakers of the small cemetery, yielded the inscription, "Maynard Sumners, December 3, 1870–April 17, 1895."

III

At the bottom of the small foothill leading up to the cemetery, Finley met a caravan of old cars and pickup trucks moving slowly along the gravel road. The caravan was following a large black hearse. The hearse turned into the narrow road leading up to the Peace Lutheran Cemetery, and the caravan of cars and pickup trucks followed close behind, like a procession of small insects led by a large black beetle.

Finley parked on the gravel shoulder and stepped out of his car to watch the funeral procession wind slowly along the narrow road. Near the top of the foothill, the large black hearse climbed over a ridge and disappeared from sight. The other cars and pickup trucks followed right behind until they too disappeared over the top of the ridge, leaving the foothill empty except for the bales of hay that were scattered on both sides of the narrow cemetery road.

Finley looked back in the direction of the church steeple and water tower rising out of the distant prairies. Then he pulled John J. Sylvester's letter out of his pocket. As he looked at the small town on the distant horizon, Finley tore the letter into tiny pieces, threw them into the wind, and watched the last words of John J. Sylvester disappear over the empty prairies.

Then he stepped into the Studebaker and drove immediately back to Danvers. Susan Hampton's light blue Chevrolet was parked in front of the General Store when Finley arrived back in town. He parked his Studebaker next to the Chevrolet and stepped out onto Main Street. Susan Hampton was sitting at a small table in the front window of the General Store. She was drinking a cup of coffee and looking out the window at the abandoned stores on the other side of the road. Finley waved and gestured for her to wait for him. Then he walked quickly across the street to the County Building.

He walked up the small flight of stairs to the County Recorder's Office on the second floor. The County Recorder was talking to a farmer at the front desk as Finley entered the hallway. When he was finished with the farmer, the County Recorder looked over at Finley who was leaning against the other end of the counter. "What da ya need today?" he asked.

"I need to see a death certificate," Finley said as he walked over to where the County Recorder was standing.

"Who ya lookin' for this time?" the County Recorder asked.

"The name is Maynard Sumners. He died on April 17, 1895."

"Just a minute," the County Recorder said as he disappeared into the steel vault in the back of the room. He returned shortly with an ancient, brown volume. "What was that date again?" he asked as he flopped the volume down on the front counter.

"April 17, 1895," Finley said.

"Here it is," the County Recorder said as he ran his index finger along the lines of the death certificate.

"What does it say?" Finley asked anxiously.

"'Maynard Sumners...born December 3, 1870, in London, England...died April 17, 1895, in Carver County.'"

"How did he die?" Finley asked.

"'Drowned in the Little Sioux River,'" the County Recorder said, reading from the book. "'Possible suicide.'"

"Suicide?" Finley asked.

"Yup, 'possible suicide.' That's what it says here. Date of death is an approximation. Apparently they found the body 'wrapped around a dead tree' farther downstream. River almost dragged him into the Mississippi. Little Sioux River's mighty powerful that time of year," the County Recorder said as he looked up from the old volume.

"Can I read that myself?" Finley asked.

"Sure can." The County Recorder spun the volume around on top of the counter.

Finley read carefully through the death certificate. "Why do you suppose they call it a 'possible suicide'?" he asked, looking up.

"Hard to say," the County Recorder said as he closed the large volume. "People around here know enough not to fool around on the banks of the Little Sioux River in the spring. Guess they figured he should have known better. Either that or else he meant to be out there. In which case he was probably fixin' to kill himself."

Finley nodded and walked immediately down the stairs. Susan Hampton was still sitting in the front window of the General Store when he crossed Main Street. As he stepped into the small shop, a tiny bell jangled on the front door. Packages of cereal, canned foods, hardware and a variety of other grocery items were displayed on wooden shelves and small tables scattered around the room. A bald-headed, middle-aged clerk in a white apron was filling an order for an elderly woman at the front counter as Finley walked past the brass cash register. Finley walked over to where Susan Hampton was sitting next to the large window overlooking Main Street.

"Any word on Joel yet?" Finley asked.

"Nope," Susan said as she sipped on a cup of coffee. "They're still looking for him."

"Where's Aggy?"

"With my mother. Poor child. I don't know how to explain all this to her. She keeps asking questions about her Daddy."

Finley nodded as he poured himself a cup of coffee from a shiny metal pot that sat on a burner on top of the table. "I know who Maynard is," he said as he sipped carefully on the steaming cup of coffee and sat down. "He's Katharine Sumners' uncle. Oscar Sumners' brother. He drowned in the Little Sioux River on April 17, 1895. A possible suicide. He's buried next to his brother in the Peace Lutheran Cemetery just south of here."

"Wasn't Maureen McCarthy committed to Farmington around that time?" Susan Hampton asked.

Finley nodded. "Three days earlier."

"And he's the brother of one of the men who signed to have her committed," Susan whispered. "It can't be coincidence."

Finley nodded again. "I know."

"What does it all add up to?"

"I have some suspicions. I'll let you know more about them later. Did you bring the envelope and the photograph?"

"Yes," Susan said as she opened the purse and handed the envelope to Finley.

Ned Finley and Susan Hampton sat in silence for a time as they looked out onto the Main Street of Danvers. "You said you had some other things to tell me," Susan said finally. "Have you found out anything more about Judd McCarthy?"

"Yes." Finley removed his beret and ran his fingers through his prematurely white hair. "I've found out *why* he disappeared. Part of the reason anyhow."

"What happened to him?" Susan Hampton asked.

"He was set up. He was carrying a phony payroll when he disappeared. He worked for a group called the Hanley Brothers Construction Company. They were involved in the Little Sioux Water Reclamation Project. Along with John J. Sylvester, a local banker, they bilked the people of this town out of their savings and then set McCarthy up so they could divide the real payroll among themselves. In fact, I'm pretty sure that's why Joel attacked Jim Morris. There's a slight physical resemblance between Jim Morris and John J. Sylvester."

"How do you know all this?" Susan asked.

"I had a talk with John J. Sylvester."

"He's still alive?" she asked, surprised.

"He was. He killed himself right after I talked to him!"

"Why?" Susan asked, more and more puzzled.

"He was afraid the people of this town would find out about his past. It was important to John J. Sylvester that the people of Danvers believe in him. He gave them dreams and they worshipped him for it."

"How did they kill McCarthy?"

"Apparently, they didn't kill him," Finley said.

"You just said they set him up?"

"They did. But someone else killed him. Sylvester said he didn't know who it was. His partner told him someone else despised Judd McCarthy. Someone he, that is Sylvester, didn't even suspect."

"Who?"

"That, I think, has something to do with Maureen McCarthy. Sylvester left me a letter before he died. He quoted his partner, Fred Hanley, apparently a man much older than Sylvester, as making some statements about an Irish woman who lived in Danvers in the 1890s. It has to be Maureen McCarthy. Hanley hated her. I don't know why. Maybe it was just his nature. Sylvester described him as a sick, vindictive man who would apparently go to any extremes to gain revenge."

"What is the connection between Maureen McCarthy and Judd McCarthy?" Susan asked, trying to comprehend what Finley was telling her.

"I think she was his mother."

"You're sure?"

"No, I'm not sure."

"Who was the father?"

"I don't know," Finley admitted. "Maybe Maynard Sumners."

Susan Hampton paused briefly to consider everything Finley had just told her. "That still doesn't explain why my husband is taking on the personality of someone who lived in Carver County in the 1920s."

"No, it doesn't. But I have my suspicions."

"What are they?"

Finley looked across Main Street at Benny who was industriously rolling the green awnings out over the sidewalk. "Susan, I know this sounds bizarre. But Judd McCarthy meant to do something when he got back to Danvers. Something so important to him that his spirit leaped across time and is working on your husband to complete whatever it was he left undone."

Susan Hampton looked strangely at Ned Finley. She spoke nervously. "What is he trying to do?"

"I don't have the slightest idea. Maybe revenge. But if that is the case, Sylvester was lying when he said everyone involved in the plot against McCarthy is dead. Still, it could be revenge."

"It would explain why Joel is so violent."

"Yes."

"Do you suppose McCarthy's spirit is trying to turn my husband into a killer to gain revenge?" A note of confused anger crept into Susan Hampton's voice.

"It's possible, Susan," Finley admitted again.

Susan Hampton shuddered as she tried to control her emotions. "Dr. Finley, do you know how hard it is to remain calm and rational about this whole thing when all I want to do is scream at someone and demand that they give my husband back to me?"

"I know," Finley said reassuringly as he patted her forearm. "Maybe on the way back you should do just that. Open the car window and scream as loud as you can. It might help."

"Maybe it wouldn't be so bad if we had a lousy marriage," Susan said somewhat bitterly. "But we were truly happy together. And that's a very hard thing to come by." Susan Hampton's voice trailed off into an incomprehensible whisper.

"I know," Finley comforted her. "I know."

Lost in thought, Finley drank coffee and stared out the window of the General Store for more than an hour after Susan had left. The store was quiet until suddenly a red-haired teenage boy burst through the front door. The boy tore off a brown topcoat as he walked quickly behind the counter.

"Where ya been?" the clerk asked.

"I was at Mr. Sylvester's funeral," the boy responded as he placed the coat on a metal hanger and tied a white apron around his waist. "Got later'n I thought."

"I couldn't get away," the clerk said somewhat apologetically. "Wanted to. But just been too busy. Listen, you better get at those orders. Seems everyone in Carver County wants a delivery today."

"Where are the lists?" the boy asked.

Suddenly, the notes of "Amazing Grace" poured mournfully out of the fire siren across the street, drowning out the conversation behind Finley.

IV

After burying the hospital uniform between the moist black furrows of a newly plowed field northwest of Danvers, he had walked the rest of that night beneath a black, star-filled sky. In the distance, on all sides of him, he could see twinkling farm lights etched against the horizon. Occasionally, a lonely farm dog barked at the moon, and the distant, plaintive lament drifted across the brisk, late October night. Sadly he remembered the other dog. He hadn't meant to kill the poor beast.

He stayed to the empty fields, avoiding the denser clusters of trees where people might still be living. When he reached the Little Sioux River, he walked a few miles north along the riverbank. Then he stopped to unlace the stiff leather boots he had stolen from the store in Danvers. He sat on a dead log next to the river's edge and let the cool waters gently massage his bloody feet. He leaned back on the log and watched the stars roam freely in the black sky.

And he remembered how it had been at night with Kate by the river. So much had changed. Abandoned farmhouses, barns, and sheds were buried in the foliage along both sides of the riverbank. Graham, Johnson, Tobin, Mosley—he remembered the names of the families that had once lived in these deserted farmhouses. And he had memories, both good and bad, about his contacts with them. Somehow, he felt they were still there, staring out at him from the gables in the thick clusters of trees. He alone had been spared. Why? He did not know. He only knew he had to go back to a time that once was....

He sat up on the log and tried to put on one of the stiff leather boots, but it would not fit. His feet were cut and bruised and infected to the point where, once released from the stiff leather boots, they had swollen to twice their normal size. His feet throbbed and the pain shot up into his legs.

He was angry with himself for having taken off the boots. He could have handled the pain and he would have been in Carson later that night. Now he would have to find a place to hide, while he waited for his feet to heal.

For a moment, he thought of walking barefooted along the riverbank until morning. But he knew at some point his feet would fail him. Besides, after having waited so long, what was another day or two? He could wait.

He picked up the boots and limped barefooted toward one of the clusters of trees near the river's edge. The farmyard in the middle of the trees was deserted and completely covered with large, dead weeds that grew several feet high next to tilting, ancient sheds and barns. In the darkness, the moonlight sent strange shadows across the farmyard.

He entered one of the old sheds and walked to the back wall where he lay down on a small pile of straw. Throughout the night, he listened to an owl hooting somewhere in the darkness, far beyond the deserted farmyard. Far beyond the moon itself, or so it seemed . . .

In the morning, if it was safe, he would soak his swollen feet in the river. Then, the next night, or the night thereafter, he would continue up the Little Sioux River, keeping always to the riverbank, for they would be looking for him. Now that he had come this far, he could not fail.

Farther north, he would walk across the empty fields toward Carson. And he would start out as he had thirty years earlier, walking south along the Sioux Line Railroad toward the outskirts of Danvers—and Kate.

Only this time he would make it. And then he would know and he would have his revenge.

He patted his pocket to reassure himself that the knife was still there.

"Kate, Kate," he whispered to himself. "I'll come back to you. This time no one will stop me."

V

When Finley awoke, the first thing he saw was a large black spider spinning a web across the dirty white ceiling of his hotel room. The spider had managed to attach several filaments to a small crack in the middle of the ceiling, but it seemed unable to expand the web beyond the boundaries of the crack. The spider crawled frantically back and forth across the surface of the ceiling. Then it returned to the center of the web and remained motionless, gazing into the darkness of the crack. It was still peering into the crack in the ceiling when Finley sat up in bed.

While he was eating breakfast, Finley made a decision to spend the day in the newspaper office searching through the old newspapers. He hoped that perhaps something in the earlier editions of the *Danvers Sun* might provide the clue he needed. He was at a dead end. He had no logical course to follow now that he had moved this far into the reasons behind McCarthy's disappearance. He decided to trust his intuition— and his intuition told him to look in the old newspapers. When and if Joel showed up here, he had to know.

The steady beat of the keys of a typewriter clacked out of the back room of the newspaper office as Finley walked through the front door of the *Danvers Sun*. As the bell jangled loudly above the front door, the rhythmic beat of the typewriter keys continued uninterrupted. Harmon was probably hard at work on the next issue of the newspaper, Finley decided, so he opened the door next to the front counter and walked down into the darkness of the basement. He pulled on a long string in the center of the ceiling, and the dark room was quickly bathed in the harsh glow of the lone light bulb.

Finley walked over to the stack of newspapers he had sorted through earlier. He placed the papers on top of the table in the middle of the room and began reading through them one by one. Occasionally, he would stand to pace around the room as he tried to think of any question he hadn't asked himself, any clue he had overlooked. Then he would sit down again and read indiscriminately through the yellowish-brown newspapers.

He began quoting aloud from the newspapers. "'Nina Jensen was an afternoon dinner guest of Florence Hagen. . . . Mr. and Mrs. Stanley Walsh were overnight guests at the Ed Flanigan home. . . . The Herbert Swensen family returned from a two week fishing trip in Canada.'" Finley shook his head in disgust. "Everytime someone opens their front door, it gets into the *Danvers Sun*," he said with mock sarcasm.

Finley stood and began pacing around the room again. "Maybe that's it?" he speculated. "If Katharine McCarthy is really Katharine Sumners. And if she left town shortly after Judd McCarthy disappeared. Then her mother would have had to put that news in the paper. Especially if she wanted to stop any gossip about the reasons for her daughter's decision to leave."

Finley returned to his work with a renewed vigor and enthusiasm. Much later he pointed excitedly at the small print and read a passage out loud. "'Katharine Sumners left Sunday morning for an extended vacation with her uncle and aunt, Mr. and Mrs. Christopher Walker of Chicago, Illinois'!"

Finley looked up from the newsprint. In the window well on the other side of the basement, a salamander that had struggled so mightily against the glass window pane lay dead beneath a pile of damp leaves. Although the body had curled over and fallen to the base of the window frame, one claw remained flattened out against the glass, as though even in death the salamander was still fighting for its freedom.

"That's it!" Finley said emphatically as he stood up from the table and quickly walked up the flight of stairs leading out of the basement. The rhythmic beat of the typewriter keys filled the newspaper office as Finley stepped out of the basement and into the sunlight pouring in through the front window of the *Danvers Sun*.

Finley walked immediately across the street to the General Store. The bell on the front door jangled loudly as he stepped into the small shop and approached the back counter.

"You deliver groceries here, don't you?" Finley asked the bald-headed clerk as he stepped up to the counter.

"Yup. Only store in town that does."

"You must deliver to Gina Walker, then?" Finley asked.

"Every Wednesday," the clerk agreed. "She leaves a list for us on her mailbox Tuesday. We pick it up and deliver the next day."

"Could I . . ."

"Even the big supermarkets in the cities can't make that claim," the clerk continued, interrupting Finley.

"Could I see the last grocery list she gave you?" Finley asked.

"Why?" the clerk asked suspiciously.

"I'm her brother," Finley lied. "She thinks you sent her some things she didn't order."

"I double-check everything. But, sure, just a minute." The clerk disappeared into the back room and reappeared a few seconds later. He handed a small grocery list to Finley. "Here it is."

"Mind if I sit down over there and look this over?" Finley asked, gesturing toward the table next to the front window.

"Suit yourself," the clerk shrugged as he started packing canned goods into a cardboard box.

As Finley walked over to the table next to the front window, the bell above the doorway jangled loudly behind him and an old man shuffled into the store. Finley sat down and pulled the dirty envelope out of his pocket that Susan Hampton had given him the previous day. He laid the envelope flat on the table and placed the grocery list next to it. He moved his eyes slowly back and forth between the envelope and the grocery list. Then he stood up and walked back to the counter.

"Thanks," Finley said, handing the grocery list back to the clerk.

"Everything in order?" the clerk asked.

"Yes, Gina ordered all of these things. She must have forgotten."

"Well, you tell her to bring anything back if she don't need it. Don't need no receipt either."

"Thanks," Finley said.

"You know," the clerk said, testing his memory. "I didn't know Miss Walker had a brother. Didn't know she had anyone around these parts."

"Oh, she has many relatives," Finley said. "Some that she hasn't seen in a long time!"

Chapter Thirteen

I

Finley turned his Studebaker into the old ruts of the gravel road leading up to the Sumners' farmhouse. At the end of the narrow road, he parked the car beside the lath fence that surrounded the ancient Victorian home. Through the open window of the car, he could hear the rusty windmill as it groaned high overhead. On the other side of the house, the tornado-damaged silo rose ominously above the dead foliage of autumn. The silo reminded Finley of a huge, gray tombstone weathering in an abandoned cemetery.

Finley walked up the stone pathway. The stones had obviously been set in the ground decades earlier, for the annual frosts had caused many of the angular rocks to sink inches below the surface of the farmyard, while others protruded above the dead grass at awkward angles. Finley picked his way carefully through the stone pathway.

As he stepped up onto the porch, he thought he again heard the music of a gramophone. But the sound was so distant that it could have been almost anything, perhaps even the wind blowing through one of the ancient window casings or whispering through the wood shingles overhead.

Finley knocked on the door, waited several seconds, then knocked again. When Gina Walker finally answered the door, she blinked out cautiously at him. As before, she reminded Finley of someone who was wandering between reality and the inner world of her dreams.

224

"Yes?" she inquired gently of Finley as she opened the door.

"Katharine Sumners," Finley replied boldly, testing his suspicions, "I think we have something to discuss with one another."

"What do you mean?" she asked blandly, without emotion.

"Katharine Sumners, I know who you are. There is no need to lie to me."

"Who are you?" she asked quietly.

"My name is Ned Finley. I'm a clinical psychologist at Farmington."

"What is it you want?"

"I need some information about someone you once knew when you still called yourself Katharine Sumners. Your secret is safe with me."

The old woman studied Finley carefully for a few seconds, then opened the door wider. "Come in, please." She immediately turned her back on Finley, shuffled down the parlor, and disappeared into one of the side rooms.

As Finley's eyes adjusted to the semi-darkened parlor, he could see that the interior of the house had been preserved in the styles popular much earlier in the century. The wallpaper, furniture, and curtains inside the house were seemingly untouched by time, just as the exterior of the home was a monument to the passage of time and the changes created by the seasonal cycles.

By the time Finley entered the living room, his eyes had adjusted to the lighting inside the house and he could see that the woman who called herself Gina Walker was dressed in the styles of the 1920s and 1930s. She was sitting in a rocking chair and was ever-so-gently rocking back and forth on a patterned, tapesty rug. Behind her, an ancient gramophone sat on a small table.

Finley sat down on a small couch located on the edge of the tapestry rug. Next to him, on a small tea table, he noticed a framed newspaper photograph of two huge, perspiring men smiling broadly and shaking hands. He recognized the smaller of the two men as Judd McCarthy. The larger man he assumed was Farmer Tobin.

"How did you find out?" the old woman asked nervously as she continued rocking back and forth.

"I was only guessing," Finley sighed, realizing that his assumptions were correct, "until I read in the *Danvers Sun* that you vacationed in 1926 with your uncle and aunt, Mr. and Mrs. Christopher Walker. I knew it had to be more than coincidence that you had the same last name as Katharine Sumners' uncle and aunt. Then I checked the handwriting on a grocery list you wrote last week. It matched the handwriting on an old envelope you had addressed many years ago."

"Why am I important to you? I'm only an old woman, living in a house full of memories."

"You aren't important to me. But you might be important to someone else. Someone we both know."

"I don't understand."

"Katharine . . ."

"I haven't been called by that name in a long time," she said, interrupting him. "I had almost forgotten what it sounded like."

"Then you are Katharine Sumners?" Finley asked as though to reassure himself that his conclusions were correct.

"Yes, but it's been more than thirty years." Katharine Sumners looked off into space, daydreaming. "I never thought I would ever hear that name again."

"If you are Katharine Sumners, then tell me, who is buried in the grave next to your mother and father?"

"I don't know," she replied weakly.

"I don't understand." Finley spoke gently so as not to intimidate the old woman.

"I left the Walker home and moved into a boarding house in Chicago. There were other girls there. Most of them had no families."

Katharine Sumners paused briefly to collect her thoughts.

"Then what happened?" Finley asked, prodding her gently.

"I decided to destroy Katharine Sumners. I put every piece of identification I had on a bureau and walked out the front door. Two days later the boarding house burned to the ground. It said in the newspapers that everyone was killed."

"So another girl probably picked up your identification cards. And her body was sent back here for burial."

"I suppose," Katharine Sumners responded sadly. "I go

out there every once in awhile to put flowers on the grave. The poor thing. She was probably just a young girl who had no one to turn to when she got into trouble."

"Trouble?"

"Most of the girls who lived there were unwed mothers from poor families. Some of them had no families."

"So your mother and everyone else in Carver County thought you had died in that fire?"

"Yes."

Finley paused to look briefly in the direction of the newspaper photograph on the tea table. The smiling faces of Judd McCarthy and Farmer Tobin stared back at him.

"Before Katharine Sumners died, what part did a gold locket play in her life?" Finley asked cautiously, remembering the song Joel had sung while under hypnosis.

"What do you know about that?" she replied, startled by the question.

"Please, you tell me," Finley answered.

Katharine Sumners stood quickly and walked out of the room, disappearing into the darkness of a rear hallway. When she returned, she was holding something softly, tenderly, in her hands. She placed a gold pocket watch with a long chain on the couch next to Finley.

"We took a trip to Carson together, several weeks before he disappeared. I admired a locket in one of the store windows, and he promised to buy it for me when he had the money. I, in turn, said I would buy him a new watch. That old watch of his made so much noise and he tied it to his trousers with a piece of baling twine." Katharine Sumners avoided mentioning McCarthy's name as though there was still too much pain in the memory.

"Who was 'he'?" Finley probed gently.

Katharine Sumners ignored the question and walked over to the gramophone. She wound the crank and what sounded like a distant instrumental version of an old Irish ballad poured out of the black horn of the gramophone.

"Do you see the eagle on the back of the watch?" Katharine Sumners asked as she sat back down and began very slowly rocking back and forth on the tapestry rug. "He was like an eagle. Always trying to be free. I thought I had changed him, but I guess I didn't."

"Was his name Judd McCarthy?"

"How did you know that?" she asked, surprised.

"I know a great deal about you, but I know very little about Judd McCarthy. I need to know more. Who was Judd McCarthy?"

"I thought he was the gentlest man I had ever met," she began. "Mother called him an uncultured scoundrel, but he was really a most gentle man. Oh, he was a nobody really. A common laborer, a very powerful man physically. That's a picture of him on the tea table next to you."

"Yes, I know," Finley responded. "I saw the copy of the *Carson Chronicle* that this came from. Tell me more about Judd McCarthy."

"Judd McCarthy came here in 1925, along with many other drifters and itinerant construction workers. They built most of the buildings on the Main Street of Danvers. Then they came out here to work on the Little Sioux Water Reclamation Project. You could see the men and machinery from that very window right over there. . . ."

II

It was July of 1926. The men who worked for the Hanley Brothers Construction Company were gathered on both sides of an open trench located next to the Sioux Line Railroad. Money was changing hands on both sides of the trench. The boisterous, good-natured group of men were surrounded on all sides by construction tents, heavy machinery and equipment, and teams of horses feeding during the mid-day break.

At the bottom of the trench, a huge, shirtless, dark-haired man was carefully wrapping a rope around his wrists. Judd McCarthy projected a boisterous cheerfulness, and a fierce determination and proud masculinity. The other end of the rope was attached to a small black and white horse that pawed nervously at the mud and rain water at the bottom of the trench.

"Ain't no man can whip a horse in a tug-of-war," one of

the construction workers said emphatically as he stared down into the trench.

"Five dollars says Mac can do it," *another construction worker challenged.*

"You're on," *the first worker replied enthusiastically.* "Might as well get out your money now, 'cause this thing's 'bout good as over."

At the bottom of the trench, McCarthy had finished curling the rope tightly around both forearms. He carefully braced both feet for the initial impact of the horse's charge up the embankment. A small man in a floppy white hat held the horse by the bridle as it continued to paw nervously at the mud and rain water. The owner of the horse stood nearby, ready to whip the animal once the signal was given.

"Now remember, Mac," *the small man holding the horse volunteered,* "if this horse gets you over the top of the ridge, you lose."

"Got it. Get with it, Scotty. Turn 'em loose."

The small man with the floppy white hat let go of the bridle, and the owner of the horse began whipping the animal furiously. Through a Herculean effort, McCarthy managed to hold his own for a few seconds as the horse slipped in the muddy trench. Then the animal gained its footing and suddenly charged up the side of the embankment as McCarthy, refusing to let go of the rope, was dragged belly-down through the mud and water, all the time sputtering and yelling incoherent phrases.

At the top of the ridge, the horse once again lost its footing in the slippery mud. As the horse slipped backwards several feet, McCarthy managed to get to his feet. He braced himself once again at the bottom of the trench. Suddenly, in a state of panic, the horse reared up on its hind legs, lost its balance, and began to fall backwards. Seizing the opportunity, McCarthy yanked mightily on the rope, and the horse tumbled down the embankment and splashed into the mud and water at the bottom of the trench.

"Well, I'll be gawd damned," *one of the construction workers exclaimed as he looked down at the horse lying flat on its back in the open trench,* "he did it!"

"Shit," *another construction worker uttered as he slapped a wad of bills into a dirty extended hand.*

McCarthy and the rest of the construction crew were momentarily stunned by what had just happened. McCarthy was a comical sight standing at the bottom of the trench, his brown eyes peering out from a face completely caked with mud. As McCarthy looked up at the many faces peering down at him, his eyes focused on a young woman giggling shyly and looking down at him with nervous excitement. It was the first time Katharine Sumners had ever set eyes on Judd McCarthy. She was always to remember him like that, standing at the bottom of the trench, caked with mud and looking up at her like a little boy.

As Katharine Sumners peered down into the trench, a loud laugh boomed out of the mud-covered figure staring back at her with his large brown eyes. It was a laugh that seemed to challenge the entire universe as it boomed out of the trench. Still laughing loudly, McCarthy fell back into the mud and allowed his body to sink slowly into the goo as the crowd erupted wildly and enthusiastically. Before he disappeared beneath the thick mud and water, McCarthy smiled and waved one last time at Katharine Sumners, who stood giggling at the top of the trench.

Later, as the bets were being paid, McCarthy pulled himself out of the mud, climbed up the embankment, and began wiping himself off with a large rag. A few feet away from him, the horse he had pulled into the bottom of the trench was limping noticeably.

"Goddamn worthless animal!" the owner of the horse yelled bitterly as he raised a whip to bring it down across the animal's head. "Cost me two hundred bucks, will ya!"

McCarthy stepped quickly between the horse and its owner. He brought his huge hand down across the owner's forearm, stopping the whip in midair. "The horse didn't make the bet, mon. You did!" McCarthy said in a menacing tone.

"This is none of your business," the owner replied defiantly, trying to extract himself from McCarthy's powerful grip.

"You ain't beatin' this animal, mon!" McCarthy issued an even sterner warning.

With his free hand, the owner of the horse suddenly reached into his coat pocket and pulled out a small revolver. He pointed it at McCarthy's stomach.

"This horse is my property. You'd do well to stay out of this."

As McCarthy stepped back, the owner again raised the whip over the horse's head.

"What's the horse worth ta ya, mon?" McCarthy quickly interjected before the owner could bring the whip down across the animal's head.

"Two hundred bucks," he replied tersely.

"Give me the money, Scotty," McCarthy said to the small man with the floppy hat.

"You can't, Mac. Not on a lame horse, for Christ's sake."

"Give it to me, Scotty!" he said firmly.

"Christ's sake, Mac," Scotty said as he handed McCarthy the money, "everytime we get something you just give it away."

"Here's your two hundred dollars, mister," McCarthy said, handing the wad of bills to the owner of the horse. "But I don't want no creases in me horse's forehead."

As the owner of the horse stuffed the wad of bills into his coat pocket, McCarthy's right arm suddenly snaked out and tore the small pistol out of his hand. Then McCarthy picked up the owner of the horse by his belt buckle and pitched him into the trench, where he did a belly flop and slid several feet across the thick mud.

"Any mon who beats a horse is no better'n a lizard," McCarthy yelled after him as the owner slid across the bottom of the trench. "Slide around in there for a while."

Almost as an afterthought, McCarthy pitched the revolver into the bottom of the trench where it too sank into the mud. Then he walked back to the lame animal and patted it gently. Under McCarthy's gentle caress, the horse began to calm down.

"There, ole buddy, we know I didn't beat ya," he whispered gently into the horse's ear. "Ya only slipped or I'd still be followin' ya 'cross the prairies."

As he stroked the horse's head, McCarthy saw Katharine Sumners standing nearby. "Now, ole buddy, who'd ya suppose that pretty lady might be?" he said loudly.

"Katharine," she whispered shyly.

"Ah, Kate it is. Such a pretty name for such a pretty lady. Now what's a pretty lady like you doin' out here 'mong these hooligans?" he asked, pretending to admonish her.

"I live right over there," Katharine Sumners said shyly, pointing at a farmhouse in the distance.

"Well, here's a present for me Lady Kate," McCarthy said, handing her the horse's reins. "An' let me help ya get him home."

As the heavy machinery behind them howled and screeched and work commenced on the Little Sioux Water Reclamation Project, Judd McCarthy and Katharine Sumners walked toward the distant farmhouse. The horse limped along behind them, its reins held loosely in the tiny hands of Katharine Sumners.

III

Judd McCarthy and Katharine Sumners were together almost every day from July to October of 1926. With her mother visiting relatives in the East, Katharine Sumners had the run of the family estate for the first time in her life. This was Agnes Sumners' first vacation away from the farm since her husband's death in 1920, and she stayed in the East until early fall, thus giving her daughter the freedom to do things she had never had the courage to do in her mother's presence—things as insignificant as visiting the Hanley Brothers Construction site. Under the ruling thumb of Agnes Sumners, who had kept her young daughter a virtual prisoner in the family home throughout her teens and early twenties, Katharine Sumners had never really grown up. Instead, she retained a charm and innocence that gave her a childlike appeal, at the same time that it made her extremely vulnerable and naïve about men. McCarthy immediately recognized this in her, and he made a pledge to himself not to violate or harm that childlike innocence in any way, for she was too much like the innocent birds and animals of the prairies with whom he felt a deep kinship. McCarthy was more accustomed to the hard-drinking women who frequented the taverns in the small towns throughout the Midwest, but he had long since tired of their company and the pleasures they had to offer. He

grew to cherish and love the twenty-seven year old child that
was Katharine Sumners, at the same time that he taught her
to grow as a woman, without taking her to the ultimate
pinnacle of love and intimacy. With every other woman in his
life, McCarthy had progressed well beyond that point after
several beers and one or two Irish ballads. But 'Lady Kate'
was something special to Judd McCarthy, and he meant to
keep it that way.

By August of 1926, Katharine Sumners knew she was
deeply in love with Judd McCarthy. He would come over at
night, after the day's work had ceased at the construction
site, and they would sit on the porch and talk while the
gramophone played in the house behind them.

"What do you know about the stars, Judd?" Katharine
Sumners asked him one night as they sat on the porch.

McCarthy looked up at the stars glowing brightly in a
clear sky. "Nuthin', Kate. Only that they're up there. And
they're free." As he spoke, several Canada geese flew across
the moon in V-formation.

"Some people think the stars aren't up there at all,"
Katharine Sumners continued. "Some scientists have been
saying they're only explosions and all we're seeing is the
light."

"Don't make no difference, does it?"

"Why do you say that?"

"It don't matter if somethin' is or isn't, just so long as
you believe it is."

"I don't understand."

"It's thinkin' somethin' is or thinkin' ya can do somethin'
that's important. Nothin's impossible when ya believe in it.
Ain't no prison can hold ya then. Those stars, even if they're
not in the sky, they're still beautiful. No one's told them 'bout
it yet. They still believe in themselves. Long as they keep on
shinin', what difference does it make what some scientist says
about them bein' up there or not?"

Katharine Sumners looked off into the distance at the
little clusters of twinkling farm lights on the dark horizon.
"How long do you plan to keep drifting, Judd?" she asked
him softly.

"Why do you ask?"

"*The world's changing. You just can't muscle your way through it forever. You've got to set down some roots, have some goals. You can't drift all your life.*"

"*I don't know no other way, Kate.*"

"*I'll teach you,*" she said, "*if you'll let me.*"

He turned to kiss her gently on the cheek. "*I'll try, Kate. But I ain't no prize, girl.*"

"*You don't have to be a prize. I'll only demand one thing from you, Judd McCarthy.*"

"*What's that?*"

"*You have to stop calling me 'Kate.' It reminds me of the kind of name you'd give a mule.*"

"*I'll try, Kate, but it'll take some gettin' used to,*" he laughed.

"*There's a whole different world out there, isn't there, Judd?*" she said, changing the subject. "*A whole new world of things to experience, people to know.*"

"*It ain't quite as pretty as it looks from here,*" he said, looking out at the twinkling clusters of lights on the horizon. "*But, if you'll let me, I'll protect you from the bad parts.*"

"*Is that a promise?*"

"*That's a promise.*"

"*I guess we decided something important tonight, didn't we, Judd?*"

"*Yes, Kate, we sure did.*"

"*There you go again,*" she said, laughing and grabbing his huge hand in her two smaller ones.

McCarthy sneaked back into the construction camp late that night. He didn't tell the other members of the work crew he was seeing Katharine Sumners, because he had a reputation with women, and he didn't want them making crude jokes about his Lady Kate.

In the morning, he slipped out of the construction camp shortly after daybreak and made his way back to the Sumners' farmhouse. It was a Saturday and Katharine had planned a picnic for the two of them down by the Little Sioux River. The picnic basket was on the front porch when Judd McCarthy walked up the stone pathway to the Sumners' home. Nearby, Katharine was sitting in the swing that hung from the huge oak tree. She was very gently pushing herself back and forth, back and forth, when McCarthy sneaked up behind her and *began pushing her higher and higher into a clear blue sky. An early frost had already turned the leaves overhead into various shades of reds and yellows, and Katharine Sumners' golden hair sparkled as the sunlight sifted through the dancing leaves and illuminated the individual strands of her blond hair. She laughed and leaned backwards as McCarthy propelled her higher and higher into the blue sky.*

Suddenly McCarthy pushed her too hard and she fell out of the swing and landed in a heap several feet from the oak tree. She lay motionless as McCarthy rushed over and knelt beside her.

"Kate, are ya all right?" he asked, a note of panic in his voice.

"I think so," she said, sitting up slowly.

"God, I'm sorry, girl," McCarthy said as he picked her up gently and carried her over to the softer grass beneath the oak tree. "Sometimes I don't know me own strength."

"I'm all right, Judd. Really, I'm all right," she insisted.

"I'm mighty sorry, Kate," he said, kissing her tenderly.

She returned his kiss passionately as they lay back on the soft grass. She would always remember the leaves rustling overhead as the child that was Katharine Sumners became a woman under the huge oak tree, and the swing swayed ever-so-slowly in the autumn breeze and the windmill whispered gently to the clear blue sky.

Afterwards, Judd McCarthy was remorseful, for he had crossed a barrier he had promised himself he would never cross. "I'm awful sorry, Kate," he whispered gently.

"There's no need to be sorry, Judd. We've already made an important decision, now haven't we?" she said, stroking the back of his neck.

"We sure have, Kate. We sure have," he repeated reassuringly as he held her in his strong arms.

IV

A few weeks later, Agnes Sumners returned from the East. She was furious when she learned that her daughter

*had been seeing a common laborer during her absence. She
insisted that Katharine stop seeing Judd McCarthy immediately. Katharine Sumners, who was terrified of her mother,
put up a brief struggle, then acquiesced to the matriarch of
the Sumners family—for a few days. But her love for Judd
McCarthy was too strong, and soon she was stealing forbidden hours with him.*

*It was during one of their meetings on the banks of the
Little Sioux River that Judd and Katharine made plans.*

"Mother will never accept you, Judd," Katharine said to
him as they sat on the leaf-strewn banks of the Little Sioux
River and watched the waters drift slowly southwards. "It's
no use. She has dreams of her daughter becoming the wife of
a senator or a governor."

"Is that what you want, Kate?" he asked softly.

"No, I don't even like going to small parties. How would
I fit in with that kind of life? I'm . . ." She paused abruptly.

"You're what, Kate?"

"I'm kind of a misfit, I guess. Not too many men ever
paid attention to me before you, Judd. I'm not really as pretty
as you think I am."

"I don't want to hear that kind of talk, girl. You stop that
nonsense."

"I'm. It's just . . ."

"What is it, Kate?"

"I'm twenty-seven years old and I never truly knew a man
until a couple of months ago when I met you. And, Judd,
that's all I want. There's nothing else that could make me
happy now."

"That settles it then, girl," he said emphatically.

"What do you mean?"

"I get paid this Saturday. Three months' wages. It's
enough to get us a start."

"What about mother?"

"Ya can't live for your mother all your life, Kate. Someday you gotta make a choice. It might as well be now."

Katharine Sumners watched the waters of the Little
Sioux River drift slowly past the embankment where they
were sitting. "Where will we go?" she asked softly.

"They're buildin' a dam south of here. Down by the
Mississippi. They'll need help. We'll get married, save some

money, and buy a place. Maybe over in the Dakotas. Land's still cheap there."

Katharine Sumners thought the offer over carefully. "I'll go with you, Judd," she said firmly.

"Next Saturday afternoon, Kate. I have to make a trip to Carson for Fred Hanley. Then I'll collect my wages and meet you right here."

"Just one thing, Judd."

"Yes, I know. I'll learn ta call ya 'Katharine.' It just takes some gettin' used to, that's all."

"No, just be here next Saturday." She kissed him lightly on the cheek, then stood and ran in the direction of her home.

Katharine Sumners was to see Judd McCarthy only one more time before he disappeared. On Saturday morning of October 12, 1926, he stood on the tracks of the Sioux Line Railroad and waved to her as she watched him from one of the distant gables of the Sumners' home. He did an awkward dance step for her benefit on the railroad trestles, then smiled broadly and disappeared in the direction of Carson.

Katharine Sumners waited for him by the banks of the Little Sioux River for several hours, long after the sun had set. When it became apparent that he was not coming back for her, she sadly picked up her large white bonnet from out of the dead leaves and walked across the barren fields back to her home. Her mother greeted her at the front door.

"Where have you been, Katharine?" Agnes Sumners demanded.

"Down by the river," Katharine said, brushing past her mother and entering the parlor.

"You were meeting Judd McCarthy, weren't you?" Agnes Sumners asked sternly.

"Yes."

"I thought I told you not to see him anymore."

"Mother, I'm twenty-seven years old. I have a right to live my life the way I choose," Katharine yelled at her mother.

"He didn't come back to get you, did he?" Agnes Sumners asked coldly.

"No." The early firmness in Katharine Sumner's voice changed to fear and then she began to cry softly.

"And you're in trouble, aren't you?"

"Yes," she answered tearfully.

"Go upstairs, Katharine. We'll talk about this in the morning."

Katharine Sumners slept fitfully that night. Once she awoke to what she thought was the sound of horses neighing and what sounded like men talking in the yard below. Another time she thought she heard McCarthy calling to her from somewhere in the darkness. But each time she awoke, she only heard the rustling of the autumn leaves as the evening breezes blew steadily through the trees outside her window.

In the morning, a black Ford coupe was waiting outside the gate of the farmhouse. As Katharine Sumners walked down the stone pathway, she looked briefly in the direction of the Sioux Line Railroad where McCarthy had disappeared. Then she climbed into the car and shut the door behind her. The Ford coupe chugged down the narrow dirt road, turned east at the entrance to the Sumners' home, and quickly disappeared behind a small foothill. . . .

V

The elderly Katharine Sumners continued to rock back and forth as she finished her story. Ned Finley sat across from her on the small couch. The gramophone had long since quit playing.

"It must have been a sad trip for him," she said quietly. "So much was changing. He could have gone through life fighting men like Tobin, but the world was changing all around him. I think he wanted to change with it, but he was a free spirit and needed room. They think he fled into the Dakotas."

"Yes, I know," Finley said softly. "I read the newspaper account of his disappearance."

"When he didn't return that evening, mother insisted that I go back East. Judd McCarthy was the only man I had ever known. This farm was my only home. When I left, I gave up my entire world."

"And then you had a baby boy and signed the adoption papers 'Katharine McCarthy'? And after your mother died, you came back here to live?"

"How did you know it was a baby boy?" she asked, startled.

"I will tell you everything I know. But first, tell me, did anything unusual happen the night you were planning to leave with Judd McCarthy?"

"No, not that I remember. Mother was very angry. She knew I was going to have a baby. I think she knew long before that night."

"Did anything else happen?"

"No. I already told you I thought I heard horses neighing and men talking outside my window. But it must have been a dream. Please, tell me what you know about the baby?"

"Katharine Sumners, there is someone who needs you very much!"

VI

It was late evening when Finley arrived back in Danvers. The hotel lobby was dark except for the one light that glowed above the back counter and the lights that filtered in through the windows overlooking Main Street.

Finley passed the gleaming blue eyes of John J. Sylvester that stared out at him from the center of the gold-leaf frame on the eastern wall. In the back of the lobby, Finley paused momentarily to study the smiling face of Judd McCarthy. Then he walked toward the flight of stairs next to the desk.

"Just a minute, Mr. Finley," the desk clerk said, turning around suddenly behind the counter.

"What is it?" Finley asked.

The desk clerk reached beneath the polished white stone counter and pulled out a small package. The edges of the package were folded over and carefully tied with twine. "Got something for you. Marsha Williams dropped it off earlier this afternoon."

"What is it?"

"Don't know. She wrote a note for you. It's on the back."

Finley turned the package over and pulled a tiny white envelope out from between the strands of twine. He opened the envelope and stepped closer to the overhead light to read Marsha Williams' note, which was penned in small, dainty letters across unlined paper:

Dear Mr. Finley,

I was going through some things in the basement this morning and I found this. The grandchildren of Frank and Helga Graham donated many books to the library several years ago. This was among them. Since you had asked earlier about Maureen McCarthy, I thought you might want to read this.

Marsha

P.S. Please return the book when you have finished with it.

Finley struggled with the tight knots on the package as he climbed up the two flights of stairs to his hotel room. Finally, he pulled out his pocketknife and cut the twine. Then he unfolded the brown wrapping paper and pulled out a small book bound and covered with green velvet. A tiny strap with a brass clasp at the end dangled beneath the book. A small brass lock was firmly set on top of the green velvet cover.

Finley turned the volume over in his hands as he walked through the darkened hallway toward his room. Once inside the room, he quickly switched on the light and opened the front cover of the book. The handwritten title, "The Diary of Maureen McCarthy," leaped out at him as he closed the door to the outside hallway.

Finley sat down in a chair next to the front window and started reading through the small diary.

July 20, 1893

Today I arrived at the home of Frank and Helga Graham. I will work for them until I save enough money to go north where there are better jobs and more opportunities.

I have come a long way to this strange land. I

am already homesick for Ireland, but my mind is set. I will not return.

As I travelled from New York to Danvers, I was overwhelmed by the many moods of America. It is a powerful land, one that is savage and gentle at the same time. But it is now my home and from this day on I will speak nothing but good things about my new country.

The Grahams are very stern, uncompromising people. I hope I shall be accepted here. . . .

VII

He had rested for one entire day and part of the following evening. Most of the time, he had remained inside the secluded shed buried in the weeds and foliage of the abandoned farmyard, though periodically he would hobble down to the Little Sioux River to soak his swollen feet in the cool, gentle waters. He had watched the blood pour out of his wounds and flow away with the river, and he had felt the swelling subside.

Toward nightfall, he forced the leather boots over his swollen feet. He laced the boots tightly, then hobbled back to the banks of the Little Sioux River.

At first the pain was almost unbearable, but he dared not take the boots off. In spite of the pain, he had to get to Carson. In time, as he walked, the pain changed to a moist numbness, and he lost all feeling in his feet.

He followed the river north for several miles. Then he headed east across the empty fields toward Carson. He wanted to see the old railroad town at night to see if it was as he had remembered it. Then he would find a place to hide, and, in mid-afternoon, at precisely the time that he had started back to Danvers on October 12th of 1926, he would walk back to the railroad embankment and begin the long journey home.

There were very few lights glowing along the streets of the old railroad town. He remembered the rumors that the Sioux Line Railroad planned to pull out of Carson in the

1920s. And he knew that must have been what happened. It was all so very different. The once-teeming city was almost a ghost town.

He stood in the shadows and watched the few lights glow weakly along both sides of Main Street. The road itself was badly in need of repair. Large holes had opened up in the dirt surface and barriers were set up on several side streets. Above the street, a large wooden sign hung from wires anchored into two buildings on opposite sides of the road. The name "Carson" was painted across the large wooden sign in faded white letters.

He glanced briefly at the sign. Then he remembered something else. He crossed the pitted dirt road, stepped over one of the barriers on the side streets, and walked toward the old railroad yard. Again he glanced up at the stars. For some reason, he could not keep his eyes off the stars that glowed brightly in the distant black skies. They seemed to be beckoning to him, calling to him from beyond the darkness of space.

He walked over to the western side of the old depot where another small light glowed on the wall just below the gable. He glanced down at a thin layer of straw spread lightly over a flat open area of dirt and rocks.

And he remembered how he had wrestled Tobin right there, and how Tobin had sweated and grunted and cursed as he rolled through the dirt and the rocks and the straw.

The thought brought a smile to his lips, and he looked back up at the stars.

Whatever had happened to Tobin, he wondered? Whatever had happened to all of them?

"What are you doing back here?" a voice suddenly demanded from behind him. As Joel turned in that direction, a state trooper stepped out of the shadows next to the railroad depot. "What are you doing back here?" the trooper demanded again. "Who are you?"

"Judd McCarthy," Joel answered without thinking.

"Who?" the state trooper asked suspiciously as he walked over to where Joel was standing in the middle of the thin layer of straw. In his right hand, the trooper held a service revolver. The moonlight gleamed off the polished black barrel as the trooper pointed it in Joel's direction.

Joel did not move as the state trooper cautiously walked over to where he was standing.

"What's your business back here?" the trooper demanded, stopping a few feet away from where Joel was standing.

Joel remained silent.

Suddenly, an owl hooted from above one of the small gables of the railroad depot, and the state trooper glanced instinctively in that direction. As he did so, Joel's right arm snaked out and twisted the trooper's wrist, causing the revolver to fall into the thin bed of straw.

"Why is it ya be sneakin' 'round behind me back?" Joel demanded angrily as he picked the trooper up and slammed him against the rotting walls of the abandoned railroad depot.

"Who are you?" the trooper inquired meekly as his shoes beat harmlessly against the thin wood siding. Even in the darkness, Joel's eyes glowed with a fierce, almost insane inner fire. "Are you the escapee from Farmington?" the trooper asked almost apologetically.

Joel tightened his grip on the man's shirt. He was reaching for the knife in his pocket when the sound of human voices drifted across the night air from the street on the other side of the railroad depot.

Joel listened carefully to the sound of the voices. Then he loosened his grip on the trooper's shirt, allowing the terrified man to slip slowly to the ground.

"Help! I'm back here!" the trooper yelled as he tore loose from Joel's huge hands and scrambled up a slight incline, disappearing around the corner of the railroad depot.

Joel stared at the piece of cloth he had torn from the trooper's shirt. The sound of human voices was growing nearer and more threatening as he reached down into the straw and extracted the revolver.

He had carried a revolver with him that day as he journeyed from Carson to Danvers. It was much heavier, more awkward than this one. But if he had carried a weapon, why had he been unable to protect himself?

As Joel thrust the revolver into the waistband of his trousers, two more state troopers suddenly appeared around the corner of the railroad depot. Joel heard several muffled threats and two sharp warning shots as he leaped into a nearby thicket of small trees. He scrambled quickly down an embankment. Behind him, the shouts and warnings grew more distant as he disappeared into the darkness of the prairies. . . .

Chapter Fourteen

I

The next day Finley made a hurried trip back to Farmington. He wanted to try to persuade Aurther Schlepler to accompany him to the Sumners' farm, in the hope that the retired psychic could help him answer the remaining questions surrounding the life and strange disappearance of Judd McCarthy. Finley also hoped that Aurther could help him find Joel and rid the young man of the terrible demon that was gnawing at his soul and threatening his life.

The diary of Maureen McCarthy and Finley's conversation with Katharine Sumners had provided most of the remaining pieces to the elaborate puzzle that constituted the mystery of Judd McCarthy. There were only three questions that he still could not answer. He still did not know what had happened to Maureen McCarthy after her escape from Farmington. Nor did he know *precisely* how Judd McCarthy had been killed and what it was that kept Judd McCarthy's powerful spirit lingering on in the memory of Joel Hampton more than three decades later.

As he walked through the front gates of Farmington, Finley spotted Aurther Schlepler in a distant corner of the hospital grounds. Finley turned and walked across the dead grass toward Schlepler.

Schlepler was standing next to the dead vines on one of the red granite walls. His hands were thrust deeply into his coat pockets and he wore an oversized, wrinkled gray hat that came down over the top of his ears. Below the brim of the hat, Schlepler's sad eyes gazed out at the many leafless vines and tendrils that clung to the red granite walls.

"You were right, Aurther," Finley said softly as he walked up to Schlepler. "Your flowers were dying."

"No," Schlepler said, pointing toward the red granite wall, "they are only becoming a part of the vine. All along this wall, wherever the flowers have died, they leave a little notch in the tendrils. In the spring, out of these notches will grow other stems and other flowers, and out of those still other stems and other flowers. And so it goes, year after year, decade after decade, century after century, until the vines and flowers will cover this entire wall. Of course, it won't happen in my lifetime. Nor in yours, Ned. But, nonetheless, it will happen."

"I've figured out most of the Hampton case," Finley said softly. "Except for one or two things." He paused momentarily. "I need your help, Aurther."

"You still don't know what happened to Maureen McCarthy, do you?" Schlepler asked.

"No," Finley admitted.

"It's not important that you know anything more about her, Ned."

"Why do you say that?" Finley asked, somewhat puzzled.

"Every puzzle has pieces that do not fit. It would be inhuman to pretend otherwise."

"What are you trying to say?" Finley asked.

"Maureen McCarthy is one of those people who disappear into the human race and are never heard from again. It is what was meant to be. Neither you nor I can change it."

"Are you saying that I should forget about Maureen McCarthy?"

"She was wrongly judged and suffered for it," Schlepler said solemnly. "But her soul is free. Your concern must be for that young man who wanders alone out there." Schlepler gestured toward the front gate and the empty fields beyond. "He harbors a soul that has yet to be freed from this world."

"That is why I need your help, Aurther. I want you to go with me to the Sumners' farm."

"You do *not* need me, Ned," Aurther Schlepler said, interrupting Ned Finley and looking up at him with his large compassionate eyes. "You need only return to the Sumners' farm yourself. Your answer will be waiting for you there."

"Aurther, please!" Finley pleaded.

"It will be waiting for you, Ned," Schlepler repeated. Then he gestured toward the front door of the mental institution. "Susan is waiting for you in the front lobby. Take her with you. You need her help, not mine."

Schlepler suddenly shuffled away, moving slowly through the dead leaves until he disappeared behind a bend in the granite wall.

Ned Finley watched Aurther Schlepler disappear. Then he turned and walked quickly back across the dead grass and leaves toward the front door of the mental institution. As he reached the sidewalk, Susan Hampton rushed out, bounded down the steps, and met him at the bottom of the staircase.

"They've found Joel," she gasped, almost out of breath.

"Where?" Finley demanded.

"Someone reported seeing him in Danvers two nights ago. Last night a state trooper found him wandering through the streets of Carson."

"Did they capture him?"

Susan shook her head. "No, he got away before they could make an arrest. They're looking for him north of Carson. They think he fled in that direction."

"He'll be coming south, along the Sioux Line Railroad," Finley said emphatically. "Come on, we have to get back to the Sumners' farm."

Finley grabbed Susan's arm and half-dragged her toward the front gate.

"Wait! I couldn't find a baby-sitter for Aggy," Susan gasped as she tried to match Finley's long strides. "One of the orderlies took her over to a park while I talked to Security."

"We'll pick her up on the way," Finley said as they stepped through the front gate. "I also have some things to tell you. I think I've figured out most of what happened on October 12th of 1926."

II

The day was almost as he had remembered it. Signs of late autumn were all around him. The stubble of recently harvested wheatfields poked out of the parched earth alongside the railroad embankment, and dead leaves, propelled by steady autumn breezes, hopped and skipped across the fields. Hen pheasants clucked contentedly in the nearby brush and heavy weeds, while an occasional cock pheasant emitted a shrill mating call that echoed across the Midwestern landscape. And he was walking, walking along the Sioux Line Railroad, moving south toward Danvers and Kate.

Only the sky was a different color than he had remembered it. It had been blue—bright blue. Now, as he looked to the west, the sun attempted to break through a gray overcast sky, but it was quickly covered by a layer of clouds.

The boots he had stolen from the store in Danvers crunched through the weeds and matted vegetation that covered the crossties and rusty tracks of the old railroad line. His eyes moved constantly across the landscape, searching for any movement in the brush and clumps of trees on both sides of the railroad embankment.

As he walked, he remembered the song. He had sung it many times before, but the words were only a distant memory. He hummed the tune as his boots moved steadily through the brush and matted vegetation that covered the old railroad line. The song brought a smile to his lips, and he knew it had once made him happy. Very happy. Why, then, could he not remember the words?

A few yards ahead of him, in the waters of the marshland, the early-evening crickets began to chirp contentedly, and frogs leaped off fallen logs and splashed into the shallow slough. On the edge of the marshland, dead reeds swayed back and forth as the steady autumn breezes arched the vegetation gracefully toward the earth.

He remembered that something had happened to him in the marshland. He had killed something. He had thought

someone was hiding in the thick grass and weeds, and he had
thrown a rock into the marshland. Then he had reached
slowly and cautiously into the reeds with his huge, callused
hands.

In the middle of the dried vegetation, a cock pheasant
lay dying. He remembered placing his hand on the bird and
feeling a convulsive movement in the animal's chest as it
shuddered and gasped and died. It had saddened him, and he
had buried the pheasant in the thick black soil alongside the
railroad embankment. Then he had stood and walked through
the rest of the marshland.

As he stepped out of the marshland, the gray haze
parted slightly, revealing the sun as it moved steadily toward
the western horizon. He watched the sun cast shadows across
the stubble of the wheat fields and cornfields. In the distance, the Little Sioux River curled around the small town
and continued on its course southwards toward the Mississippi.

It was off to the side of the railroad embankment that it
had happened. As he had looked in that direction, a sudden
gust of wind blew through the thicket of trees, sending dead
leaves tumbling out into the prairies. Someone was waving to
him from the edge of the thicket. As she stepped out from the
shadows, he recognized who it was and he walked over to her.

"So, at last we meet, Mr. McCarthy," she said to him.
She smiled strangely and gestured for him to join her at the
edge of the thicket. "Do you know who I am, Mr. McCarthy?"

"Yes, ma'am," he answered politely. "You be Kate's mother."

"Yes, I certainly am." She introduced herself by holding
out one tiny, limp hand. He had felt uncomfortable trying to
shake her small, wrinkled hand in his huge callused paw. "I
understand you are about to become my son-in-law?" she
said. He could not tell if she was being sarcastic or was
simply trying to make him comfortable. Something about the
way she said it was not right.

"Yes, ma'am," he answered, again politely.

"Do you think I disapprove of your marriage to my
daughter?"

"That be what Kate says, yes."

Agnes Sumners sighed deeply and again the strange
smile spread across her lips. "Mr. McCarthy, I do not disap-

prove of you marrying my daughter. What I disapprove of is
the fact that you feel you must sneak around behind my back
to do it. I know that you are on your way to meet Katharine,
and I know you are planning to run away together. That is
Katharine's decision, of course. But if I am not to be a part of
your wedding plans, could you at least give Katharine something from me—so she will know I approve? Then the two of
you can decide whether to go ahead with your plans, or
whether you would prefer to be married right here in
Danvers—with my blessing."

He studied Agnes Sumners' sharp, piercing green eyes to
determine if she was telling him the truth.

"Don't you trust me, Mr. McCarthy?" she asked, almost
teasing him.

"Yes, ma'am, I trust you. Do you want me to go get
Kate?"

"No, like I said, Katharine can make up her own mind
once you bring her something from me. I have a family
heirloom I want you to give to Katharine—a silver plate that
has been used in the weddings on my late husband's side of
the family for more than a century. When Katharine sees it,
she will know my true feelings. Then the two of you can
decide."

"Yes, Mrs. Sumners, I'll bring it to her."

"Very good, Mr. McCarthy. Please, come this way with
me. The plate is back at the house."

Then they had walked away from the thicket. In the
distance, the old Victorian home rose out of the prairies. As
they walked across the empty fields, he felt the fading sun
against the back of his neck, and he knew Katharine would be
happy that her mother approved of the marriage.

"I will only keep you for a minute, Mr. McCarthy,"
Agnes Sumners said as they stepped up to the gate that
surrounded the old Victorian home. "Please, come this way."

III

Ned Finley directed the Studebaker toward the church
steeple and water tower that rose out of the prairies several

miles in the distance. Aggy sat in the back seat watching the countryside roll by the rear window, while Susan Hampton sat in the front passenger seat next to Finley.

Ned Finley had been strangely quiet for the first few miles of the trip to Danvers, and Susan had thought it best not to interrupt his thoughts. Finally, he spoke.

"Susan, I just talked to Katharine Sumners," Finley said softly as he glanced out the side window at the dust rolling out into the empty fields.

"She's alive?" Susan asked, surprised.

"Yes."

"I thought you said she was killed in a fire in Chicago."

"That was someone else. Another young woman. Katharine Sumners, for many reasons at that point in her life, wanted everyone in Danvers to think she had died in the fire in Chicago."

"Why?"

"She was pregnant with Joel at the time."

"Are you certain she's Joel's mother?" Susan asked.

"Yes. Joel is the son of Katharine Sumners and Judd McCarthy. She signed the name 'Katharine McCarthy' to the adoption certificate even though she wasn't married."

"What was she able to tell you?" Susan asked.

"Katharine Sumners was pregnant with Judd McCarthy's son when he disappeared somewhere between Carson and Danvers. She was waiting for him down by the Little Sioux River. They were planning to leave together. But someone got in the way of their plans."

"Sylvester and the Hanley brothers?"

"No, someone else. Someone who despised Judd McCarthy even more than the Hanley brothers."

"Who?"

"That part of the puzzle goes back to the 1890s," Finley said as he again glanced out the side window. "Marsha Williams, a librarian and museum curator in Danvers, found the diary Maureen McCarthy had kept during her first two years in this country. She gave it to me. It answers a lot of questions."

"Was she Judd McCarthy's mother, as you suspected?" Susan asked.

"Yes. Maureen McCarthy came to this country to tend

house for Frank and Helga Graham. She planned that it would be a temporary job, only until she could save enough money to move farther north. She came to this country full of idealism, but she found something quite unexpected when she arrived here. Most of the people in Carver County were not like her. She was an independent young woman, a free spirit who loved to drink with the men in the Danvers saloons. She was also Irish in a predominantly Scandinavian and British county. The social elite of Danvers looked on her with scorn, especially when many of their husbands became enthralled with this charming, free-spirited Irish girl. Later their scorn turned to anger and finally to hatred when the community began to whisper about her pregnancy. Any errant husband could have been the father. So they had her committed to Farmington."

"Who was the father?" Susan asked.

"Let me fit in some of the smaller pieces of the puzzle, Susan, then I will insert the final piece. Maureen McCarthy was hated by two groups of people in Carver County. The very proper, stern-faced men and women whose portraits now hang in the Danvers library thought Maureen McCarthy had the morals of a prostitute. Then, of course, men like Fred Hanley hated her because she would have nothing to do with them. Apparently Hanley tried in every way to coerce her into a relationship, but Maureen McCarthy was a shrewd judge of character. She hated Fred Hanley and spit in his face. Hanley threatened to kill her, but she laughed at him. On the surface, Maureen McCarthy might have appeared to be promiscuous. But the reality is that she knew only one man."

"Maynard?"

"No," Finley said, shaking his head. "Maynard only allowed himself to become the object of the community's scorn and accusations. After all, he was a single man, and it was better that he be the father of Maureen McCarthy's child than some married man with a family. In the process, Maureen McCarthy fell in love with Maynard, even though she was carrying another man's child."

"Is that why he killed himself?" Susan asked.

"Maynard befriended Maureen McCarthy during the early months of her pregnancy. But his compassion brought

the wrath of the community down on him. He knew who the
real father was, but he never revealed his name. He was
protecting someone very close to him. And he undoubtedly
loved Maureen McCarthy himself. When the community
succeeded in getting Maureen McCarthy committed to
Farmington on some trumped up moral charges, Maynard
became extremely depressed. He went to the one man who
should have stood beside Maureen McCarthy. But that man
refused to get involved. Feeling totally powerless to help and
knowing the living hell Maureen McCarthy would experience
at Farmington, Maynard ended up committing suicide. In
spring, when the ice was breaking on the Little Sioux River,
he threw himself off a bridge into the icy waters. They found
his battered body wrapped around a dead tree miles downstream."

As he spoke, Finley directed the Studebaker through the
narrow Main Street of Danvers. Within seconds, the car sped
out into the countryside northwest of the tiny village.

"Who was the father of Maureen McCarthy's child if it
wasn't Maynard Sumners?" Susan asked as the car picked up
speed on the other side of town.

Finley paused briefly, then continued. "Judd McCarthy's
father was Oscar Sumners," he said, glancing over at Susan.

"My God!" Susan Hampton blurted out. "Are you sure?"

"Yes, I'm sure. Maureen McCarthy describes the relationship in her diary. It was a relationship she came to regret
after she met Maynard Sumners."

"That makes Judd McCarthy and Katharine Sumners
brother and sister! Joel's parents were brother and sister!"
Susan uttered in disbelief.

"Half brother and sister," Finley corrected her.

"Did either of them know that?"

"No, they were innocent victims of fate. I doubt that
Maureen McCarthy ever told her son anything about his
past. And of course Oscar and Agnes Sumners wanted to
forget the whole thing. They didn't want to taint the family tree by acknowledging an illegitimate son. So obviously they never told their daughter she had a half brother.
It was just pure coincidence that Judd McCarthy drifted
back into the lives of Katharine Sumners and her family."

"Did you tell Katharine Sumners that McCarthy was her half brother?"

"No."

"Why?"

"I didn't know about it then. Even so, she's lived too long for those dreams," Finley said thoughtfully. "It would serve no purpose to take them away from her now."

"What does all of this have to do with McCarthy's disappearance?"

"Sylvester and the Hanleys wanted McCarthy out of the way for obvious reasons. Somehow Fred Hanley knew Judd McCarthy was the illegitimate son of Oscar Sumners and Maureen McCarthy. How he found out, I do not know. Hanley seemed to have ways of finding out what he needed to know about people, things he would then use to his own advantage. Whatever the case, Fred Hanley told Agnes Sumners that Judd McCarthy was the illegitimate son of her husband and Maureen McCarthy. Agnes Sumners was none too stable anyhow. When she heard this and was told that McCarthy was coming back from Carson alone to get her daughter, who was also pregnant, she found a way to get rid of him. In fact, I think that's why your husband threatened to take your daughter's life. It was the name Aggy that provoked him. He associated it with Agnes Sumners. A simple nickname concocted by the children in your neighborhod is what almost cost your daughter her life."

Susan Hampton had been so involved in her conversation with Ned Finley that she had forgotten Aggy was sitting in the back seat of the car. Susan glanced at her daughter who was looking out the window, seemingly oblivious to the conversation taking place in front of her. Aggy smiled innocently at her mother.

Suddenly, Susan thought of something else. "If Joel and Aggy are the products of an incestuous relationship, what does that mean?" she stammered.

"It was an *accidental* incestuous relationship," Finley corrected her. "Neither Judd McCarthy nor Katharine Sumners knew they were half brother and sister. There is no moral issue involved."

"Still," Susan pondered, "aren't there physical and psychological consequences?"

"Yes, there can be a kind of Jekyll-Hyde effect. Virtues and vices, strengths and weaknesses are all accentuated. Great talents and also mental defects have accompanied incestuous births."

"And madness?"

"Yes."

"Is that Joel's problem?" Susan asked.

"I don't know, but I think it's more than that."

Susan glanced back at Aggy who was still looking innocently out the side window. "What about the second generation?" Susan asked, looking over at Finley. "How will Aggy be affected by all this?"

Finley glanced quickly over his shoulder at the little girl. She smiled strangely back at him. "I don't think anyone knows how the second generation is affected by an incestuous relationship in the family tree. Theoretically, the effects of the incestuous relationship should be nullified by the second and third generations. But that's no guarantee. It bears watching in your daughter." Ned Finley turned sharply onto a gravel road leading toward the Sumners' farmhouse. "We're almost there," he announced. "Katharine Sumners should be expecting us."

Remembering what they were talking about earlier, Susan looked over at Finley. "You said Agnes Sumners was responsible for McCarthy's disappearance. How did she get rid of him?"

"That's what we plan to find out," Finley said as he turned the Studebaker into the narrow dirt road leading up to the Sumners' farmhouse.

IV

The dust from the gravel driveway billowed out on all sides of Finley's Studebaker as it came to a skidding halt next to the ancient wooden fence that surrounded the Sumners' farmhouse.

"Katharine Sumners is waiting," Finley said, turning toward Susan. "I told her we'd be out."

"Dr. Finley, that's Joel over there!" Susan Hampton screamed as she pointed out the window.

Finley looked quickly in the direction where Susan was pointing. Joel was standing on the other side of the wooden fence, gazing up at the old Victorian farmhouse.

"Come on!" Finley said. "Grab Aggy! Let's get over there!"

"Is it safe?" Susan asked as she reached into the back seat for her daughter.

"Yes, I think so. Come on."

Finley helped Susan and Aggy out of the car, and the three of them walked over to the wooden fence.

"What's wrong with Daddy?" Aggy asked softly. "He looks funny."

"Sh," Susan said, quieting the little girl.

Joel looked puzzled and dazed as he moved his eyes back and forth across the farmyard. A slight breeze blew, rustling the dead leaves that littered the lawn and causing the rusty windmill to groan high overhead. Joel studied the tornado-damaged silo, the swing dangling by one rope from the branch of the oak tree, and the wagon, shorn of one wheel, weathering in dying, waist-high vegetation. . . .

It was different. The trees were in fuller foliage then. Red and yellow leaves dancing in the sky and tumbling out into the nearby fields, while the windmill whistled a much gayer song overhead. Underneath the dancing leaves, the girl with the white linen dress had soared higher and higher into a blue sky as he pushed her from behind with his great strength. She had soared higher and higher as the sunlight sparkled off her golden hair and her laughter rang out beneath the dancing autumn leaves that filled the huge oak tree. . . .

Joel heard the sound of the gramophone coming from the farmhouse, and he looked cautiously in that direction. Katharine Sumners was sitting on the porch in an old swing that creaked on its rusty chain and hinges as she gently pushed herself back and forth, back and forth, in slow, delicate movements. She looked weary, sad, and seemed not to notice her visitors as she pushed the swing back and forth, back and forth. . . .

As Joel Hampton walked up to the porch, he grew

increasingly eager and excited. He approached the swing
with an unrestrained joy, then leaned over to look closely into
the eyes of Katharine Sumners.

"Kate, me lass," he teased her in a thick Irish accent,
"why so sad? Would ya take a penny fur yur thoughts now,
girl?" He reached into his pants pocket as though to extract a
coin, all the time continuing to tease her with his large brown
eyes.

"Who are you?" Katharine Sumners asked, completely
bewildered.

"Come now, lass. I got a present for ya. But first I gotta
see me Lady Kate smile."

Katharine Sumners reached slowly out to touch him, but
Joel leaped playfully out of the way and did an awkward
dance step on the porch.

"Judd, is it really you?" Katharine Sumners asked softly.

"Who'd ya think it was, lass? That little pup down the
road yur mother wants ya ta marry? Yes, Kate, it's Judd
McCarthy himself, bigger'n, meaner'n anyone else in the
county. That is, till he met you, Kate."

"You'd better learn to call me Katharine, Judd McCarthy,"
she admonished him, playing his game, though a little
reluctantly. "You know how I hate the name Kate."

"Sorry, Kate, I keep forgettin'. But I'll get it right one of
these days." He leaned over, still teasing her. "I gotta present
for ya, girl. Ya want ta see it?"

"Judd, did you? You went to Carson, now didn't you?
Where'd you get that kind of money, Judd?"

"Wrestlin'," he proclaimed proudly, rising again to his
full height. "I beat the Farmer Tobin, Kate. Fair'n square.
Had 'em on his back in five minutes. Told ya there weren't no
Norwegian alive could whip Judd McCarthy."

"You told me you'd stop that foolishness, now didn't
you?" Katharine Sumners admonished him gently.

"I said *after* we were married, Kate," he corrected her.
"Now you take this and wear it for me."

"Will nothing ever tame you, Judd McCarthy?" she
asked, shaking her head in mock disgust.

As Joel searched in his pants pockets, his actions suddenly
became more frantic, and his mood changed from joviality to
confusion and finally to anger.

"It's not here, Kate! Where did . . . Where did I put it?"

"Judd, please . . ."

Suddenly he leaped off the porch and ran to the corner of the farmhouse. He paused briefly, looking wildly in all directions like a cornered animal.

Something was not right. When he had walked up to the old Victorian farmhouse with Agnes Sumners, he had expected her to go right up to the front porch. But instead, she had taken him around to the back of the house.

"Mr. McCarthy, I hope I will not shock you when I say I know Katharine is pregnant with your child," Agnes Sumners said as they walked around the corner of the house. "I think it is very noble of you to marry her when you could very easily have said to yourself that it was just another easy conquest."

"Kate never told me about that," he said. The statement surprised him. "Course it don't make no difference, but she never told me. It's just all the more reason for us to get married."

"She never told me either. But we mothers have a way of knowing about those things." Agnes Sumners stopped and looked back at him with her sharp green eyes. "Maybe Katharine was afraid to tell you—for fear you'd leave her?"

"It'd never cross me mind to leave Kate."

"As I said, that is a very noble gesture, Mr. McCarthy." Agnes Sumners started walking toward an embankment behind the house. "Now, I've had this silver tray in storage for years and years and I just didn't want to go down there by myself. The rats, you know. I'm terrified of them . . . ."

Joel Hampton pointed emphatically in the direction of an embankment behind the house. "It's back there!" he yelled angrily.

As he spoke, Joel drew the state trooper's revolver out of the waistband of his trousers. He raised the revolver to shoulder height and turned slowly toward the farmhouse. He pointed the revolver menacingly at Finley, Aggy, and the two women who were gathered in front of the house. Then, as though venting his rage on the old Victorian farmhouse, he fired six shots into the gable above the porch. He continued squeezing the trigger long after the last shell had been spent, until the monotonous metallic clicking of the firing pin seemed to pull him out of his trance. As he lowered the revolver, the look on his face changed from anger and bitterness to a confused sadness. Tears filled his eyes and he stared at the revolver as though contemplating some deep, impenetrable mystery.

Suddenly, he reared back and threw the revolver out into the weed-strewn fields. Almost in the same motion, he bent over and extracted a rusty iron fence post from out of the leaves that covered the farmyard. Grasping the fence post in his right hand, he ran quickly around to the back of the farmhouse.

As Joel disappeared, Finley quickly approached Katharine Sumners. "What's back there?" he demanded of her as he pointed toward the back of the house.

"Nothing . . . an old cellar," Katharine Sumners stammered.

"I don't know why my husband didn't just bury this old cellar and be done with it," Agnes Sumners said as she led him over to a large wooden door protruding out of an embankment behind the house. "But he always said we needed the storage space. And, of course, it is protection against tornados. Now, Mr. McCarthy, if you will just lift this door for me."

He remembered how the door creaked on its hinges as he lifted it off its concrete foundation and watched it flop open against the ground.

Several small concrete steps led down to a second, much larger door at the bottom of the staircase. Three large pieces of lumber stretched across the door, fitting snugly into huge metal clamps bolted into the concrete walls of the staircase.

"My husband had this reinforced several years ago," Agnes Sumners said as she inserted a key into one of the two large padlocks attached to the door. "We have many valuable pieces of silver down here. . . ."

Finley grasped Katharine Sumners firmly by both shoulders. "Were the men working back by the cellar the morning you left to have the baby?"

Katharine Sumners searched carefully into her memories. "No. But mother must have had it buried sometime before I left. She said it was a haven for rats. It was only in the last year or two that the rains washed away the dirt. . . ."

"Let's get back there!" Finley said, grasping Katharine

Sumners firmly by the hand and pulling her out of the ancient porch swing.

"Dr. Finley, what is it?" Susan Hampton pleaded as he led the two women and Aggy around to the back of the house.

"Let's get back there," Finley repeated, ignoring the question.

As they approached the half-buried cellar, Joel Hampton was beating on the heavy wooden door with the rusty iron fence post. Then he forced the iron post behind the lock and tore it off.

"Joel, what are you doing?" Susan Hampton pleaded as her husband dropped to his knees and tore madly at the dirt blocking the entrance to the cellar.

"Leave him alone," Finley said firmly, restraining Susan Hampton.

When the dirt was removed from the bottom of the doorway, Joel Hampton leaned over and tore the door from its ancient hinges. He plunged quickly into the darkness of the cellar. There was a loud crash as the second door collapsed. Then there was a hollow echo from somewhere in the darkness, and finally a deep, overwhelming silence.

The second door of the cellar had creaked open slowly. Almost immediately, he heard the soft padding feet scurrying across the dirt floor.

"As you can see," Agnes Sumners had said, "it has certainly become a haven for rats."

"Yes, ma'am," he replied. "Do you have a lantern?"

"No, but I can tell you where the tray is. It's in a large box, right in the back there. Can you see it?"

"No, ma'am." He could not see into the darkness.

"If you'll just go over there, I'm sure you'll find it. I wouldn't ask you to, but I know it'll mean so much to Katharine. Just bring the box out here and we can go back upstairs and look through it."

He walked into the darkness, brushing aside the cobwebs as he felt his way slowly across the dirt floor. He could feel nothing against the other wall except the cold concrete.

"There's nothing in here except an old bench and some jars, Mrs. Sumners," he said as he groped around in the darkness.

"Oh, I think that's where you are wrong, Mr. McCarthy," he heard her say behind him. The tone in her voice had changed. *"You're in there, now aren't you? And so are the rats!"*

"What?" he asked as he turned to face Agnes Sumners. Her body was silhouetted against the bright sunlight outside the cellar door. A strange, evil smile spread across her lips as she looked back in his direction.

"You didn't really think I would let you marry my daughter, now did you, Mr. McCarthy?" she asked scornfully.

"What do you mean?"

"Katharine is too good for you, Mr. McCarthy. You belong in here—with all the other rats."

"Why?" he yelled as the door started to close, blocking out the sunlight.

"Why?" she repeated, taunting him from the other side of the thick wooden door. He heard the heavy pieces of lumber fall into the metal slots. Then he heard an insane, muffled laugh. *"Why? Because she's your sister, Mr. McCarthy . . ."*

"So she lured him in here," Finley said softly, staring into the darkness of the cellar.

"What?" Susan Hampton uttered, not comprehending. "Dr. Finley . . ,"

"Katharine," Finley said gently as he turned to face Katharine Sumners, "your mother tricked Judd McCarthy into this cellar the night you were to meet him by the river."

"What are you trying to say, Dr. Finley?" Katharine Sumners whispered.

"Your mother lured Judd McCarthy into this cellar," Finley repeated. "She must have made up some excuse. Probably told him she would accept the marriage, then asked him to get something for her out of the cellar. He probably sensed something was wrong. But he wanted to make peace with your mother. And he went in here anyhow, most likely against his better judgment."

"Oh, my God!" Katharine Sumners exclaimed.

"Then she locked the doors and Fred Hanley buried the cellar, probably that same night. Even with all of his strength, Judd McCarthy couldn't break down that door and dig through six feet of solid earth," Finley said softly.

Finley suddenly turned away from the two women and

walked down the concrete steps into the darkness of the cellar. From the light filtering through the open doorway, he surveyed the contents of the small room. A broken bench, numerous, smashed crates, the butt handle of a knife, and a .45-caliber revolver littered the dirt floor. Unable to free himself from his prison, Judd McCarthy had instead vented his rage on the contents of the small cellar, destroying everything before he died.

Joel Hampton lay prostrate on the dirt floor next to the broken bench and wrecked crates. He did not move. He did not even appear to be breathing. Nearby, a large human skeleton was half buried in the wreckage. A canvas bag lay next to the skeleton. Its contents, worthless pieces of paper cut to the size of currency, were dumped in a heap and scattered over the dirt floor.

But it did not end there. It was days later. Maybe weeks. Maybe even months. It did not matter. Surrounded by the impenetrable darkness, time ceased to exist. Except as measured by his failing strength, his dying will.

At first he lashed out frantically, until the blade of the hunting knife shattered. When that failed he fired the revolver into the darkness. He watched the orange flames spit out of the barrel as the muffled gunshots echoed harmlessly all around him. Still it did not end.

And each time he fell the rats would scurry over to sniff at his mildewed clothing. Bolder they became with the passage of time, until he would lash out with the butt end of the knife, sending them scurrying back into the darkness. But always they came back. Relentlessly. And he grew weaker.

Sometime, near the end, he heard the scream. Loud and shrill, it echoed in the darkness. First in anger, then in agony. Growing weaker as his strength failed him. When it too failed, he again heard the soft padding of tiny feet scurrying about in the darkness. Moving ceaselessly. Relentlessly.

When the end came, he was lying face down. The rats sensed that he had lost his will, his strength. He heard them padding softly across the ground to where he lay. They sniffed at his clothing and brushed against his cheek. Then a sharp pain tore through his arm like a thousand needles penetrating the flesh. But he was too weak to care. And he lay there, enduring the pain until it turned into a moist numbness.

As the life poured out of his body, he was filled with rage at the horror of how he had been duped. And even as his life yielded to the darkness that surrounded him, his soul held firm against the night and refused to accept what had been left undone.

It was then that he thought of the locket. The locket for his beautiful Lady Kate. He reached toward his pocket to see if it was still there. But the numbness had spread over his entire body and his arm would not move. . . .

"Jesus, he tore this place apart trying to get out of here!" Finley exclaimed as he knelt down to examine the worthless paper currency scattered across the dirt floor. As he did so, the figure suddenly opened one eye. He blinked twice in the direction of the light streaming through the open doorway. The bodies of the two women and Aggy were silhouetted against the streaming rays of sunlight that entered the dark cellar for the first time in more than three decades. Susan Hampton held her daughter close to her chest as she peered into the darkness.

He raised himself slowly to one knee, stood, and walked awkwardly toward the open doorway, blinking repeatedly against the bright sunlight as he stepped out of the cellar and turned to face the women.

At first he did not appear to recognize them. Susan clutched her daughter, not knowing what he would do. Then slowly he reached his hand out.

"Susan, Aggy, I love you," he whispered gently, pulling them close to him.

They stood for a minute locked in each other's arms. Then Susan turned toward Katharine Sumners and said, her voice filled with tears, "Joel, this is your mother, Katharine."

Joel Hampton turned slowly toward Katharine Sumners. Then he reached out his hand as the sunlight burst between the distance separating them. Katharine Sumners also reached out her hand toward him. As they were about to touch, Joel Hampton paused, his hand a few inches above hers, and he dropped the locket he had found on the dirt floor into her open palm. The chain dangled from his hand into hers, connecting the two of them, as the sunlight sparkled off the golden links and the music from the gramophone wafted gently from the interior of the farmhouse.

Behind them, Ned Finley stepped out of the darkness of the ancient cellar. As he glanced overhead, a lone bull goose, delayed in its departure from the north, spread its magnificent white wings against the sky and echoed a lonely mating call at the departing sun as it flew southwards—following, or so it seemed, the course of the Little Sioux River to where it bent into the Mississippi, and from there into the Great Sea beyond. . . .

The things that are meant to be—will be. The spirit confined in this cell refused to die in its own lifetime, but rather lived on into the next generation to place a locket in the hand of his Lady Kate.

THE END

ABOUT THE AUTHOR

DENNIS CLAUSEN grew up in Morris, Minnesota, a few miles east of the South Dakota border and a few miles west of Sinclair Lewis' home town of Sauk Centre, Minnesota. During his childhood and adolescence, he grew increasingly fond of the vast loneliness of the prairie and the lives it harbored and occasionally destroyed. Although he now does freelance writing and teaches at the University of San Diego, he has never lost this fondness for the Midwest. It is the prairie towns and the characters who live in them that provide the inspiration for much of his work.